SECURE THE SHADOW

ALSO BY MICHAEL HENSON

Ransack

A Small Room with Trouble on My Mind

Crow Call

The Tao of Longing and the Body Geographic

The Dead Singing

Tommy Perdue

The True Story of the Resurrection and Other Poems

Maggie Boylan

SECURE THE SHADOW

A NOVEL

MICHAEL HENSON

SWALLOW PRESS / OHIO UNIVERSITY PRESS
ATHENS

Swallow Press
An imprint of Ohio University Press, Athens, Ohio 45701
ohioswallow.com

Printed in the United States of America
Swallow Press / Ohio University Press books are printed on acid-free paper ∞ ™

30 29 28 27 26 25 24 23 22 21 20 5 4 3 2 1

Library of Congress Cataloging-in-Publication Data
Names: Henson, Michael, author.
Title: Secure the shadow : a novel / Michael Henson.
Description: Athens : Swallow Press / Ohio University Press, [2021]
Identifiers: LCCN 2021011100 (print) | LCCN 2021011101 (ebook) | ISBN 9780804012355 (paperback ; alk. paper) | ISBN 9780804041171 (pdf)
Classification: LCC PS3558.E562 S43 2021 (print) | LCC PS3558.E562 (ebook) | DDC 813/.54—dc23
LC record available at https://lccn.loc.gov/2021011100
LC ebook record available at https://lccn.loc.gov/2021011101

Secure the shadow ere the substance fade.

—Nineteenth-century
photographer's advertisement

1

A SERIES OF black-and-white photographs: set on the streets of a city. The streets are background, out of focus. But in each we see a haze of old brick and old cut stone. In some of the pictures, windows mirror the streets and the people who pass on them. In corners or in the distance, we see cars and buses. These are busy daylight streets. They throb with poverty; they shimmer with human density.

The photographs are all of the same person, a woman. It seems they were all taken on the same day. In some she appears to be almost a child. In others she seems to be very old, very hard. She might be from these streets; she might have her home in some other place. Anything made clear in one picture is undone and redefined in the next.

The subtle muscles around her eyes seem tense; she seems at once to look and look away. Below each eye is a thin gray moon.

A hint of bruising? Worry? Days without sleep? Drugs? Could we give those dark places a name or a history?

In each she wears a peacoat. So the weather was cool when the pictures were taken. But it was not winter. Some of the people walk by in light jackets. No one hunkers his shoulders against the hawk of a wind. No one blows into her hands for warmth.

Something in the light says November. Something in the light hints of the sea. The light sandy grays in the walls and sidewalks contrast with her peacoat and the dark moons under her eyes. She stands at or near the center of each photograph, a clear darkness, painfully sharp against the background of streets, against staircases, gangs of people, signboards.

In one picture she leans back against a blank brick wall. Her eyes gaze off camera, her dark hair falls loose to her shoulders, her mouth is slightly open. Her tongue just touches her teeth as if she has just lost the word she would have spoken. Her hands at her sides are flattened against the wall. The peacoat is buttoned. Heavy, it makes her dark, breastless, a bell.

Another: A torso shot. The same peacoat. The same streets surrounding. She stands against a wall covered with tattered bills and posters. Her face turns toward her shoulder. Her eyes are cast to her left, and down. Her collar is open and we see the muscle and shadow in her neck. Her skin is smooth as stone, shadowed in the cheeks and eyes. Strands and wisps of her long dark hair trail back, pulled perhaps by the wind. But for the coat with its dark fraying collar and the hair that crosses her cheek, she could be taken for a museum marble. But the eyes are not the passive eyes of the museum woman. The brows are cinched together in a knot. The eyes are determined; they brood and pierce.

Another: She wears a wide Kansas-girl straw hat. It frames her face like a ball of sun. Her face is open in a wide sunflower smile. The smile cinches the hollows under her eyes into wrinkles like an old woman's or like a small child's squinting into the light. The wall, her face, and her hands are full of light. Light dances under the hat. Light dances even against the darkness of her eyes. Her eager shoulders lean forward. Her hands fold around a coffee mug. The picture carries a sound of laughter.

Another: The hat is gone; she embraces a child. Her arms cross the little girl's back. The girl's face is half-buried in the peacoat. The woman's hair is tousled, roped up, thick. One hank has fallen across her face and partially obscures it. But we still see her worried eyes. Her brows, very black, flex together. Her lashes, very black, hang low. Her hair stretches across the face of the child like a raven's broken wing. Has she embraced the child? Has she staggered and fallen against her?

Another: Alone: freeze-frame: in profile: hatless, head back, her hair strung back over her shoulders. She holds a bottle of cheap wine aimed like a pistol at her mouth.

FALL 1995.

Every day, Amy Taylor hiked the same stretch of streets to get to school, streets that were first broad, then narrow: first rational and stark, then crazy with living patterns. Every morning, she traveled with her mother from the almost-suburb where they lived, downtown to where she went to school and where her mother worked. She was seventeen and studied at a special high school for the arts and was destined to study in New York, Los Angeles, or Chicago. Anywhere would do, just so it was big and would get her out of this cramped city. She was eager to get on with living, eager to get moving. But for now she trudged every day with her books and portfolio through the vivid, dense, transforming streets.

Her mother could have dropped her off each morning at the front door of her school, but they had settled into this pattern a year ago when she transferred to the special school in the neighborhood called New Town, just north of the central city business district. Their schedule was so tight and the parking garage was so near the same building that housed her mother's office and those tiny neighborhood streets were so complicated that she finally said, "Oh, Mom, I can walk. Just drop me off at your work."

Her mother objected, but did not insist. So, unless the weather was very bad, Amy hustled through the blocks from the downtown parking garage to her school, a daily routine. She had even grown to like it, in spite of the heavy portfolio she had to carry some days and the camera bag she carried for photography class on others. And in spite of her uneasiness about the winos and the crackheads and the young men on the corners who watched her with half-lidded, predatory eyes.

It was a borderline neighborhood, White to one side, Black to the other. But here, in these few blocks, it was a meeting ground where Black and White and Hispanic and Asian all crossed, as well as artists, musicians, and other people of the fringes. Nothing here was bland; nothing was borrowed from fashion. When she crossed into the neighborhood, she entered into something vibrant and primal. She felt she entered into the roots of all things.

Even the weather did not bother her. She lived in a city known for its sudden turns of season, where summer and fall can sweep in with day-long rains, where winters alternate periods of cold, brilliant, bitter snow with long stretches of slush and damp, where spring means bursts of flower and leaf constantly threatened by sudden frost. Winter was hard. Spring was tenuous. She embraced it all.

Her walk started outside the door of the parking garage, cut past the last of the downtown office towers, switched across a wide parkway split by traffic islands full of flowering trees and park benches, then plunged into a dark canyon of small brick buildings where the upstairs windows were tightly shaded and little bars and carryouts and cluttered laundromats and furniture stores and storefront churches occupied the first floors.

On her route, she crossed Broad Street, where the little shops and neighborhood bars had died and been reborn as art galleries, coffee shops, and nightclubs, which all, at the hour she daily passed them, were deathly silent, as if sleeping off a hard night. At the far end of Broad, she could just catch a glimpse of the bus station. On winter mornings, when it was still not fully light, she could see the glow of the neon running dog and the big block letters. She crossed Broad quickly, then walked three more blocks through the narrow, dense streets before she reached her school.

The denseness of these streets ran right up to the door of her school like a crested wave. Her school, a massive brick headland, stood alone in its block, surrounded by a wide concrete yard. Stone curbs fitted with wrought-iron fences protected the yard.

The alleys that broke off from her route glittered with broken glass; they darkened with brick and shadow. She knew better than to use the alleys. She stayed out on the streets, where there were more people and therefore greater safety. But some mornings even the main streets were nearly empty. If the weather was cold or harsh or if the winter darkness was still on them, she might see no one at all but for an early morning prostitute, or children running to school, or the little boy named Jonathan, or the one she liked to call the Rag Man. Or the one she knew as the Dealer. She was afraid on those days (though she never told her mother), for even though she saw no one and heard no step, she felt herself watched and followed.

But if the sun was out or if it was warm or—as she later learned—it was check day, or even for no good reason at all, the streets could swarm with people of all ages and colors. The tightly shut windows would fill with elderly watchers. Children—who should have been heading toward school just as she was—might sit on the stoops or jump rope in those same alleys that had loomed with threat just two days before.

~

The first time Amy saw the Rag Man, he had blocked her sidewalk with his cart. He was a large man in a heavy coat with large white hands and wide, pasty eyes. But he seemed so soft and so intent on what he had found in a large wire waste can that she saw no threat in him. She stopped, unsure whether to go out into the street to get around him or to wait. He was dissecting an old radio, for the copper, she supposed. His face was pale as butter, passive and unperturbed. Two men came up from behind him, talking loudly and gesturing widely and emphatically with their hands.

"Crazy motherfucker," one said. "Blocks the fuckin sidewalk like he owns it."

The other pulled back his fist, shifted into a boxer's stance, and faked three, four quick punches at the Rag Man's head. She winced.

The Rag Man, as if deaf to all, as if blind to all but his work, continued to pry into the metallic heart of the radio.

Furious at the two men, Amy shouted at their backs, "Bullies!"

They glanced back. Would they come back at her? She caught her breath for fear. But they laughed. What she said had struck them as hilarious. One of them pointed at her and they laughed even louder; they strutted down the street, laughing and gesturing widely. Her word bounced off their backs and broke up in the street.

She looked around. Had anyone seen her? The Rag Man had dropped the black magnet and copper heart of the radio into his cart and started pushing toward the next waste can. She cast her eye down the long valley of the street. A prostitute sighed and stepped to the corner. A group of children argued fiercely past her, dragging their coats and backpacks. A wino sat in a doorway and measured the remains of his bottle. A tall boy, about her own age, leaned against a wall and gazed out to the street with a steady eye that seemed to stare past her and yet to see everything of the street, an eye that did not blink or deflect all through her encounter with the Rag Man and the two cursing men. He wore a thick jacket zipped up to the neck and a stocking cap pulled down to his eyes. She looked back; he turned toward her and the morning sun came full in his face. His lip rose to expose a tooth and a spike of gold shot from it.

~

"Hey, wassup," she heard a man call to the gold-tooth boy one morning. The man limped down the sidewalk toward the boy like the prodigal come home. "Wassup, my brother," the man called again when the boy did not look his way. She was right behind the man, so she could not see his face, but she could sense the nervous need in the jerkiness of his elbows and the shaky give in his knees. "What you got . . ."

A movement of the boy's eyes silenced the man, who looked back over his shoulder, not so much at her as at the whole threatening street. The man huddled next to the boy on his wall, muttering into his ear and darting his eyes to each side.

She passed them, moving to the curb to give them as wide a berth as she could. But still she felt the tension rise off them. She felt their eyes all the way past Broad Street and up to the door of her school.

~

After that, she saw the gold-tooth boy nearly every morning, standing in nearly the same place, grim and immobile as the stone facings of the buildings around. She tried to ignore him, for she soon figured out what he was doing. She saw the lean and desperate people who came to him. She saw him count the money. She saw the gold chain at his neck and the glinting gold tooth.

~

On another morning, one of the winos she had come to recognize stumbled into the gold-tooth boy just as she came near. The boy drew up as if to gather energy. His lips wrenched small and his nose twisted into a sneer. His brow narrowed. He erupted with curses.

"Cheap winehead motherfucker. Don't you *ever* bump your pissy self into me." He flashed back his fist and the man ducked and stumbled. The boy shot six hard punches to the air behind the man's head.

"Cue-ball-headed, red-nose, snot-sleeve bum," he spat. "Keep your dribbling ass off my block."

The man, still veering side to side down the sidewalk, kept his head down and his shoulders pulled tight as if he ran under a hard rain.

The boy, in turning on the wino, had blocked the sidewalk. She waited until he went back to his wall, then started around him to pass. She wanted to speak. But this close, and given the outburst she had just heard, she felt safe only to glare. She met him eye to eye and held her pose as she passed him.

He raised his lip, exposing the gold. She turned and continued her march to school.

Across the street, she saw a smaller, younger boy, his hand in a bag of chips. He had dark hair that slanted across his dark and narrow eyes. His mouth was pulled to one side like that of a hooked fish. She saw that he watched her until she crossed Broad Street, that his dark, narrow eyes switched back and forth from her to the Dealer.

~

The children in these streets amazed her. Singly and in clusters, they trudged to school like soldiers in an army that had been, not yet defeated, but shot up and scattered. Undaunted by the harshest winter days, some passed by her in the thinnest of jackets slung back on their shoulders. Others were bundled into thick pneumatic winter coats like pieces of fine china packed for shipping. They ran, or slogged, dragging backpacks torn at the corners, complaining or laughing, daring one another to fight or whispering together, and—something which always amazed her, having been schooled on the virtues of proper nutrition—munching, first thing in the morning, on candy bars or potato chips or even pickles, or sucking on bottles of pop.

She began to know and recognize some of them as, day by day, she passed them on her way to school. "Wassup," one might say.

"What's happening," she might call back.

One morning, the large black leather portfolio slung from her shoulder caught the attention of one smallish boy. He separated himself out of a group to turn and follow her.

"What's that big thing?" he asked. He was dark-haired and squint-eyed, the same boy, she realized, who had watched her encounter with the Dealer. His mouth was still pulled to one side, the side with which one eye squinted. His brow was furrowed.

She did not answer right away, so he said, "It's okay, man. I ain't gonna do nothing. What is it?"

"It's a portfolio."

"A poor what?"

"Aren't you supposed to be going to school?"

"It's okay. I got time. What did you call that thing?"

"A portfolio."

"A port-o-foldo."

"Something like that. Don't you know you're going the wrong way?" Her school, the special school for the arts, lay on one side of New Town. The school for the neighborhood children waited on the other.

He dismissed the notion with a wave of his hand. She had expected the sideways pull of his face and the wrinkling and furrowing of his brow to have relaxed by now. But his forehead seemed etched into position and his mouth seemed permanently pulled to the side. "I'm cool," he said. "What's in that port-foldio thing?"

"It's my art."

"You mean, like, pictures and stuff."

"Yeah, I put my pictures in it."

He nodded impressively and continued to walk alongside her. "You must have some big pictures, man. When we do art, it's like these little pictures, like . . ." He held up his hands in a letter-size frame.

"Here's my school. Where's your school?"

"It's over there." He pointed vaguely back in the direction they had just come.

"Don't you think you need to get going?"

"Let me see some of your pictures, man."

"I don't have time. First bell is coming up. Your first bell is coming up too."

"I'm all right. I got excused from first bell. Come on, man."

"Why do you always call me man? I'm a girl."

"Come on, man."

She had to wait for a WALK light before she could cross to the front lot of her school. A group of her friends was gathered on the wide front steps. In a moment, first bell would ring. The boy began to pry with his fingers along the edges of the portfolio, looking for a latch. It had a zipper that started at the bottom, but he didn't know that. She pulled it away from him.

"Come on, man."

"You don't just put your hands on other people's stuff," she said. The traffic light was a long one; it still had not turned.

He waved his hand again. "You just don't want to show me." The light changed and she started across. He continued with her as if he intended to follow her all the way to school. "That's cool," he said. He shrugged his shoulders and looked deliberately ahead. "Be like that."

The kids perched on the steps of her school, with their own backpacks and portfolios, watched her with this strange little boy from the neighborhood in tow. And she was sure they wondered, *Where did she pick up that little thug, that little grit from the neighborhood?* But she decided she did not care. *People can be such snobs,* she thought. She figured she would lose the boy at the school door, where the security guard stood.

But suddenly, in the middle of the crossing, the boy turned on his heel.

"Later, man." He slapped her on the shoulder and disappeared into the streets that ran toward his own school.

~

She liked these streets for their liveliness and for the little dramas that played across them: arguments, celebrations, drug deals, intoxication, romance, struggles for survival, loneliness, supplication. She had come to hate her static and set-piece home.

Gradually, she felt herself become a part of the life of these streets. Old winos would tap their foreheads, say, "Good morning, missy," and did not even bother to bum her for change anymore. Little kids might slap five with her or invite her to watch them in double Dutch. The skinny balding man who played the same scratchy bluegrass records over and over would bob his head and wave from his window. The prostitutes would eye her coolly and, just barely, nod. And the Rag Man, pushing his enormously stacked cart full of rescued trash, would steadily, and in spite of all her attempts to say a friendly word, ignore her as if she were air.

In just the year that she had been going to the downtown school, she had seen little shops spring up and die. Others, like the barbershop that seemed it had always been there, suddenly stood vacant, padlocked, and bare. Storefronts were boarded over with plywood sheets that looked fresh one week and the next week were covered over with graffiti and the next week chipped and buckled with weather and the next week ripped off altogether and the shop window shattered.

She knew now, when she saw such a one, that if the shop were not filled soon, it would stand emptier and emptier and the apartments above would begin to empty out and the building itself would die like a tree blighted in a forest.

It was in one of those storefronts, where he had recently set up shop, that she first met the photographer who was to become her teacher. And it was in that shop that she had first been startled by the series of photographs of the woman in the peacoat.

And it was on those same streets that she first saw the woman herself.

~

The boy with the strange mouth told her his name was Jonathan, though he told her many things she could not trust. In spite of her lectures about truancy, he continued to follow her to school once or twice a week like Mary's little lamb. He called to her when he saw her on the streets and gave her a special cool-guy wave when she responded.

"Come here," he waved to her one day.

"You come here if you want me." She had a good two hours between the end of school and the time she had to meet her mother.

Usually she stayed at the after-school study hall her mother paid for; she could do most of her homework and kill the time with her friends. But lately she had begun to find excuses to sneak out early, to take her time walking down to where she met her mother. Today she was looking for a store where she could buy a pop and some chips.

The boy was studying something like a book in his hands. When he saw she really did not intend to come over, he complained, "Aw, man." But he crossed the street to her. "You got to check this out," he said.

"What?"

"Look at these old pictures I got."

She was skeptical.

"For real, man. Look." He held out a stack of twenty or more sepia portrait photographs. Individuals, couples, and families, shots that went back, judging from the styles of clothing and hair, to the thirties and forties. Some had been hand-tinted: blushes of red on the cheeks of the Whites, brown shine on the faces of the Blacks. None of the people looked prosperous or sophisticated; they all looked as if they had been brushed up and dressed up to their best for the portrait. Each had put on his bravest, her most hopeful face.

Cool, she thought. The photographs in her fingers were like living things.

"Where did you get these?"

"That old man up on Main Street's gonna close up. He said I could have them. 'I'm gonna cash in,'" the boy quoted in deep mock solemnity, "'so you might as well have these.'"

"Come on."

He showed her the portrait studio on Main Street that had closed. A painted sign above the door still read,

FRANK CARLUCCI

PHOTOGRAPHER

Through a window, she could see pale patches on the walls where framed portraits, samples of his work, had once hung. A pile of dusty prints lay on a table.

What a piece of history, she thought. "Where is he now?" she asked.

"Where's who?"

"The photographer! The guy who ran this shop?"

"He's gone. I ain't seen him since the day he give me those pictures."

"So what are you going to do with them?"

"Keep them."

"Just keep them?"

"For real. I collect old stuff, man. I got all kinds of stuff. Pictures, old books, old keys, nickels with Indian heads on them. I got stuff you never even heard of."

"And you didn't steal any of it?"

He shook his head derisively and waved his hand. "What you take me for?"

"I don't know, but I just know that last week you told me you lived in Alaska for five years and California for seven and since you're no more than ten—"

"Eleven."

"Whatever you are, it doesn't add up. So: I got to wonder."

He looked at her with his odd, side-twisted look and said, "Man, you're a trip."

~

A week later, at the beginning of second term, the boy flagged her down again. "What's in there?" He pointed to a bulge in her backpack.

"It's none of your business."

"Come on, man."

"It's a camera. And don't follow me or you'll be late for school again."

"Let me see it."

"And if you're late for school again, then you'll have the truancy people all down on you again and you'll have to spend another six months in lockup."

"Who told you that?"

"You did. Just last week. Not that I believed you."

"So take my picture."

"I can't."

"Why not?"

"Because I've got to get to school and so do you and if you keep following me to school I'm going to get a boyfriend just so he can beat you up."

"Aw, man."

~

"So hey. Come here," he called on a sunny day after school.

"You come here," she said. "You want me. You come here."

"No, for real. I got something to show you."

She was less inclined to doubt him this time, so she followed. At the corner, he raised his hand to stop her.

"Come on," he said, pointing back down the street they had come. "We can't go this way."

"Why not?"

"That's my cousin."

She recognized the Dealer, standing in his usual place.

"I ain't supposed to go around him."

"Because?"

"'Cause he tried to get me to sell drugs." He took her down side streets she did not know to another row of shops—small shops, dingy shops—until he stopped in front of one and said, "Here it is."

Whatever it was did not look like much. "So?"

"Check it out, man."

To her first glance it looked abandoned, emptied out like the Italian photographer's studio. There was nothing on the walls. There were shelves, but only half full. There was furniture, but all in a jumble.

"It's another picture store," Jonathan said finally, tired of waiting for her to figure it out.

She looked again. Behind the wide, empty windows, the shelves were stacked with boxes of paper and chemicals that had become familiar from her photography class. And among the furniture were filing cabinets and a light table. And on the floor and leaning against the walls were photographs matted or framed and not yet hung.

"He's pretty cool," the boy said with a shrug. "He don't let you skip school or bring in no food."

"Who?"

"The guy who runs this place."

"Where is he now?"

"I don't know. He don't tell me where he's going."

~

The photographer's shop had nothing to advertise itself. That was no big deal. Several stores in the neighborhood bore no sign or title, and it was only by watching who went in or out that she could recognize each as a place where she could get snacks or bottles of pop. So she was curious about this new shop that was neither thrift store, candy shop, furniture store, wine store, nor shooting gallery.

She began to cut past it on her way back downtown from school. Gradually, she saw the shop take shape as a studio: More photographs went up on the walls. Equipment emerged from the jumble of crates and wrappers and stood on tables and shelves. Eventually a few photographs looked out from the windows. Twice she saw the man who ran the shop. Once he was tacking together frames; a second time he was holding a set of negatives up to the light. He was a smallish, thin man with a thick, droopy mustache and hair to his shoulders. He wore blue jeans and a black shirt with the sleeves rolled up. His hands were slender and red as the claws of a bird.

Jonathan stepped to the door. "Come on in, man."

"No, not now," she hissed.

~

Twice more they stopped at the door and twice more Jonathan urged her to go in. The third time, he said, "Forget you, man." He pushed the door open with a sweep and went straight to the bench where the man was working. Dying of embarrassment but afraid to leave, she watched as Jonathan talked briefly to the man, then waved to her to come in. *Omigod,* she thought, but she stepped up, opened the door, and entered.

The man's name was Paul Lewis. He was not particularly friendly, but that was all right, because he showed her his work and what he was doing to prepare for a show, his first major recognition after many years of work. That he was gruff and spare with his words and with his time mattered less than that he was willing to teach her things about photography she did not realize she wanted to know. In fact, she had become hooked on photography. And now for the first time she had a chance to know a live, genuine artist. She had her teachers, of course. But this man had been around for years—and he was *doing* it, not just drawing a salary as a teacher. And he wasn't like the photographers who worked for her mother, who just did what they were told. He was independent. He was an artist. It changed her. Where before she had seen photography as a sideline, now it was to become her focus, her aim. She had yet to shoot more than a few rolls of film, but she began to love the smell of stop bath and fixer and the feel of a good, crisp print. She began to imagine the pictures she would do once she had learned all she could and went to work in the real world.

She arranged school credit for working with him, and after that spent every day after school and before her mother got off work helping him prepare his show. She liked his work. It was so . . . committed. And it had power too. And yet he was an unknown who made his living driving a forklift or something and had kept a darkroom in his closet until he got the grant that allowed him to rent this shop.

She thought his work was as good as anything she had ever seen. But she was not prepared for what she would feel when she came across a set of photographs by accident. He had sent her to his files to look for another set of prints when she found (and was struck dumb by) the woman in her peacoat: the black bell of her, that smile full of sun, the black wing of her hair, that bottle like a loaded pistol.

THE young man watched his street like a hawk perched on a post. He had mastered the art of seeing without seeming to look. A wire ran up from the pocket of his coat to a set of headphones that crossed from ear to ear. He had the face of a very young man, pale, clouded by acne, and tufted with blond hairs at the lip and chin. Up close, you might hear the dead-steady beat of the music that escaped the speakers. You might see the slight, nearly imperceptible nod he gave to each beat. But you could not know that he watched the street without seeming to move his eyes from the single spot on which he had fixed them. That spot might be the cracked stone step of an abandoned building, a kicked-in garbage can, a dope fiend gone to rags, a stop sign flaring with spray paint, or a stoned-out streetlamp. You could not know how, without moving, he could see the entire streetscape or any change on it, from the intersection at Broad, down the line of shops and vacant lots and empty buildings, to the bus station with the white running dog in its stiff neon stride.

It was morning. The air was full of traffic noise and diesel fumes. The sidewalks were crowded with children dragging their way to school or people stalking downtown to work, and he took it all in without seeming to see anything at all. Everything around him was in motion, but he seemed to have been carved in stone.

A girl in a loose black coat had just entered the street, lumbering down the sidewalk with her books in a knapsack strapped to her shoulders and a big black case at her side. His eyes were tagged to a fat set of intertwined initials, intricately drawn in white on the black iron tail of a dumpster. Anyone watching would have thought that the tag was all he could see. But he could see all this street. No one watching him could know it, but he followed the clumsy path of the girl in the loose black coat, clear and dark as the outline of a flying bird.

To watch the girl, he leaned back against the window of what used to be a machine shop. With the ghosts of the gray lathes behind him, he mouthed the words *Prissy little preppy bitch.*

In her loose black clothes and her backwards ball cap, the girl looked like a small black bird. Not a crow, for she had none of that sleekness, gloss, and balance. She was like some awkward, small, nervous, loosely flapping bird he had no name for.

He had watched her before; he had watched her nearly every day. And nearly every day she lugged the large black case that, with its handles, zipper and clasps, looked like a regular suitcase flattened by a steamroller. Once, on a windy day, a gust skipped her off the curb and into the street as if it were a sail. He watched her fight her way back to the curb with it and watched her fight her way down the street with it.

But on most days, as she did this day, she walked straight down the sidewalk with her face cut straight into the wind. She glanced at the winos, glanced into the windows of Ma Barret's restaurant or the no-name secondhand store or the drug store where the dope fiends bought their crack pipes; she glanced at the whores at the corner of Broad and at the little kids dragging their books to school. Her wide eyes shot here and there, to the right and left, up into the windows of the second-floor apartments, down into the alleys and the doorways. But all the time her face pointed straight forward like the point of a plow.

She was part of what he watched every day, part of what he saw without seeming to look. He knew she watched him each day, ever since that day she saw him go off on that wino. She watched him with a nervous quick glance, as if she were afraid he might go off on her as well. *Prissy little prep,* he silently scoffed at her for such a face. Day after day, he pondered such labor by such a small person, by such a black-coat sparrow, a person of such little weight that she could be blown about by any little sailboat wind.

But he was sure she did not know that he watched her. He was sure she thought he gazed right past her.

A dope fiend all gone to bones and rags emerged from between two buildings and looked over with his scarecrow eyes. The dope fiend was careful not to look too long or too directly. He scanned the street and, as his eyes passed over the young man, raised his eyebrows slightly, almost imperceptibly. The man was wearing a jacket with arms too short by an inch. The cuffs of his jeans were ragged from catching under his heels. The young man smiled a little, but he did not move his eye from the tag on the tail of the dumpster. *Rag-head,* he muttered. *Dope-fiend fool.* By the series of nods and looks, the young man knew that the man had pawned his clothes. Or stolen a VCR. Or sold some blood. And now he had his money and was ready. But the young man remained still as stone, oblivious to the man who now sagged, leaned against the hood of a truck, and cast his craving eyes over the young man several more times, to implore him for a signal.

The girl came closer. Her eyes ran from the dope fiend, across to the young man, and back. His face curled up into just a touch of a sneer.

He continued to nod with the music wrapped around his skull. One nod was special, for the dope fiend waiting, and the dope fiend knew it. He looked all around him, pushed himself up off the hood of the truck, pumped swiftly down the street, and disappeared into an alley.

But the young man waited before he moved to follow the dope fiend to the alley. He continued to stare a moment more into the tag, and to nod in time with the heavy beat of the bass line.

The girl glanced again with her little quick glance. He raised his head back with a face of stone and nodded once more, just for her.

2

PHOTOGRAPHS:

One man stands talking to another on a sidewalk. The one to the left is older, forty or more. He wears a black coat belted at the waist. Mustache and goatee are trim, sharply honed. Brows are dark and sharp. He fists a cigarette in his right hand; smoke jets out the side of his mouth. He leans forward slightly; his eyes narrow to a cutting edge; they sharpen toward some point out in the street.

The other man is younger; he wears the thick coat stitched with a sports logo that teenagers and young men favor. And there is something about him, something respectful, tentative, almost bored, the look of a young man listening to an older man. A dark stocking cap is pulled down nearly to his eyes. His hands are in the pockets of his coat, and he leans back against the frame of a doorway. His eyes aim in the same direction as those of the man beside him, but where the older man's eyes are sharp and specific, the younger man's eyes are furrowed, evasive, withdrawn.

~

Another: The same man, same youth. The man points with the hand that holds the cigarette, and he speaks to someone out of the frame. His eyes maintain their sharply honed edge. But he smiles through the smoke that still flows from his mouth.

The young man has not moved from his place in the doorway. But his eyes have shifted. His face betrays no feeling; it is like a carved mask. But he watches the talking man carefully.

~

Another: The man stands with a third man now. Between them sits a washing machine, a large block of white that escapes from the picture as if in that portion the shades have been stripped away and we see only the bare white paper. The three stand in a wider frame; we see now the whole of the front of the building, and we see the front end of a car parked in the street. The men look to the right of the frame, where the tail of a pickup truck has entered.

The youngest man, still in place against the doorframe, looks out to the street. He has pulled himself bodily away from the action. It is no business of his. His eyes are tunnels, his face a mask.

~

Another: The young man has left his post at the doorway. He is frozen in the act of helping the third man to raise the washer to the bed of the pickup truck. There is no sign of strain in his face. Were his face not such a mask, we might expect to see pride in his face, he seems to lift so easily.

The man in the black coat watches the lifting from the side of the frame.

~

Last: There are just the two again, the younger man and the man in the black coat: they have returned to their stations at the front of the building.

The older man looks with approval toward the younger; we can tell this in the softening in his brow and the set of his eye. We can tell it in the way he taps the young man on the upper arm. He speaks, again with a mouth full of smoke. It is as if he says, *You're all right. I can hang with you.*

The young man does not break his mask-like stolidity. But almost: he seems almost to smile, almost to look aside toward the man.

ROGER Nolan watched the tall boy at his left push off from his station against the wall and step into the sea of traffic. Nolan was a trim man, pencil-thin. His shoulders, elbows, and knees seemed to have been folded into him and stored like the blades and implements of a complicated tool. Though his feet remained planted, he watched the boy so eagerly that he canted over at the trunk and stood angled like the hands of a clock at half past ten in the morning. A dark half dollar sagged beneath each eye, and a parenthetical groove lined each side of his mouth. He was very dark in the eye and brow, and very pale in the face and hands. There was a blue teardrop tattoo stitched at the temple corner of his left eye. His short hair bristled in the wind. He wore a heavy black leather coat, cinched at the waist with a belt of a type that had gone out of style some years ago but that still looked somehow very new.

A man stood to Roger's right. He noted the tall boy as well. "That boy best watch himself," he said. He was dressed in gray work clothes. A short, condensed, balding, bright-eyed man, a shrunken version of a man, smooth-faced, hard as a nut.

Roger cast a sour eye at the man, then looked back out to the street. The tall boy stood waiting. A bus, then a pickup truck, then a Mercedes passed before him, then he trotted across to the opposite curb.

"That boy," Roger said, "is gonna be just fine. That boy knows where he's going. And he don't take no shit."

The shrunken man followed the tall boy with a skeptical eye.

"Ain't nothing wrong with that boy," Roger said.

"I didn't say there was anything wrong with him. Just . . ."

"Young motherfucker got more move on him than a whole lot of these young boys."

"Looks like to me . . ."

"He's takin care of his granny that's sick. He looks out for his people."

". . . like he's got himself caught up in something . . ."

". . . and he don't be chasing pussy all up and down the street. He's about business."

". . . something like to tear his young ass up."

Each could see the boy standing on the sidewalk opposite, taking dollars one by one from a woman in a blue coat. In a moment, the woman stopped, turned up her palm, and waited. But the young man tapped his stack of dollars, raised his brows, and released on her a torrent of words which, at this distance, were lost in the noise of the traffic. The woman set one hand on her hip and argued back. There was a brief flurry of arms waved, fingers pointed, and shoulders shrugged, and the woman rolled her eyes, resigned from the argument, and drew from inside her blouse five more bills that she laid across the young man's open palm. In return, he pulled up a little plastic bag, tweezered out something very small, as if he were picking spice, and placed it in her hand.

Roger ran the sour eye over the man again. "So you want this space heater or don't you?"

They argued briefly over the price as the tall boy threaded his way back through the traffic.

Then Roger stood with an open palm as the man counted out bills. He said to the boy, "You reckon you can help this man get his space heater in the car?"

The tall boy nodded briefly and turned to the space heater. The man's trunk was open. Before the man could position himself to take one end, the boy had squared himself up to the space heater. He squatted down, enveloped it in his arms, rose with it, and placed it in the trunk as if placing a baby in a bassinet.

"It's pumping that iron," said Roger Nolan. "Know what I'm saying?" He said it very quickly: *Knowmsain?* "Young motherfucker can lift a cow."

"Well, I wish him luck," said the nut-hard man. "I wish him luck." He nodded to Roger and the tall boy. They watched him drive off with his heater.

"That old man's a trip," Roger said. "Motherfucker got something to say about everybody."

"He's all right," the boy said.

"Oh, he's all right," Roger said. "I don't say nothing bad about him. I give him that stove for less than what I got in it. He's all right with me. But he's like everybody else. He's got his good side and he's got his bad side. He ain't no different than anybody else."

The boy nodded.

"They all got a good side and they all got a bad side. That's why you got to watch."

The boy nodded again, and continued to nod, as if in time to music.

"'Cause no matter what's going down, it don't matter what, you got to watch so it don't turn on you. You see . . ."

The boy was nodding still, but he looked to where the man held out his hand.

"It's like this dollar bill."

He stretched out the wrinkles and held the dollar out, green side up. "It's got a light side." He turned it over. "It's got a dark side."

He turned the dollar over again, dark side and light side. He waited for the boy to see.

"You see it? One side's printed green, one side's printed black. Light side. Dark side. Every dollar that's made got it, dark side and light side. Life on one side and death on the other. And it's all one dollar. Knowmsain? Everybody wants that dollar. They think of all the good stuff that dollar's gonna get them. Big house. Big car. Women. Groceries. Rent. Something to keep the rain off your head. That's the bright side. But every dollar's got that dark side. Bright side. Dark side. The more money you got, the more dark you got. The more life, the more death. Knowmsain?"

The boy nodded.

"That's why I don't worry none about the money. You been where I been, you learn that. It ain't about the money."

The boy continued to nod.

"It ain't about the money."

The young man seemed to understand, for he tightened his lips and nodded more deeply. He seemed ready for more talk of light and dark, but Roger Nolan nodded toward a slight scrap of a boy on the opposite sidewalk. He asked, "Ain't that some kin of yours?"

The young man said nothing, so Roger said, "He's your cousin or something, ain't he?"

"He's a little buster," the young man said.

"A little buster?"

"He's a nosy little wet-nose punk."

"Whatever he is, he's coming this way."

The young man shifted his eyes, his only sign of impatience. Then he watched with Roger as the boy scanned the traffic for a break. He feinted a run several times, as if hoping to bluff one of the cars into stopping, but none would take his bluff. He had to wait.

"Little motherfucker's like to get himself killed," Roger said. The boy had gotten halfway across and was standing on the yellow line as contending lanes of traffic moved around him.

The young man seemed to steel up at the remark.

A break in the traffic freed the boy and he ran up to their curb. "Hey, wassup," the boy called to the young man.

The young man nodded, barely, in recognition.

"What's up, little man," said Roger.

The boy nodded to him and said to the young man, "Where's that two dollars you owe me?"

"I don't owe you no two dollars."

"Yeah you do. 'Cause you said, if I swept out Granny's hall . . ."

The young man pulled up a pad of bills from his pocket and peeled off two singles.

"How about five?"

"Two dollars, you sniffly little dusty-headed motherfucker." But he stripped off three more bills.

The boy took the bills and wadded them in his fist. He looked around as if ready to go.

Roger said, "Don't I know your momma?"

The young man's eyes shifted.

"I don't know." The small boy looked to his cousin who was looking out to the street.

"Her name Sylvia?"

The boy nodded.

"Tell her I got her a stove if she wants it."

"We got a stove already."

"Just tell her for me."

The boy nodded.

"She's good people, your momma."

The boy nodded again.

"She works pretty hard, don't she?"

"She's working right now."

"Does she treat you good?"

The boy shrugged. He nodded.

"What's up with that coat?"

The boy looked himself over. The seam was broken in the left shoulder and the zipper had ripped loose halfway up the front.

"That coat ain't gonna get you through no hard winter. Skinny little guy like you gonna freeze right up. You let me get you one of them big down coats like the players wear."

The boy's eyes widened. But he was unsure what to do. He looked to his cousin.

"He's all right," the young man said to Roger. "He don't need no coat."

"Well look at him," Roger said. "That thing's going all to rags on him."

"Buy him a new coat, it'll be a rag in a week."

"Man, that coat looks like it's been pecked over by the crows."

"He's all right, man."

"I just want to do him a favor 'cause I know his momma."

"He don't need no coat, man."

"But . . ."

"His family got his coat, man."

"Whatever." Roger had finished his cigarette and was lighting another. He leaned back against the window of the shop and watched the traffic.

The boy looked from one to the other.

"Go on, man," said the young man. "Get your hind end to school." It was already ten o'clock in the morning.

"I don't got school today. I got . . ."

"Get your lying ass to school before I beat you blue."

"Aw, man," the boy complained. But he left in the direction of the school.

The two men watched the boy until he turned at the corner, then they turned to watch the traffic.

"Think about that coat," the older man said. "I'll help you out on that coat if you want."

The young man nodded, and continued nodding, as if in time to music.

"MOM!"

Ann Taylor shut the car door and hit the keyless remote; the alarm twittered briefly. The car—a BMW—was new, and the sound of the built-in alarm each time she locked the door still made her jump. Both sounds, the boom of the door and the twitter of the alarm, echoed against the concrete walls of the parking garage, then lost themselves among the sounds of other cars cruising for space, other car doors slamming, and other alarms.

"I said, Bye, Mom!"

"Oh. Yes. Have a good day." They kissed briefly, and Amy smiled. They touched hands, then Amy turned and headed toward her separate exit.

Ann watched her daughter go, thinking, *When she's that friendly, she's up to something.* The girl struggled toward the exit door in her bulky black clothes, lugging that huge portfolio, weighted by that backpack stuffed with textbooks, passing one by one the gray pillars of the garage like stations of the cross.

I'll find out soon enough, she thought. It was time to worry about work. She dropped her keys into the depths of her bag and slung it to her shoulder. For a moment, the weight of it unbalanced her. The shoulder bag was loose and bulky and things were forever tumbling out, but she liked the look of it and she liked to have her hands free. She grabbed her attaché case off the garage floor and headed for the stairs.

She needed to move quickly. She had not had a cigarette since she left the house; she never smoked in the car with Amy, and normally she would light up as soon as she got out the door of the car. But today she was running late. She decided to grit it out until she got to her office. She gritted it out for a block and a half, then decided she was not so late after all and it would really be nice to have some caffeine.

She stopped in front of a coffee shop, dug in her purse, found the cigarettes, and lit up. She smoked it up as she waited in line, then, with her coffee in her free hand, stabbed out her cigarette on the sidewalk and walked the half block more to her building.

The guard in the lobby stood behind his wide counter with its shiny Formica surfaces. His arms were stretched wide and his hands gripped the corners of the counter like a preacher at his pulpit. "Good morning, Miss Taylor," he said in that country accent he could not quite cover up with the clipped professional script she was sure they taught him in security guard school. He nodded toward the sign-in book. No one ever got by without signing in. God only knew why; no one ever signed out.

"G'morning," she answered. Where was the pen? The counter was empty. Why couldn't he ever keep a pen ready?

"Here we are." He smiled and handed her a ballpoint. The top had been chewed; there was no cap. She took the unchewed portion in her fingers and signed.

The guard was a short block of a man who walked, when he left the back of the counter, with a limp that rocked him like a metronome. He had a little thin mustache and sideburns out of the early seventies which wouldn't have looked good even then. His shirt was starched so bright it hurt her eyes, but there was a hint of yellow at the cuffs and a half dozen threads were spinning loose at the collar.

"Have a good day," he told her.

She stepped onto the elevator and the door closed on her before she could reply. It was already crowded, and a lawyer, one she knew, had been holding the door open for her. He was one of a pair from her same floor. There were also a couple of the lawyers from the third floor (this building was thick with lawyers), the corporate headhunter from an office on the fifth, a pair of secretaries from wherever, and the bond market manager from the floor directly above hers.

"Is that your daughter I saw you with this morning?" someone asked.

"Hmmm?" It took her a moment to realize who was talking to her. The lawyers were staring straight at the elevator door. The secretaries were whispering to each other in the corner. The bond man, she saw, had edged closer. He was tall and had eyebrows that raised like toggle switches. He was leaning toward her. Not too close, but definitely leaning; one switch was raised.

How did he even know she had a daughter?

He anticipated her question. "She was carrying a portfolio?"

She nodded.

"And a big pack on her back?"

"And . . ."

"And wearing a big black coat."

She raised her own brow. That awful-looking thing. But Amy would wear no other. It was what all the art school kids were wearing.

"I see her coming out of the parking garage most mornings. I never realized until today she was connected to you."

"Yes, she's very connected."

"Does she catch a bus downtown?"

"Oh, no. She walks from the parking garage."

The elevator stopped for the third-floor lawyers. They nudged themselves closer to the door and, as it opened, stepped in lockstep into the hall. The headhunter shifted to the middle of the car. The secretaries, still in the corner, paused and looked around them.

"She walks? Is it far?"

"No. Just over in New Town." She realized that, as he had leaned slightly toward her, she had turned her shoulder a half turn in his direction. She looked at her watch and squared herself to the door.

He seemed to ponder this a moment, then he squared himself to the door as well. In silence, the elevator swept them to the fifth floor. The headhunter left and the bond man shifted a half-step back to take advantage of the space. The secretaries resumed their whispering as if they were high school girls.

"She seems like a nice kid," the bond man said.

"Yes," she replied. "I suppose she is."

Four more floors and she was ready to get off. He stepped aside with a nod and a flip of the toggles of his brows.

At the office door, Rebecca the receptionist, was rearranging her station and grinding up a fresh stick of gum. Rebecca tidied her desk every evening before she left and rearranged her family pictures every morning when she came in. The children, her husband, and even the family dog smiled out from ceramic frames, arranged in a row at the side of her desk as if they had all just sat down to TV.

"Hey," Rebecca called. "Don't try to sneak past here. You've already got a couple messages."

Ann set down her attaché, scooped up the messages, and looked them over. "Who are these people who start work so early?"

"It may be that somebody else starts . . ."

"I know. I know." It was already eight forty.

Ann took a quick glance to the floor-to-ceiling picture window that took up one whole wall of the reception area. As she feared, a man stood facing it, staring out at the city below. He was dressed in a gray suit and wore a gray hat. He stood with his feet squared and his hands behind his back; he had an overcoat hooked onto one arm and a satchel leaned against one leg. An out-of-town client, but no client of hers and really none of her business. But he bothered her anyway, framed against this solid wall of window and, by the motion of his head, taking in every inch of New Town. The view fascinated newcomers to the office. But it was only New Town, so she hated it. She had never liked this office and had always wished the company had taken a south-side instead of a north-side view. They were on the ninth floor, after all, so if they were going to pay the money they ought to have gotten a decent view. But it was not her decision. She had not even been asked. A south-side view would have been much nicer for clients. The southern skyline was big and dynamic, even inspirational, crowded with Manhattan-like towers, a landscape of upswept glass and concrete and steel that conveyed power and vision. People looking at such a view would have become more energized, more focused.

But to the north there was nothing like that at all. Developers liked to prattle about New Town's historical architecture, but from here she could only see a jumble of little red-brick apartment buildings and narrow, confusing streets. Occasionally a warehouse or an old factory building stuck out among them. Thorny church spires and power lines and billboards advertising malt liquor and little barren lots where buildings had been pulled down and filled with junked cars and broad-leafed, jungle-looking trees all created a picture that was busy, intricate, and baffling. Among them was the trendy Broad Street stretch of coffeehouses and galleries and nightspots, but she could not have told where. They were all to her like pebbles on a beach.

"Rebecca, will you . . ." She was about to ask her to do something to distract the client from the window. Offer him coffee, give him a donut, whatever. Whenever waiting clients began to stare for long out that window, they would become moodier and more withdrawn, or even a little dazed. She could get no sense out of them. So she would do whatever she could to draw them away: offer them cappuccino or suggest they look over the mockups. She never left them by that window if she could help it.

"Rebecca . . ." she started again.

But she was not able to complete her sentence. Richard, the lab tech, came up with a handful of proofs. "Ann. Can you give these a quick look for me? We have to get . . ."

"Richard, can this wait?"

Rebecca warned, "Careful, Richard. She hasn't had her cigarette."

"You hush."

"We have to get the finished copy to McAlister's by two o'clock. We're already . . ."

She snatched the stack of proofs from him. A little more abruptly than she wanted. She did not want to be rude. He was trying, really. But still. Like this, before she had even time to get her attaché off her shoulder or get a cup of coffee. Or light a cigarette.

"Look," she said. She tapped the corners of the first proof. "See this border? If you let it flare like that, it'll spike out like a barb-wire fence when it's printed."

He nodded.

"It's the same with every one of them."

"I can play with it," he said. "I think I can get it right."

She handed him the stack. "It cannot," she paused for emphasis, "go out like that."

Richard nodded and headed off to the lab.

"I know what you're going to say." Rebecca handed her another message.

She glanced at it and stuffed it into the pocket of her jacket. "What am I going to say?"

"That you didn't have to put up with that sort of thing in New York and just because we're in the Midwest doesn't mean we have to go second-rate and why can't they get it right the first time?"

"Well, at least they could get the basics right."

She looked back to the window and saw that a marketing person had come up from the back and was pumping the man's hand and making ready to drag him back to an office.

Relieved, she looked down to check the new message as the marketing person marched the gray-suit man to the back. For just a moment, as they passed, she felt something like a chill, so she looked up. His face was obscured by the brim of the hat, but it was obvious he was staring right at her as he followed the marketing person. Just for a moment, but it was so clear that Rebecca said, "They're all wired the same, aren't they?"

With a nod, she went back to her office to settle in. She set down her attaché, pulled her planner from it, and set it out with her stack of messages as if dealing out a game of solitaire. Then she drew a pack from her jacket pocket, ripped off the cellophane, tore back the foil, and tapped out a cigarette. Under a blue veil of smoke, she set to work.

AMY Taylor's mother had worked for years as a fashion model in New York and still had that New York model elegance and control. She still looked, at times, as if she had stepped off the cover of a magazine. She still seemed, at times, to be posing. She had long, slender legs and arms that she settled into odd positions like those of a store window mannequin—positions, Amy assumed, her mother had learned in New York and which, though impossible to others, were now natural to her. She had a model's narrow, unreadable face. Her wide-set eyes seemed to focus on nothing at all, though Amy knew that they saw nearly everything. Her penciled eyebrows were her punctuation, capable of forming, together or one at a time, brackets or daggers or question marks made of fine-spun steel. She smoked cigarettes one after another like bullets whenever she was busy, and long, slow cigarettes whenever she was thinking. When she was discussing a thing and thinking it through, her willowy, long-fingered hands turned over cigarettes as if they were well-cut jewels. She drew slowly on her thoroughly examined cigarette between question and answer as if she were deep in thought, as if the cigarette were a crystal.

So, when Amy brought up the question after supper, her mother leaned back against the chair, pulled up a cigarette from a new pack, then asked, "Now what's this plan you have?" Amy was sure she would have to listen to an hour of lectures and questions, sure that her mother would sigh and ponder and say, "I have to think this over." She would never get a clear yes; she would never get a clear no. And it would die right there on the living room floor. But she decided she would try. She told her mother that she had been recommended for the project by her art teacher at school. She had covered herself by asking the teacher if she could get class credit for helping with the printing and arrangement of the works for an exhibition. Her teacher even knew of the photographer and his work and thought it was a fine idea. "You'll learn a lot," she had said. Amy told her mother that, and a number of other things besides.

Amy was not sure whether her mother bought the story or not, for she immediately leaned back with her cigarette and began to ponder. She asked, "Does he plan to take pictures of you?"

"It's not a job as a model. I'll be an assistant. The pictures are already . . ." She had explained this, but knew that her mother would ignore her.

"So what does he . . ."

"He's been given a retrospective. His first real show. He's been taking pictures for years and now he's finally getting, like, recognition."

"And what sort of pictures has he taken?"

She had already explained this as well, but knew her mother was probing for more.

"Social issues, mostly. Like I said." Her mother did not appear to take note of the dig, *like I said.* "Like, people being evicted. And there's a few, just scenes of people and places and stuff."

"And he . . ."

"He did a thing on, like, farmworkers, and he's done strikes and homeless people before it was, like, the thing to do, and he's done ecology and street scenes and all kinds of stuff."

"No studio work?"

"I didn't see any."

"Personal things?"

"What do you mean?"

"Say, portraits. Explorations of an individual? Abstracts?" Her mother rolled her cigarette over in her fingers.

"I don't think so."

Her mother eyed the smoking ruby at the tip. "Because it sounds as if he's just a journalist."

So what if he is? she wanted to say. Instead, she said, "That's not all." She thought of the photos of the woman on the street.

Her mother drew deep and slow on her cigarette. Her quizzical eye and wire-thin eyebrow hooked toward her.

"There was some stuff I really liked. But I don't think they'll turn up in the show."

"Why not?"

"I don't know. He's really touchy about them."

"Touchy?" She tapped her cigarette on the ashtray and shot the eye at her.

I should never have said that. There was no hope of turning away her mother now.

"He got sort of mad when I talked about it."

"Well, are they something to be embarrassed about?"

"No. They're really powerful. Like, they're . . ."

"Powerful?"

"Yeah. Out of all the work I saw . . ."

"I thought you just met this person?"

"I did. I mean, I looked around some . . ."

"Go on."

She knew, when her mother said, *Go on* and drew slowly on her new-lit cigarette and arched, ever so slightly, her left eyebrow, that her mother was onto something, and that she had filed away some slip of incriminating information.

"Go on," she said again.

"Go on with what?" She had been thrown off.

"Go on with what was so good about those photographs?"

"Well, they . . . I don't know . . . *Mom.*"

The plea was not enough. It never was. The eyebrow and the cigarette arched and rolled. Amy struggled and smoldered, thinking, *This isn't even worth it.* But she was now too deep to back out.

Go on, her mother nodded through her smoke.

"Well, you'd have to see them."

"But from what you're saying, that doesn't sound possible." She let the words hang in the smoke around her, then flicked an ash and said, "I'm just trying to point out to you that if this person doesn't even want anyone to see his best work, there's something very strange about him. Or so it seems to me."

She drew deeply one more time and stubbed out cigarette and conversation. "I'll have to think about this," she said.

~

Amy knew that *I'll have to think about this* meant she would never bring it up again. Amy did not want to wait for her mother to think, and she did not want to be denied. She scratched a practiced imitation of her mother's signature onto the contract that her teacher had drawn up.

So every hour she spent in the studio was stolen.

AT a certain corner along Amy Taylor's path to school, a group of men gathered every day to pool their money and share their wine. In the warmth of the sun, watchful of police cruisers, they stood in clusters on the sidewalks or sat with their bottles wrapped in paper bags on the gloomy granite steps of the buildings where they lived. In other weathers, they huddled together against wind or cold or curious eyes. There were seven that Amy came to know by sight, men of mixed and largely unidentifiable races and accents, with complexions that ranged from the palest of pink and into a sable gloss like that of an old-style telephone, with faces arranged in a variety of rounds and angles and slopes and sharpnesses, supported by a range of heights and variants of backs straight and stooped, all of which seemed to be shared among them like the bottles, so that she could never be sure which complexion or bend of back belonged to which angle of nose or which shock of hair but only knew that each belonged to this ageless council of mismatched, shrunken, and battered men. Amy thought it odd that they should laugh as much as they did. They had so little to laugh about, with their secondhand coats and their handout sandwiches. But they did laugh—hard, raw laughter that seemed at times to stem from sheer joy and at others to shiver with malice.

"Hey there, little sister," one might call as she passed. "Come here a minute. Tell me a little something." But if one stepped toward her or reached out a hand to her shoulder, the others would grab him back; they would push down the arm and drag him away. She crossed the street each time she saw them, and she watched them carefully from the corners of her eyes as she passed.

She never saw a woman with them and had decided that she never would. But one day, a week after she had started at the studio, she heard from the corner a woman's gravelly laughter. She slowed—not enough that anyone would know but so that she could watch more carefully—and was stopped as suddenly as if she had hit a stone wall.

Directly across the street stood the woman from the photographs, the one in the peacoat.

It had to be. Unmistakable.

The woman stood with all seven winos in a huddle, and even from across the street Amy recognized that face, that smile. It was the same face she had studied in the prints, battered some by years and broken in the veins across the cheeks. She could not mistake that face of the woman in the nun-like peacoat, the face that, in the photos, squinted girl-like into the bone-colored western sun, that was now squinting girl-like into the midwestern morning light.

Amy stood stone-still on the sidewalk and stared.

In spite of an early fall snap in the air, the woman wore no coat, only a sweatshirt and plaid slacks that left her ankles bare. She was smiling again, as in the photos. Each time her smile widened, her eyes disappeared into the recesses of her cheekbones like birds into a cave.

The woman leaned against a wall as she and the men laughed together, murmured in a huddle, laughed again, then broke apart.

Amy knew she risked being late for homeroom. But she wanted to see. So that she could watch without seeming to watch, she leaned back against a utility pole and pretended to look in her backpack for something like a bus schedule. It was unnecessary, for none of them bothered to look back at her once they noticed she was watching. They were wrapped up in their laughter.

She could not tell what was their secret until the three men laughed out into the street, shouted, and spun in winish circles, singing, pointing their hands back to where the woman from the photographs stood against her wall, laughing, her face asquint into the sun with her country-girl smile.

When the men moved away from the wall where the laughter had pinned her, the girl could see what had caused the last burst of laughter. The woman had wet herself, or seemed to. Perhaps it was just a spill of wine. But a wet patch made an embarrassing, black, circular flower against her slacks.

The woman and the men all, in that moment, glanced over to where Amy stood.

Omigod, she thought, and turned her eyes away. Digging into her book bag, she could feel their silent eyes on her for a full discernible moment. Then they laughed again, all together, and shambled together toward the alley and were swallowed into the sea of their laughter.

~

Amy went back to the studio that afternoon as soon as she could get free from class, went straight to the file of photos, and flipped through them until she found the photographs of the woman. She was tucked in among the street scenes, demonstrations, industrial landscapes, family portraits, and documentaries: among these, and in no particular order, the black bell, sea light, wounded wing, bottle like a pistol.

The woman was the same woman, but not the same. The girl felt herself take a turn.

~

Something had broken loose in her the day she first saw the photographs of the woman. The prints in the file were not in good shape. Many had been wrinkled or cracked. One was stamped with the print of a shoe. But there was a power and an awfulness to those images that excited her like nothing else had ever excited her. She had barely been able to hold still the afternoon she saw them; she had barely been able to face going back to her mother's intricately laid-out and untouchable home. She was struck by the starkness, the graininess, the white and black, the spine and bone of the photos. What did they mean? What story did they tell? Why did they pull on her so strongly?

She had not been able to talk to anyone about them that day. Paul, the photographer, was too busy and too grim. And it was late before she got back home. No one at school, she was sure, would even understand. So she slept on her excitement and waited for the chance to talk after school with Paul.

But Paul had no interest in talking about these pictures at all. "That's some old stuff," he grumbled.

"But they're good," she said. "They're really great. I mean . . ." He would have let her finish. It seemed he wanted to hear what she said. But she had run out of words that would have stood up to the pained, off-putting look that had crossed his face. She tried again, on another tack. "You really ought to put them in your exhibit. I think they're as good as anything else you've done. They're as good as anything I've ever seen. I mean . . ."

"That's not what I want to focus on now," he said abruptly.

She wanted one more chance to persuade him. "But these are the really great ones. These are . . ."

"I don't even have the negatives," he said. "They're long gone. I don't even have a decent print to work with." He turned and stalked into the darkroom and began to loudly shuffle boxes.

She dropped it for the time, but she did not forget the pictures. At odd moments, when she thought he would not notice, she went back to that file and studied them again.

~

Two weeks later and first thing in the morning, as she walked half-asleep to school, she saw the woman on the street. Later she would remember her rush of excitement, as if she had come face to face with someone famous.

But what broke in her later (and began the moment the laughing of the winos started) broke more slowly and continued to break minute by minute for hours and days, so strange and sad and so early in the morning were that shared bottle of cheap wine, that black flower of urine, that mockery and laughter.

3

PHOTOGRAPHS:

A broad, furrowed Salinas Valley field. These are black-and-white photographs; the leafy green lines of the planted furrows are gray. Perfectly parallel, the leafy gray lines alternate with black. The lines are ruler-straight; the flatness of the land is nearly geometric. In the distance, as the lines converge, small figures scatter over the furrows; they stand or bend over their work. Beyond the convergence of the furrows, at a great distance, dappled skies, dappled hills.

~

The blade of a hoe. It rests, as after a long day, along with other tools on the bed of a truck. Clots of dirt are clustered in the joint where the blade is riveted to the gooseneck that connects the blade to its handle and in the borders of the rivets. But the blade itself is clean, honed silver-sharp as the blade of a knife. Light is sucked down into various small pits in the surface of the blade; small sabers of light form across the blade where the hone has caressed it.

~

Farmworkers in a field. They are bowed over their work among the furrows. Large baskets in the furrows. We cannot see the faces of the workers; we cannot tell if they are men or women. They are arms and legs and backs and baskets.

~

A single worker. He is standing at the edge of a field; a dirt lane crosses behind him; the field extends out before. His hands are at his sides and his back is to the camera. The lane is cut and rutted with tractor tracks; water pulls light into one of the rutted tracks. The field that extends out before him stretches endless as the sea.

~

A farmworker stands in a field. Behind him extend long rows of lettuce heads and, in the background, hills in their dusty distance. He is stocky, his legs slightly bowed. His blue jeans are shiny at the knees; he wears a belt buckle with a union logo. We note his bucket-solid torso and the western styling of his chambray shirt. His sleeves are rolled up to expose his forearms. The arms are so solidly muscled that the veins stand out; each carries its own sliver of shadow. His hands are thick with muscle and callused; they fold around the top of a hoe. His white straw cowboy hat, creased for style and for protection from the sun, is split at the peak from wear. All of this is clear and detailed.

But not his face.

The face of the man is hidden within the shadow of his wide-brim hat.

The man's body is tired; he leans into the hoe for support. But still his body holds power and tension. His body is patient with the camera, but tense and potent, weighted and compact as a battery. The rows of lettuce stretch out behind him, and if he waits too long to return to his labor, the man knows the heat of his muscles will begin to leave him; they will stiffen; they will rebel all the more when he returns to his row.

But he has paused; he seems to trust the camera.

UNDER the red light of the darkroom, Paul was showing Amy how to burn in an image. A heap of cast-off prints filled and overflowed the trash can. Other attempts to capture the image were pinned to the wall with their exposure times marked at each gradation.

The first image had been hopelessly obscure; the man and the fields behind him had seemed wrapped up in gloom. "We missed him," Paul said. "But he's in there. I know how to find him." Gradually, he had adjusted the timing of the exposure and had played with his hands around a scrap of cardboard over the image cast down by the enlarger until the form of the man in the lettuce rows took shape. But it was still wrong. The man stood there, a perfect strength-of-labor image. But he had no face. In each image they had cast, his face was still hidden in the slant shadow of his hat. She thought Paul could do no more.

Besides, it would soon be time for her to go. She had not wanted to break his concentration by going out to check the time, but she had become bored with running one sheet after another into the developer bath. "It's too bad," she said. "That would have been a good shot."

He said nothing. He reached to start the timer, and again the image fell from the enlarger onto a new sheet of paper. Checking his calculations, he repeated the steps that had gotten him the image with the shadowed face. Finished, he reset the timer again, but this time he covered all of the image with his arms, then folded his hands to allow only a beam of light the size of a quarter to fall on the page. He moved the coin of light around slightly, careful to keep the center of the image always in the light, for the full minute the timer would allow.

When the light clicked off, he handed her the paper. "Let's see who we've got."

She placed the paper in the stop bath, rocked the basin to agitate the chemicals, then flipped it over.

This was the amazing moment. She loved to watch it every time. It was this miracle, this blank snowfield that filled suddenly with faces or front porches or buses or factory gates. Each time, it was as if she had just opened her eyes, as if, each time, she experienced the miracle of sight to the blind, in which snow-blank paper enlivens, and the figures of yesterday afternoon or of fifteen years ago appear like a visit from family or like a tug of guilt. And now, there, suddenly on the blank page: the long rows and distant hills, the tired electric body, the logo at the belt, the broken hat, and, as if he had just stepped out of shadow, the lean jaw and skeptical eyes of the man.

"Wow," she said. "Awesome." She looked up to see if Paul was as excited as she was. But he had turned and was reaching for a broom. So, without saying more, she moved the man to the stop bath and then to the fixer while Paul swept up the scraps around the room.

FINALLY, after much dodging and burning and much wasted paper, he had gotten the print he wanted. It was a waitress he had known in California, staring at him square-jawed and narrow-eyed. Her brows had been plucked narrow as the blade of a penknife, and he wanted that detail as much as the woman had wanted it for herself. But in print after print the brows had escaped him. Either they faded away or they grew out thick and woolen. So he dodged light and burned paper, and spent light and paper for one hour, then another. Then, finally, he had those plucked and penciled brows; he had the precise bar of her eyeliner and the shadow of her mascara. He had every thin hair that crossed her jaw line. She was, for him, an icon of defiant beauty, Venus of the griddle, square of jaw, shoulder, midriff, hands; there was nothing soft about her, yet she was so solidly herself that he felt such a harmony in her that he felt her as he would a stave of music. She neither invited nor teased; she set her distance. She had her business to take care of, thank you. So he hung the print to dry and started the next.

Again, the same process. He had to focus on the little frame of light under the enlarger, then on the parts. Over and over, until each element was right. So much wasted paper, so much lost time, such a delirium of concentration that when he finally emerged into the studio, he was dazed with all-around light. He was still dazed when the girl hit the door, crossed the studio without a word, headed straight for the filing cabinet, jerked open a drawer, and called out, "I saw her today."

"Saw who?"

She was nodding into the files, flipping through the prints.

"This woman in the peacoat."

This girl had done good work in the two weeks since she started helping him out. This was his first exhibit that was not in the corner of a bookstore or a coffeehouse, his first recognition outside the magazines, his first chance to show what he had been doing all these years. But he had not realized how much work it would be. He needed help if he was to make it by deadline. So when she showed up with this idea of working for school credit, he thought nervously for a minute, for he had never had anyone help him before and distrusted what having a helper might do to his thinking. He figured that if he ignored her hard enough she might get the idea and not come back. But she had come back. She had come back every day and even on the weekends. And she worked hard and well, so he was glad of it. But she could be strange. Kids could be strange. People in general could be strange. So it came as no surprise that she would be strange at times.

~

"There's a lot of people in that file."

"This one," she said. She held up a print that looked like a crow in the rain. "The one I talked about before," she said. "The one in the peacoat. There's about a jillion of her."

Not a jillion. Maybe three dozen. And no, they had never been published. And no, he had never tried. And no, he had no plans to do it.

~

On the afternoon when she first found the photographs of the woman, she had asked him, "Wow, when did you do these?"

"Years ago," he said. He spoke slowly and grimly, as if the words came out with an effort, as if he were shoving something away with the words.

"Where?"

He looked shifty for a moment before he answered. "San Francisco."

"Wow," she said. "Back in the day. They're awesome, man. They're, like, the best pictures I've ever seen, anywhere."

He nodded as she talked, and smiled a little, but it was a very little smile and it was not a smile that he seemed to feel. His face became an unreadable mask with that little smile painted across it. He nodded as if moderately interested, but she could tell that was not real either. They talked for a short time longer about the pictures. But she could tell by the way his eyes retreated that something had retreated within him.

"Anyway," she said. "I just now saw her. Just, like, around the corner almost."

"It's not her."

"Yes it is. I saw her."

He shook his head. "That was a long time ago. And half a continent away."

"But it is her. I swear it."

"I don't think so."

"Why shouldn't she be here as well as anyplace else?"

He shrugged.

"Really, she could be here. Strange stuff happens."

He leaned into his print, shifted it, and seemed to get it where he wanted it. "Was she drinking?"

She nodded. "I think so."

He pondered this a moment, then shook his head. "There's thirty years between those pictures and whoever you saw on the street. There's a lot of damage done on those streets."

She waved another print at him. "I've looked at these pictures every day for two weeks. There's no other face like it."

He looked at her very sharp, as if what she had just said had offended him. Then he looked back to his print. "The street does that. They all have that look."

She went silent. She was absolutely and radiantly sure. *What is the deal with him?* she thought. *Why is he so mad?*

His face, which seemed to have tensed with skepticism moments before, now settled, like that of a sleeper. He asked, without raising his eyes from the print, "Who was she with?"

"It was, like, a bunch of winos."

The stone of his face broke for a moment. "Same old same old," he said, and turned away. "If that's her," he said, "which it isn't. Either she's drunk herself to death or she sobered up and married a dentist."

More curious now than before, she followed him to the darkroom, where he began to shuffle boxes of paper and bottles of chemical.

"So she's an alcoholic?"

"It isn't her."

"Because if she is, then that just shows you it was her, 'cause . . ."

"It wasn't her."

"So tell me," she said. She felt a little surge of power she had not felt before. He was uncomfortable with this conversation. It showed in the way he stared up into the shelves above the sink, in the way he peered at the labels. It showed in the way his hand hesitantly stretched as if to grab something. It was clear he only wanted to appear to have a project. She liked the impact her question had on him and the edge it had put on him. She was surprised by how much she enjoyed that small power.

"What do you want me to tell you?"

"Who is she?"

"What do you mean, who is she?"

"You could start with her name."

"Her name," he nodded to the photograph in her hand, "is Jenny." He continued to pull down small cartons and to search them, one after another.

"Jenny?"

"So what else do you want to know?"

"Who is she?"

"I don't know who she is."

"You know her name. You took her picture."

"You're really into this, aren't you?"

"I'm curious. I mean, it's wild. The pictures are so awesomely good. There's a lot of them. You obviously spent some time with her. And now she shows up, just a few streets from here. So how do you explain that if you don't know her?"

"I don't explain anything. I don't even know if it's her."

"But it's not like I'm accusing you of murder."

"So you could just drop it."

"I'm only asking. Who is she?"

"She's what you see on the streets. She's what you see in the prints."

"Come on."

He had given up on the cartons. He held both hands gripped on the edge of the sink as if it were the rail of a ship. "I could tell you a lot more about her," he said. "And some of it might even be true. But all I know is what's in the prints."

There was a voice inside her that said, *You better drop it.* Instead, she followed another impulse and asked again, "But you must have known how she got from wherever that place is . . ."

"San Francisco."

"From San Francisco to here. So . . ."

"I don't have a clue as to how she could have gotten here. I don't have a clue if that's her. I don't have a clue if she's even alive. She's just someone I took some pictures of a long time ago. So look." His voice was so calm it embarrassed her. "We're just people working together on a project. I don't owe you intimate details from my personal life. So I don't mean to be rude, but we're going to close this little conversation."

"Okay," she said. Then, feeling defeated, "I hear what you're saying."

~

All that next day, Amy continued to feel defeated and dejected. She thought for a moment she should quit. She was barely able to drag herself in to face him; she was embarrassed to think she might have offended him. After all, people don't just talk out their whole lives to people they have barely met. Even people who are close hide huge sections of their lives from one another. She should know.

Great swathes of her own life were wrapped in secrets, vagueness, allusion. Amy knew that her mother had brought her back from New York City when she was small, too small to have a memory of the city and where they lived within it, too small to know what could have happened to her mother there, too small to know her father, who was now (she knew from bits of overheard conversation), at this moment, somewhere on the road doing small-city one-night stands with his band.

Whenever she asked about her father, all she got were hints and evasions. All she got were her mother's vague statements ("He's not a person you can really get to know"). All she got were the movements of her mother's hands to select a cigarette, tap it on the side of the pack, light it, inhale on it, and flick off the ash of it with a single tap like the period at the end of a sentence.

Amy had long ago stopped asking.

~

A memory: from when she was small:

She knew the phone call was from her father. She did not hear her mother speak his name, but she knew from the way her mother's face resettled itself after the word *Hello,* the way her features hardened, the way her mother nodded so sharply, like someone striking a flint with steel. She did not remember what sort of small talk went on for the first several minutes, but she knew by the nervous way her mother fumbled through her purse with the phone clamped between her shoulder and her ear. She knew by the way her mother struck, struck, struck at her lighter. She knew by the way her mother used the (finally) lit cigarette like a lance, by the way she thrust the tip of it into the air and slashed it toward the ashtray, by the way she swept a cutlass of smoke through the air. She knew by the way her mother paced back and forth through the kitchen that was so cluttered and comfortable in the days before they could afford the cleaning lady and the trim Spartan furniture that now pinned down each room.

Up and down, across the kitchen, through the little hall that was no bigger than a closet, into the living room a half dozen paces. Then back. As far as the phone cord would allow her.

Amy, playing in the living room so that her mother passed her on each round, talked loudly to her dolls so she could pretend not to be listening. But she heard, through her own loud chatter, every word her mother said.

"So you're in town, and . . ."

She strained to hear her father's voice, but her mother had cupped the phone closely to her ear. She heard no word: she heard only a tone, a rhythm, a few loose syllables.

"So you want to . . ."

"You want to see her?"

At this, her mother broke stride and turned suddenly back into the kitchen so that Amy would not hear (though she continued to hear, even through her dolltalk, every word of her mother and, more muted, the tone and rhythm of that stranger, her father).

"Don't you think it's a little . . ."

"A little abrupt . . ."

Abrupt. She did not know what the word meant then, but she could tell it broke something loose for her mother.

"Yes, abrupt. Like five years and no contact at all, not even a birthday card or a dollar. And all of a sudden you want to play . . ."

"Right. And now you want to play Nice Daddy, just because you've got a gig in some sleazy bar in Clifton . . ."

There was a pause.

"Okay. Okay. So it's not a sleazy bar. I'm real glad to know you've got a good gig. Yes. I'm glad to know that."

Her mother emphatically stubbed out her cigarette, then picked up her pack and tapped out a new one.

"But I don't see how that changes anything . . ."

"Right. I don't see how it changes a thing. In fact, I think it makes it even worse. If you're playing concert gigs, you must be getting decent money. So you could send a buck or two every now and then."

Her mother had achieved some control by now. The angry energy ran off her in smooth, masterful lines. She smoked her cigarette slowly and tapped the ashtray firmly.

"What can you do to prove yourself?" She snorted.

"Well . . ."

"You could show some commitment for starters."

"Yes, commitment . . ."

"What the . . . ? What do you think it means? It means a lot of things you never learned back in New York. It means you could have been doing something other than leaving me stranded with a kid while you ran after groupies . . ."

Stranded. Her mother stranded with a kid. She, and her mother, stranded. Abandoned. Desolate. Stranded. The word stuck with her like no other. She built a picture in her mind and came back to it again and again. In that picture, her mother was an island castaway leaning at the water's edge, her hands shading her eyes, scanning the sea for ships.

And in that picture she herself was always ten paces behind. Under a little tent. Or sitting small-shouldered and alone on a driftwood log.

~

When she was very small, she had been happy to wear the clothes her mother bought her for school, the nice clothes to play in, and the special dresses her mother bought her for special days. New, they had a stiffness and a shine, a brightness, as if they had just been pulled from the pages of a glossy magazine.

She liked them too because she knew it pleased her mother to see her in them. She would show her pleasure with an elaborate and professional inspection, not just as a mother who would always want her daughter to look good, but objectively, like a designer or an editor. Her mother would reach out to adjust a collar or a belt, would tweak her pleats just so, then stand straight, place her hands on her hips, and run her eyes up and down and over her edges.

And as soon as she had spun herself around like a world, her mother would nod and smile. "Very good," her mother would say. "Very nice."

It pleased her to please her mother like that.

She pleased her mother often and she pleased her well. She got good grades. She went to parties with the nicest children. She kept her room neat and rarely disobeyed. She would never have thought there was any other way to be, but for the edginess she heard in her mother's voice on the day her father called. She knew from that edginess, from that failure of her mother's crisp tone, that her father was a power. For nothing else had so shaken her mother. Nothing else had put a quaver in her voice or had challenged the power of her gestures. She had been told for years (and with half a heart believed it) that her father was irresponsible and uncaring, that he was the cause of her feeling empty and alone, that he had chosen other lives over her own. But she wanted to see that power again. She wanted to know what her father's power was made of. And a desire came up in her, sudden and irrational and wholly without precedent or history: she wanted a power like that. She wanted to be able to put that quaver in her mother's voice. She wanted to learn how her father could do that with nothing more than a phone call.

But her father was untouchably and perpetually on the road, sharing his power with strangers. She never overheard another phone call. She never saw her mother shaken like that again. So for a long time her desire for a power like that disappeared. It crawled up into the cliffs and slept like a bear.

~

There were moments she felt hollow and terrified.

There were whole days and sometimes weeks when she felt as if she were nothing but a tinted shell and that the outfit that she wore that day—with its crisp color and its just-off-the-hanger smell—was her entire self. She was a smile to front it and a rack to hold it and nothing more. She imagined escaping like a vapor from within the dress and that the dress, with its starch and its crisp outline, would continue walking, standing, doing its homework. She would float above it all like smoke.

And not a soul would notice.

~

She could not tell when she changed. When it was no longer enough to follow her mother's desires while she felt like smoke in a chimney of starch. She knew it was not a sudden thing; she knew it had been a yearslong, gradual change and that only her awareness of it had been sudden. But what marked the change and what made it feel so sudden and so much like a deluge of transformation was the rage with which she began to press against her mother's power.

Suddenly, at fourteen, she felt anger surging from the center of her belly out to the tips of her fingers. When she first felt it, she thought she might end up breaking furniture or smashing windows. But the anger was silent as a cat and willing to wait. It purred through school and through visits to the houses of friends. It licked its fur and stretched its muscles and gathered strength. And no one but her mother ever knew of it, for no one but her mother ever saw it pounce.

~

The first flash: Suddenly, and for no good reason, she hated the clothing her mother liked.

One day she could wear an outfit her mother bought her. The next day she could not. It was as sudden and simple as that.

"It's too preppy," she spat. She did not recall even having the thought before she spoke, but once she said the words, she had become utterly convinced. The clothes had gone totally over. The party dress was laid out on the bed like Peter Pan's shadow. They had picked it out together from a shop downtown, and she had liked it then. But suddenly, as if someone had switched dresses (or as if she herself were the changeling), she saw how tacky and childish it was, with its white bodice shiny with starch. It looked like funeral clothing. It looked like something someone would wear to an office.

She had not thought she was picking a fight when she spat out the words, but she felt a thrill when her mother drew back. She knew that, with that one sentence, something had changed, and in that moment she felt something like elation and something like terror. "Pardon me?" her mother said. She realized her mother had heard, but needed that moment to gather force. Uneasy, she braced herself.

Her mother shook her head as if she still wanted to pretend she hadn't heard, then leaned forward to hear it again.

She mustered courage and defiance. "I said it's . . . preppy." She wanted to say *too damn preppy.* She wanted a word with more force. She wanted a word that would sting and make her mother jump back. She wanted to say it with a sneer. With a flounce. With a curl of the lip as she shook the dress as if it were a stubborn child and tossed it back onto the bed.

Later she would realize that the moment in which her mother drew back, that moment in which she shook her mother's power, was to be the only victory possible to her at that time. And later she would realize that, to win, she would have to fight in a totally different way. But at that moment, the only weapons she had were insult and rage which, as weapons, were useless and trivial against her mother's renewed composure.

Like her father, she could shake, but not shatter, her mother's power.

~

"So what are you going to wear to the party?" Her mother asked smoothly.

"It's a stupid party; I don't even want to go."

Her mother had by this time brought her cigarette slowly to her lips. She drew on it slowly and drew on it deeply so that the coal flared at the end of it. She leaned back against the bedroom wall with one arm across her chest and the other holding up the cigarette. "So where will you stay if you don't go to the party?"

"Mother! I'm fourteen! I don't need a babysitter. I'm able to stay home on my own. I've done it before."

She expected her mother to make a huge argument. She expected to hear about her mother's worries and her mother's concern for what she would do at home alone or what people at the party would think. Instead, a strange serenity came over her mother.

"Well," her mother said, "if that's what you'd rather do . . ." She tapped at an ashtray and left the room.

So Amy stayed at home and stormed within. She stayed at home and fretted. She stayed at home and felt her belly tighten as if she had been kicked.

~

She reasoned: Everyone fights her own mother. She thought all her friends' mothers were nice, but each of her friends hated and fought her own mother. Each of them had the same storm within her. Each of them flashed with the same adolescent lightning. "You never let me do anything," they all cried. "You're always telling me what to do." Each of them felt her own mother was possessed of a unique hunger for absolute power, aimed solely toward her.

So she thought it only natural that she should hate her own, that she should fight her own. What surprised her was how easily her mother won, how little her mother seemed to care for her victories.

~

The battle went on for the next three years. She plotted, at one point, to spend the weekend with a boy. She plotted a party in the house when her mother was out of town. She made plans to attend forbidden movies and dances. She found a way to make a fake ID to pass as twenty-one (in spite of the fact that she was small and slim and not yet five feet and had a habit of saying *wow* at every little thing).

But her mother broke the back of each plan. She counter-plotted on the phone with the mother of the boy. She had a friend sit in the house on the weekend she went away. She let Amy know, with a meaningful flick of her cigarette, that she knew of each of the movies and each of the dances. She handed her the fake ID snipped into stiff, useless pieces.

Nothing that Amy said, not even if she screamed it, not even if she stood in her mother's face and spat out words like buckshot, could shake her mother again as she had shaken her that day. Her victory lasted just a brief moment, just as brief as the moment she had seen her mother shaken by her father's voice.

Gradually, the fighting died down, just as it did for her friends, whose mothers had become, by seventeen, more reasonable, less venomous and irrational. But the years of fighting and losing had left her uneasy, floating like driftwood and looking for somewhere solid to beach.

IT was worth the risk that her mother would discover her lie.

After she bit down on her embarrassment and settled her argument with Paul, the photographer, she found that she could learn a great deal just by sticking to the job at hand. And the more she worked at it, the more he trusted her to do. At first her job was limited to pinning up prints, going for chemicals, sorting proofs, making coffee. Eventually he let her take on some prints. Because she did well on those, he let her do a whole strip of negatives.

"Go ahead," he said. "Make a stack of prints. Let's see what we can make out of them."

She was floating on pride when he sorted through them, picked out three, and said, "Pretty good." Then he showed her what more she could do to bring out the tones he felt he wanted. A month and a half into the project, she was doing prints on her own. Sometimes he rejected them, but not, she noticed, without studying them first, with real consideration. She felt her first flush of adult acceptance for her work. Real work, not schoolwork, but real, out-in-the-world work where they give no grades but they can flunk you for sure.

It made her feel different as she walked to school, as if she was a real working person. She now had a real claim to the neighborhood, a real, working reason to be here. No one else in her school had such a claim, not even her teachers. And, possessed of a reason to be here and of proprietary rights, she saw things differently. Things she had passed every day with an everyday bare notice began to radiate, to move with personality and mystery. The bricks themselves seemed to speak; each had a story, like the hand-painted sign that read COMMIT NO NUISANCE or the chipped granite of a doorway stoop. Or the little storefront chapel with its corny sign: Mount Nebo Holiness Tabernacle. Behind its windows on each side of the door, a white-painted wall and a white-painted counter. On each of the backdrops, a cross and scroll. On each of the counters, a vase of plastic flowers, each plastic petal fuzzy with dust, the color of each petal faded from red to pink to yellow. Before, she had shared the common contempt for small-time, holy-roller religion, with its mindless, Bible-driven money pitches. Now she wondered: *Who had lettered that sign? Who painted those crosses and scrolls? Who placed those fading dusty flowers? And how long ago? And what had they hoped for? What did they hope for now?*

~

Day by day, as she performed the tasks Paul assigned her, she learned more and more about the fine details of developing. She learned that as it is cropped, shrunk, blown up, adjusted for light or tone, printed, and framed, the same negative can create an unending variety of images, that the stormy tones of one print can become stark and desert-like in another, that the smile and confidence of one print can be tinged with doubtful weathers and shadows in the next. She stood over and learned as he tried various lights, cropping, papers, and manipulations. She watched as he watched for what came up out of the bath.

Before, she had believed that a camera cannot lie. But she had not known before how selective and multitudinous were its truths.

It was mid-November. She had a month to finish the job. She wished it were more.

~

She put the woman from the photographs into the back shelves of her mind and left her there like an old sweater. For the first few days she watched for the woman as she walked from downtown to school and from school to the shop, looking sidelong into the alleys, into the doorways of the carryouts where they sold cheap wine, and up into the windows of the cheap hotels and boardinghouses of the neighborhood.

There was life near the place where she had seen the woman; people joked and argued and made deals as usual. She heard wisps of talk or song in the doorways and from behind the windows. But she did not see the woman. She had emerged and disappeared, like a fish from a pond, in a single, silver arc.

And so she began to believe Paul was right, the laughing and debased woman she saw that day was some other woman. She no longer bothered to look for the woman. There were too many years and too many miles between here and that day in San Francisco. Besides, Amy's head was full of what she was learning, and her hands now tightened with anticipation each day at the chance to work on something that was not schoolwork, something that was real and would be seen by real people in a real place that was not school.

She still saw the seven winos nearly every day. But the fall winds were brisking up. She saw less laughter in the men gathered on the corners. She saw, instead, their raw and reddened faces or their bruised-up and darkening faces and their shabby, hunched-over backs as they counted out their change together or let the wind push them around a corner.

~

She knew the voice before she saw the face. On her way to the studio after school, she had stopped in a little, sparsely shelved narrow-front store that sold pop, cigarettes, newspapers, candy, snacks, and wine (though mostly wine). When she heard the voice, she was standing, nose-down in her purse, digging for change for a pop and a bag of chips. A boy played a video game in the back of the store. Two old Black men in ball caps leaned at the counter, arguing about Republicans with an Arab-looking man behind the counter. She had pulled her chips from the rack and her pop from the cooler and, as the men called a truce in their argument, presented them on the counter without even looking up.

"That's seventy-five cents, babe," she heard as she continued to dig in the purse.

She knew the voice, but she could not name it. She stopped a moment and shook her head as if to wake up. It had been a long school day full of quizzes and stress; she had had to dodge the normal boring flirtation and gossip. She was feeling dopey and irritated. She had been trying to shift herself to be ready for work at the shop. But the fog and gravel in the voice at the counter drew her out of that mental frame and into another.

"That's seventy-five cents, babe," the voice had said. Amy still had not looked up to see the face, but knew, with a shock of recognition and embarrassment, and even though she had heard nothing before of the voice but its laughter, who it was. It was a rough-as-cat's-tongue, whiskey-toned voice. A voice as soft as a lap: it was a sad voice, and a little tired. But it was a comfortable, cushiony voice, unlike the bony furniture of the voices she heard at home and or the voices of brass and Formica that she heard at school. The voice, in spite of the common, six-bit message it carried, stroked her, just as someone might briefly, with little attention or purpose, stroke the ears of a pet or the hair of a child.

She tried to act calm. She found her money—a quarter, two dimes, and a stack of nickels—and started to hand it over. But as her hand came near the woman's hand, she felt a chill. She did not dare yet to touch the fingers and could not find the will to drop the coins. She realized that, in spite of her efforts to stay calm and unaffected, the Arab and the two Black men and the voice all stared at her as if she were about to do something dangerous or crazy.

In this neighborhood, just to seem dangerous or crazy could itself be dangerous and crazy, so she wanted to come quickly back to normal. But she found herself pegged into place: her feet seemed nailed to the floor; her hands quivered; her head remained bowed into the face of her purse as if she were in prayer. For a time that must have been seconds but felt like minutes and ached like overnight, she could not even move.

Before, she had imagined that if she saw the woman again, it would be from some safe distance, from across the street and down the block. But standing this close and without even having seen her face, she was turned to stone. It was unfair, unexpected. She felt shamed, mocked by her immobile muscle and nerve. The boy at the video game still leaned and mumbled over the triggers of his little war. The two men in caps stood waiting, with no sign of impatience or judgment, to resume their argument. And the woman from the photographs, whose voice she knew only from three bars of laughter and a store clerk's message, stood reaching out her hand for a pile of paralyzed coins.

Gradually, Amy was able to lift her head and hand to meet the eye and hand of the woman. She had to blink for a moment not to see her in black and white and had to blink again to take from her the peacoat and re-dress her in the sweatshirt and vest she wore and to tack in the crow's-feet at the edge of each eye and the web and wrinkles between them. She had to push back the bay fog to reveal the cans of dog food and boxes of macaroni ranked behind her.

Her hair was shorter and flecked with gray. Her hands were nicked by little scars and knotted with veins. She was more worn about the eyes and mouth than in the photos. But these were the same eyes and same mouth.

He's wrong, she thought. *It's her.*

When she finally dropped the coins, the woman looked her straight in the eye, as if she were judging Amy's face for recognition from some old photograph as well. Then, with a brief, nearly imperceptible shrug, the woman looked down into the coins in her hand, counted them into the tray, closed the drawer, ripped the receipt off the register, quickly bagged it with the pop and chips, and said, through the fog and gravel, "Thanks, honey."

Amy still could not bring herself to move. She still hoped for some way to bring up words, any words, to keep the woman talking. The Arab and the Black men, still silent and patient, shifted on their heels and leaned more comfortably against the counter, waiting for the woman to rejoin their argument. The boy at the video game had lost his battle. He cursed, slapped the side of the machine, and dug into his pocket for another coin.

The woman had counted up her money and she had her chips and pop, but still Amy could not move. She felt as if she were in one of those terrible dreams in which the dreamer wants to move but cannot. She knew she looked foolish; she knew she was being judged. She stuttered twice, then managed to say, "I've seen your pictures."

The woman's brow lifted. She glanced to the two men at the counter. She grinned, exposing a missing tooth.

"I think she means that wanted poster," the Arab man grinned back. The men grinned with him.

"Really. I have. You don't believe me, but I've seen them."

"Honey," she said, with something of the thick, slow-motion flow of honey in her voice. "Honey, I don't know what you're talking about." She looked again to the men; they looked back to her and shrugged. She shook her head and reached for the cigarette that lay in an ashtray on the edge of the register.

"In San Francisco, years ago. You were wearing a peacoat. It was a guy named Paul."

The woman dropped her grin and immediately looked suspicious. Her eyes narrowed and retreated. She drew nervously on her cigarette, exhaled slowly, then, staring hard, asked, "How do you know all this?"

"From Paul. You know him."

The woman glanced at the men waiting for her to rejoin their argument, then peered at Amy and shook her head.

"He lives just a few blocks from here."

"Who does?"

"Paul. The guy who took your pictures. He's got a shop. Your pictures are all in a file."

She saw the woman mouth the name *Paul.* The men looked away and began to take up the argument on their own. She put down her cigarette and leaned forward. Quietly, she asked, "Paul who?"

"Paul Lewis."

"Does he know I'm here?"

She lied: she shook her head no.

"Because he doesn't need to know."

"Well, I mean, I . . ."

"I'd appreciate it if you wouldn't tell him."

She wanted to ask why. What difference could it make? Instead, she nodded. "Sure," she said.

"Thanks, honey." The woman pushed the bag across the counter.

Amy took the receipt from the bag and folded it into her pocket as if it were a very important thing to keep. She said, "They're great pictures."

The brows lifted. The woman gazed up to the wall past her, drew once more on the cigarette, and shook her head again. *Those old things,* the gesture seemed to say.

The Arab and the Black men still laughed and argued. The boy at the video game still punched and pressed his buttons, still cursed and carried on his little war.

"So could we talk some time?" Amy asked the woman.

"Yeah," said the woman from the photographs. "Yeah, we can talk some time."

~

So Amy stole yet more time to come to the store where the woman worked and, sometimes, even to her side-street apartment, which, as it happened, was in the same building with Jonathan. And, over many visits, she heard the woman's story, a story with many strange lapses and pauses. The more she heard and the more she learned, the more she wished she could find those negatives, the more she wished she had those pictures for herself.

IT was nine o'clock in the morning and the young man was out at his station. His headphones were strapped across his head, and he was huddled in his down coat with his stocking cap pulled down close to his eyes. No one would have known, but he was watching closely as a boy advanced toward him from the corner at Broad. He was a staggered little patchwork of a boy with a tear in the shoulder of his jacket and a mess of hair that shot up at one corner and fell down over an eye at another corner and a misplaced mouth that pulled to one side. The boy's backpack tugged down one shoulder, and every few paces he looked back over his slanting shoulder. This gave him a rocking, tick-tock motion that zigged him and zagged him over the sidewalk. An old woman wheeling a wire shopping cart steered wide for him as he walked upstreet. She flattened herself against a wall to let him pass.

He's making sure his momma don't catch him, the young man thought.

Oblivious to the old woman and to the parking meter he barely missed, the boy ticked and tocked and zigged and zagged several half-backward paces, then glanced forward and startled himself to see the young man watching.

The boy called, "What's up?"

The young man did not turn to look at him. "Go home," he told the boy.

"Aw, man." The boy took one last look over his shoulder, then sidled next to him.

"I said go home."

"Hey, man, it ain't like that."

The young man nodded in the direction of the backpack. "Ain't you supposed to be in school?"

"I got out early."

"Try again."

"Naw, for real."

"Try again."

"Aw, man. You ain't been in school for five years."

"So what's that got to do with you?"

"Well, if you ain't been in school, you can't be telling me."

"I tell you what I want to tell you."

The boy was silent for a long moment. Each of them watched the traffic ranging back and forth.

Finally the young man said, "So go home."

"Aw, man."

"You know you ain't supposed to be out here with me."

"Man, she ain't gonna say nothing."

"So why you looking over your shoulder every other step?"

"I ain't thinking about her."

"Yeah, right."

"Man, I ain't no little kid."

"You're a punk."

"Man, you're all a time down on me."

"'Cause you're a punk."

"Man, I can help you out."

"You can't help shit."

"For real, man."

"How you gonna help me when you ain't even supposed to be around me?"

"I don't care what she says."

"You ain't helping me."

"Check it out, man. I can . . ."

"You ain't helping me."

The boy hesitated to speak once again.

"And if I hear about you out here trying to serve, I'm gonna personally kick your skinny ass."

"Man . . ."

"'Cause you ain't nothing but a drooly-mouth, gimpy little, raggedy-ass, candy-sucking punk." He inhaled deeply, as if to draw force. "And you can take your little sorry self out of here before I get mad and wear you out on this telephone pole."

The boy hitched up his backpack higher on his shoulder and waved the young man down. "Forget you, man."

"Get on home, you little punk." He peppered the backpack with a load of silent curses.

When the boy had passed out of range of the curses, the young man dropped into silence and began to nod his head in a rhythm.

He leaned his back against the wall, fixed his eye on a spot across the street, watching without seeming to watch.

~

Paul Lewis gazed from the window of a restaurant, slowly drinking coffee. He saw that, as the boy left, a slate-gray car pulled up and a man, a short, narrow-faced man in a belted black coat and a trim beard, got out, slapped five with the young man, and took a place beside him where he leaned back against the window of a shop. The young man and the black-coat man were shoulder to shoulder and did not face each other. The black-coat man kept up a constant action with his cigarette, checking its coal, knocking off its ash, inhaling, talking through the smoke, waving it like a painter. When he had smoked it down, he pulled a pack of cigarettes from an inside pocket, hammered the end of it on the heel of one hand, then pulled off the cellophane and a corner of foil. He let the wind take each of these away, then tapped out a cigarette and lit it.

The young man made no movement at all but a slow, rhythmic rocking of his head.

In a moment, with a word and a tap at the young man's elbow, the man walked off down the street, turned down an alley, and disappeared. The young man did not move except for his rhythmic nod, and in a few minutes, time enough for the man at the window to finish the last of his cold coffee, the man in the belted coat returned.

The young man, for the first time, looked aside. The man in the belted coat subtly slipped him a small packet. He saluted briefly, raising the cigarette to his brow, and the young man nodded back. Then the man in the black coat got into his car and left.

The young man remained, still nodding in rhythm, and Paul Lewis continued to watch him. He stood, piled money on the table for his coffee and a tip, then went to the door of the restaurant.

There, standing where he could not be observed from the street, he raised a small black camera, calculated briefly for light, framing, and distance, and took three quick shots.

4

PHOTOGRAPHS:

A man and woman stand in front of a house. It is a small house; some would call it a ranch-style house, or even a cottage. It is the house a middle-class family would own. This is a middle-class couple; we can tell by their Sunday clothing and by the comfortable manner by which they fit in that clothing, by the trim knot of his tie and the purse held close to her side. To their right, in the driveway, waits a car. Sunlight gleams in the wax of its panels and in the chrome of its bumpers and trim.

The woman looks directly into the eye of the camera. The man's eye, in a stolen glance at the moment of the click of the shutter, drifts toward the car.

~

The sidewalk of a residential street. The camera takes us down the sidewalk into the obscure distance. To the right, a line of near-identical houses. To the left, a line of parked cars. In the yard of the first house, a sapling tree, supported by ropes staked to the grass, in each of the yards beyond, a similar tree, staked in place, a similar house and porch, a similar car parked out front.

In the distance, the various lines of the cars, the sidewalk, the staked trees, the porches and eaves of the houses all merge into obscurity.

~

In various images, we see the couple—together or separately—digging in a garden, watering the lawn, at work on a carpentry project, cutting vegetables in the kitchen, walking up the steps to the house after a day at work, looking across the backyard fence at the cornfield beyond. In some, they wear their professional clothing; in others, they wear blue jeans or skirt and apron.

~

By lamplight at the kitchen table, the man and woman sit hard at work. The man is to the left, the woman to the right. Each has a pencil in hand; books and papers lie spread out between them. The curtains at the kitchen window are pulled to left and right and fastened as they might be in a theater. The man and woman are so intent on their work that they do not seem to notice the photographer, though his cheek and jaw, his human eye, and the cycloptic lens of his camera appear, ghostlike, in the window between them.

HE first saw Jenny in a burst of light. She was on stage at a concert, where she had somehow eluded the security. She was encircled in the white repetitive flash of a strobe light, a captured shadow, her dark shape haloed, framed, repetitively illuminated. In that first image, her black hair curled wide about her. Her arms were thrown wide as if for balance or as if in dance. Her face, turned to one side, had just a hint of the darkness of her eyes, of the slim line of her jaw. Her brow was knit as if wounded by the music and the thudding of the speakers. Her smile, in that first split second, was the smile of a failing angel, caught at the pivotal moment, the turning point: a fragment: a simple flashpoint, freeze-frame image.

He wanted that image. He wanted to put her into a print, to save her in the falling. Again: the light flashed around her. Again. Again. In those next half-dozen images, he saw her, in fractured motion, turn, crouch, put down a hand to steady herself, and jump from the stage and out of the track of the light.

The roadies were right behind her, their faces grim.

He knew then he had to have her in his camera. Everything before had had a political purpose: to illustrate, to document, to agitate, to explain. He had never before gone after a photo simply because he wanted to capture an image.

He had no idea who she was, and there were probably seven hundred people in the place, but he knew that, even after she slipped into the crowd, he would track her down. He would find her if it took days. But it only took a few minutes. She was easy enough to spot in her sandals and blue jeans and the white peasant blouse with wide sleeves that opened up like wings. Pure instinct guided him through the rocknoise and the elbowing crowds to where she stood, alone in a circle of dancers. He stopped a moment, fascinated by the stark and suffering beauty of that image: the black, cascading hair, the white, open wings of her sleeves, her hands pressed into her hair as if her head were in pain or as if she were trying to pull herself free of a thought.

It could have been either. It could have been something else altogether. He only wanted the image, not the meaning. Let someone else have the meaning.

In a moment, the band stopped for a break, and in place of the heavy music there was the smoky noise of the seven hundreds. She looked up, a little dazed, and he approached her.

"I've been looking for you," he said.

It was hard to talk over the shuffling crowdnoise, so he had to say it twice. "I've been looking for you."

"Really?" Her smile, as it emerged, was amused, almost silly. Her hands were still in her hair, still pressing her temples. He knew she was high. Even standing still, without the pulse of the music, she was, almost imperceptibly, swaying and rocking. What had been separate, frozen frames under the strobe light was now low, steady, and unceasing motion. He had expected that. What he had not expected was the wounded evasiveness of her eyes.

"Where did you get those eyes?"

She stared a moment before she answered. "I was born with them. I never had any other."

He already imagined close-ups of those eyes.

"So why have you been looking for me?"

"I want to take your picture."

"So take it."

"I don't have my camera."

She laughed. It was not a full laugh, like that of someone who laughs at a joke or at the craziness in life, but a half-laugh, the kind people laugh when they're thinking of something else. She began to look away, as if she had already forgotten him. This angered him. He was ready for refusal. He could handle that, because he knew he could eventually change her mind. But he was not going to lose this chance just because she was too spaced to remember what he was telling her.

But she turned back to face him. "So what are you trying to get at?" she asked.

"Just a picture, babe. I just want your picture." He could tell she was calculating, in some foggy way, what he might be about and how safe she could be in this.

"Are you into porn?"

"I don't believe in porn. It's all beauty. It's all porn. You decide."

"I mean," she started rubbing her forehead in time with a slow swaying in her body. "I mean, are you trying to get me into some kind of movie for old men to jerk off on?"

"I just want your picture. Stills. Photographs. You don't have to do a thing. I don't want you to do a thing. I just want to take your picture." He was not trying to convince her. He knew he did not need to.

"Why me?"

"Why not?"

She shrugged as if what he said made sense. Suddenly she looked at him sharply. "What kind of pictures?"

"I don't know yet."

She eyed him as if he held a snake. There was no way to predict what she might say next. There was no need. He had never felt so sure of a thing. He would have that picture. He wanted her in the failing light of late afternoon, on the streets, on the wharf, in a window, at a table, in the rain, against a telephone pole. All that where-and-when would be decided in the winds of the moment. He knew he wanted nothing staged. No studio shots. No portrait stuff. Nothing planned, in place, or set up by method. He knew that all he had to do was to follow behind her with a camera. He knew, by instinct, that she could forget there was a camera in front of her. And as she did, things would begin to happen: miracles, mysteries. He knew that what he wanted was that failing smile. He wanted whatever faces were in that face with its shadows and ancient eyes.

"Are you for real?" she asked.

"What's real?"

Her eyes narrowed in anger. He noticed for the first time the rasp in her voice. "*Something's* real," she said.

He thought for a moment. "What's real is what goes in the camera."

She kept on shaking her head. It was as if she might be puzzled over what he had said, or as if she despaired of ever making him see her meaning, or as if she were confused, or she had decided he was. He could not read her and he liked that.

"I'm going to go," she said. "When do you want to take my picture?"

"Tomorrow."

"How do I find you? Or do you find me?"

"Either way."

"Don't you use a studio?"

"Not for this."

"Well, you can find me in the neighborhood." She told him the place to be and when she would be there. "We'll see how much reality you can fit inside your camera."

~

She was drinking cheap wine from a coffee mug when he found her the next day, an hour late and a block away from where she said she would be. The light was leaving at a furious rate.

"You don't make it easy, do you?" he said.

She smiled and said nothing. Her straw hat was pushed back on her head and the cup was cradled in her hands. He shot that quickly, before she had time to move. She laughed at the sound of the click, and started walking.

He followed her through the streets and alleys for the next two hours, shooting her like a sniper among the winos and abuelas and patchwork children of the streets and alleys. She never said a word to him. Which was fine with him. He didn't want words. He wanted pictures, and he knew that what he was getting was good. As he followed her, she would dodge him, tease him, dare him to miss her. She would duck behind a wooden staircase with some old soldier to share some wine, or lean with an old neighbor woman to trade

Spanish and make sly eyes back at him, that funny man with his bag and camera slung like bandoliers. Children stopped their games to run to her and embrace her.

When he was done, she had dodged him so well that he had no more than a few dozen shots for the whole two hours. He had no idea what was actually in the box.

A cool wind had moved in from off the bay. She had pulled her coat closer around her. The coffee cup had disappeared somewhere along the way, probably returned to the neighbor woman when he couldn't catch her. The straw hat, which she had left on some steps for most of the time, had begun to look feeble. "Did you do any good?" A thin rattle had come into her voice.

He liked that sound. He liked the sound of the sand in her voice.

"Did you get any good shots?" she asked when he did not answer right away.

"I think so," he said. "I'll have to get off some prints and see."

She turned serious. The smile died; her face changed just as the bay changes on a change of wind. "What will you see in the prints?"

"I don't know. Right now it's all in the box. I can't know till I print them."

"I mean, what kind of pictures will they be?"

"I don't know what you mean."

"What will they show? What will they mean?" She moved forward on him, ready to lock on him like a badger or a debt.

"I don't know, babe. I don't know. Like I say, it's all in the box right now, and what comes out, comes out." He could answer no better than that. It was his only answer. He generally liked this kind of parrying, but her intensity scared him. "If I did know, I couldn't put it into words. It's all in the picture."

She backed down. The steam had gone out of her.

"I'll go a long way for a picture," he said.

She shrugged. She had stopped paying attention. "I'm dying," she said, looking off at the street, where a wind was shifting papers in the corners and under the staircases. She turned her eye and fixed him. "I'm dying. See if you can get that in your picture."

~

He still did not know what was in the pictures. He knew only that they made a series (shuffle them how you will), that they told a story he could neither revise, nor repeat, nor sell, nor free himself of.

He had printed up a couple dozen out of the fifty or more frames he had shot that day. The negatives, by some accident, had disappeared long years ago. Now he kept the prints of her in a file with others he had made through the years. People stopping in the studio flipped through them and, he noticed, usually stopped at one of that series, if they stopped at nothing else. But he had never tried to sell them. He had never hung them. He had never, though friends had encouraged him again and again, tried to package them in a book.

He had done many other things. Magazines, pamphlets, leaflets, and brochures for a dozen causes that had used his photographs. Within the small circle of those who knew his work, people praised, encouraged, and respected him. He could even, by way of sales and magazine gigs, make some money when he tried.

But the battered prints of the woman in the pictures stayed in his files where people, riffling through, would see them, for he found he could neither use them, nor hide them, nor throw them away.

~

She had stayed with him that night. He had taken no more pictures the rest of that day nor any more that evening after they had gone back to his apartment, nor even, after the wine and marijuana, as she danced across his kitchen floor. Not until the foghorns woke him just at dawn.

At the sound, which usually did not wake him, which he usually felt as a pressure against the temples of his sleep, he rose up on his elbows, glanced out the window by his bed, and measured the light that broke from across the mountains and was softened by the fog. Early morning light, though he only rarely rose in time to catch it, always shook him as if it were something momentous and not just the light through which people shuffled for their clothes, not just the light through which carpenters and maids and short-order cooks stumbled on their way to work. The light shook him and saddened him with its fragility, with the blue tint it gave to everything it touched, with the silence with which it dressed the edges and corners and hard places of his room or the sharpness of the streets, the way it just now softened the clutter of wine bottles and candle stubs and ashtrays and books that were stacked or standing in the room, the colors of which, under lamplight or daylight, would have harshened and hurt like a hangover.

The thought of a harsher light irritated him, so he propped himself higher in the bed and looked out the window.

Out on the street, among the stony corners softened by that light, a man in a wide gray hat stood with a duffel bag slung over his shoulder. He had a traveled, just-come-into-town look about him, as if he had just now tramped up from the railroad yards a few blocks away. The man scanned the buildings around him until the two of them met eyes for a moment. Then the traveler shook his head sadly, pulled the hat down over his eyes, and stepped into the street.

Unsettled by the momentary stare and shaking head, he watched the traveler disappear into the fog-softened light. Suddenly he took a notion. He looked around him in the room to satisfy himself that the light that the room had captured (dressed with the smell of the sea) was sufficient: she lay under a sheet with her black hair piled on the pillow. He had decided that he wanted, badly, to catch her in this light.

Still naked, he rose and picked up his camera from the table where he had placed it the night before. Inside the camera, and in the cans of film attached to the strap, lay, like a string of small dark fetuses, the photos he had taken that afternoon. He pulled the sheet from her and examined her naked form.

She was lying on her back with her arms raised above her, as if dancing. She was sleeping so deeply that the movement of the sheet had not roused her. He had fastened back the curtain so that the soft, new light from the window fell across her. It stirred in the small hairs on her cheek and across her belly. Her face was turned to one side; her mouth was open; a childlike bead of drool hung from her lip. The hollows under her arms softened with darkness. Her pubis darkened like a fold of trees along a fence line.

He wanted her then more than he had wanted her the night before. But he did not want to wake her.

She stirred, made a small shudder, and turned on her side, doubling herself for warmth against the chill in the sea-cold light.

He fingered the camera, calculated aperture and angle and film speed against the blue morning light:

And put the camera down. He did not want to wake her.

~

Paul's hometown was a small place just a two-hour drive from where he now made his studio. His parents both taught school. That meant nine months in which they worked day and night into the late hours preparing classes and grading papers, as he and his sister were nailed down to homework and class projects. Then summer came. They breathed more easily. They looked around and recognized each other again. For a month or so his parents worked on projects around the house. Then they all loaded up into the car and they traveled.

They traveled down long, narrow, pre-interstate, two-lane highways into all corners of the country. It was a project of his parents that they see all the places featured in *National Geographic*. After nine months of cornfields and textbooks, they set out to see Washington, the Atlantic Ocean, the Smokies, the Empire State Building, Niagara Falls, anything within a few weeks' drive. Those old roads brought him face to face with everything they passed. Not just the important things. And not just at a monumental distance, but right there: just beyond the window of the Plymouth: buses, front porches, cattle in the barn lots, workers at the factory gates, bums, tractor drivers, berry pickers, ballplayers. Dogs ran right up out of front yards to run full-tilt at their hubcaps, snapping and snarling until they were satisfied they had driven them off. At night, he looked right into people's living room windows, or even bedroom windows (where he hoped, just for that flash-by second, he might see something sexual and forbidden). He saw gas pumps, grazing horses, bicycle riders, junkyards, balers in the fields, signboards over country stores.

Those highways took him right into the hearts of the cities. The Dixie Highway, the old National Road, the Mohawk Trail, Route 66 were the main street of a hundred towns and Main Street of a hundred cities. They trundled in from the farmlands and small towns right down to the trolley lines and the packed streets. And there, right in the frame of that back-seat window: tenement stoops, hotels with brass-buttoned doormen: police waving the traffic on or swaggering into the faces of passed-out winos; young men in muscle shirts and pegged blue jeans, sneering into their faces. Right there.

All of it flashed right by him in a heartbeat.

He remembered, too, distant scenes: wide stretches of farmland, mountains, lakes. In his memory now, those scenes carried a phoniness and gloss like that of a stack of postcards. As a child, he wanted the motel pool and the souvenir shop; he wanted his comic books and model airplanes. He was bored with the monumental vistas his parents so wanted him to appreciate.

But what sharpened in his memory later were those scenes just outside the window of the car. The porches and gas stations, the kids in leather jackets hanging out on street corners, the old men on canes, the first time he ever saw Black people. All those scenes alerted him, whipped by, and were gone. Even if he sat up, turned, and tried to keep that ice cream stand or that boy and girl kissing in sight through the rear window, they faded almost immediately. They shrank into the growing highway distance.

What he kept were the momentary images framed in the window of the car. What he kept were snapshots.

~

They traveled once to a place called the Blue Hole, a local Midwest attraction, some miles from their home. He recalled a wide, grassy picnic area sheltered by great leafy trees. There were probably a souvenir stand and a snack bar for hamburgers and french fries. And not much else that he could remember. Except for the Hole itself: just a small opening in the earth brimming with dark water. It was surrounded by a white wooden rail so no one would fall in. No one, his father said, had been able to find a bottom to it. Blind fish swam up from its depths. There was nothing blue about it. It was a deep, luminous black. Not black like used oil. It was a different black, clear as tap water until somewhere, deep down, it lost the light and there was nothing but the blackness of a water cave. He remembered that he leaned against the rail—he must have been very small—and that, looking as hard as he could into the depths, he saw nothing. Just the dark water and the backs of the blind fish.

~

Once he saw a collie kill a kitten. He saw it all in a flash, and saw it still. Though it had been years, the image was as clear to him as a picture in a book. He had thought of collies as gentle, friendly dogs. But all dogs are hunters. The cat was short of full-grown, old enough to move around on its own, but still small. It was in a front yard of a farmhouse, the classic kind with the big white house and the big shady maples and the lawn furniture.

No one was around. It was just the kitten and the dog. He had not been watching for anything. The miles of Iowa (or Wisconsin or Ohio) farmland had bored him long enough that he expected nothing. No one had told him, *Sit up and look.* But somehow, at just that moment, he felt called to look up from his Hardy Boys: there was the moment of killing in the middle of that big green lawn: the cat made three desperate lopes across the grass and scrambled up the tree, but not fast enough: the dog made a single long arcing leap and pinned it to the trunk with its teeth.

Then they were gone. He turned to watch out the rear window, but he could not see around that tree, except for a little bit of dog-colored something that seemed to worry some other thing into the ground. The car continued to roll right down that highway. He sat with his eyes fixed on the window, which quickly filled with tall green waves of corn. His heart had stopped like a clock; his mouth was full of stones.

He supposed the cat might have got away. He supposed the cat could have spat and clawed until the dog let him go. Things are pretty hard to kill, he had learned. But at that moment, it looked so certain. The dog's jaws would surely break the cat's back. Or the dog would shake the cat to death.

It was an awful moment. He sat back in the car seat. Everyone was silent. Nobody knew. His father had his eyes on the road ahead. His mother was reading a book. His sister was dozing.

He must have been ten.

~

The girl, Amy, asked him, "What do you want to do with your photographs? What's your message?" They had gone out to pick up paper and chemicals.

"There isn't any message," he said.

"Oh, come on."

He looked at her gravely.

"I mean, there's so much meaning in your pictures. What are you trying to say?"

"Not a thing."

"But . . ."

"There is no *but.* There is no message."

"But you're in all those magazines. You've been involved. There must . . ."

He tapped her arm. "I want to stop you," he said. "That's what I want."

He pointed to a man at a newsstand across the street.

"Watch how he turns the pages of that magazine, one by one."

The man was maybe fifty, with a large gut and big black glasses. He was scowling intently into the pages of a magazine. His lower lip was thick, as if it had been punched. It folded up over his upper lip like the clasp on a purse. The Chinese man who worked the kiosk was watching him. People on the sidewalk jostled by, inches away. But the man continued to flip the pages and to peer into the spine of the magazine.

"See, he's ignoring everything else around him. Watch his eyes: they scan the pages back and forth. There's even a rhythm: flip the page, scan right to left, flip and scan again. But in a moment he'll stop." And he did. His eyes stopped dead in the center of the page. They moved corner to corner and back to center again. What he saw might have been something he would like to have, a woman or the latest model car. Or it might have been something that shocked him, like the dead stacked up from the latest war. But he had stopped.

"Just for a moment. See, he starts again. He turns the page and falls back into the rhythm. Flip, scan. Flip, scan. Until he stops again.

"That's what I want. That moment when your eyes stop. I want to stop you for that moment.

"Before you turn the page."

THE first time he held a camera in his hands was at a Berkeley demonstration. He had forgotten by now who organized it or what it was for. But he remembered the crowd gathering near People's Park, grouping and ungrouping, seeking to place themselves, to find positions. He remembered that as the march went forward, the crowd unfurled like a long, bright-colored banner and that (it was not just that he was high at the time) the people of the crowd themselves were banners, flags of their own nations.

He was watching the banner roll past when a friend pushed a camera on him and said, "Here, I need you to take some pictures."

The black, boxy, windowed thing was around his neck and in his hands.

"What do I do?" he asked, baffled by the dials and buttons, the little windows and shutters.

Randall—the friend who had slung the camera on him—showed him quickly how to focus and frame. Randall was red-maned and stark. His eyes were nervous and moist, like small black birds at a fountain. His hands were shaking and he rubbed his nose as he talked. Paul guessed that Randall was in need of a fix.

"What kind of pictures do you want?"

"I don't care. Real pictures." Randall rubbed his nose again. "That's it. Real pictures." He rubbed his stomach, then rubbed his nose, then craned into the crowd. "Just take some pictures, man." He swept his arm across the bannering rows of people. "Shoot up the whole roll. Shoot the whole world."

"So what do I do when I'm done?"

"Don't worry. Somebody'll show you." He slung a camera bag over Paul's shoulder, slapped him on the back, waved him off, and threaded himself into the crowd.

Paul tried to get a shot of Randall's desperate, hunched-over back, but Randall disappeared—even the tall red tangle of his hair—before he could bring the camera into focus. What he got in the frame instead was a boy: Probably sixteen, his face was framed by the heart-shape fall of his hair. He had been walking across the grass and into the line of Paul's vision, and he had spotted the camera out of the corner of his eye. Paul could see him pause, just for a moment, a bare instant. He could feel the boy size himself up, as if he had glanced at himself in a mirror, as if he could shape himself in the mirror of the lens. He made himself a little taller, a little more determined, a little tighter in the muscles at the side of his face. Little shadows flared in the tightness of the muscles.

Paul snapped the picture.

The boy looked elsewhere and marched on. By the time Paul brought the camera down to see him with his natural eye, he had disappeared, just like Randall, into the shifting flags of the march.

It happened that way over and over. A girl shifted the jacket she had slung over her shoulder; Paul felt her lean slightly toward him with a winged stare. He snapped her. Another boy rolled his shoulders and cracked his knuckles. Paul took him quickly, before he could even know he had posed. Each person he turned to would pause, ever so slightly, to pose, to reshape himself or herself, if only for the moment that the camera was on them. Each would go on into the march that was gathering a little changed, a little more the person they hoped to be.

~

Later he would wonder, *Were they creating a mask that had nothing to do with who they really were? Or did the mask they created remake them?*

~

Randall never came back for his camera. Paul saw him again, two or three times on the Berkeley streets, and wanted to approach him. But something always held him back. Something always stopped him. It was not greed, though it was a good camera. He had, by then, other cameras and had begun to collect equipment and material. He could live without Randall's camera. It was something else that stopped him there, a force like a hand on the shoulder that told him: Wait: Watch:

Passing among the bright hawkers' stands on Telegraph Avenue or across the gray squares of the campus: gaunt, with chiseled-out cheeks and paranoid, side-glancing eyes, Randall walked steadily into the void that lay just before him like a bait before a fish.

~

Paul had rolled out to California at nineteen on a wave of loneliness and rage. A wild loneliness and an inexplicable rage: they followed at his knees like a pair of dogs. Loneliness and rage were threaded into the wind that drove him west in that nine-day journey. He could see them stir in the heads of the Nebraska wheat; he could hear them tasseling in the corn. They stirred in the dust devils and in the eddies of the rivers he crossed. They whooped over the peaks of the Rockies and, with that wind that was rolling him, rolled him right to the Pacific edge and cast him up, like Jonah, on the streets of San Francisco.

The rage was so bearish and so unrelated to any identifiable or blamable thing in his life, it was so sudden and so alien to what he had to live, that, thinking on it later, he had trouble recognizing it as his own. But by the age of nineteen it had become his road partner, his companion, and was not to be left at home nor buried along the way without violating some sort of code of loyalty and right. The rage traveled right beside him all the way across the country. It hitchhiked alongside him and crowded the truck cabs and back seats of cars in nine states and, once he got to San Francisco, helped him find a place for them to move. It took him down the most desolate of alleys and onto the wharfs and, raging at nothing he could give a name to, out into steep, lamplit, fog-shrouded streets at two in the morning.

~

He could not remember a time when he did not feel lonely. He did not know why. He had his parents and his sister. There were plenty of relatives and friends nearby. His life was full of gatherings and socials. His aunts and uncles and cousins would gather on the lawn of his grandparents' home to eat, shake hands, play loud games of euchre, and sing old corny songs. He and his cousins played tag and red rover or conspired in the cornfield nearby. His grandfather, still in his workday clothes, as if he were about to mount his tractor, would lean on his cane and watch and grumble; his grandmother would sit with her hands in her lap and talk about her health. His aunts would pinch him on the cheek and tell him, *My how you've grown.* They were bustly, crowded times, and in them the loneliness would disappear, just as it disappeared, sometimes, in the band concerts and church socials, or at the county fair or in a basketball game. But it reappeared right after, as soon as the car door closed, as soon as he saw his cousins head down the drive.

The loneliness was like a gland, filling him with an errant hormone. He felt it saturate his blood and alter the colors and tints in his life, the lights that went off in his brain, the pace of the words he spoke (which was almost always, unless he was excited and which he nearly always regretted, slow and awkward, full of mumbles and hesitations).

As he grew older, he mastered more of the skills of talk and social interaction, so that, at school dances, in classes, on dates, or driving the small-town streets with his friends, he could talk like anyone else. No one knew the sands that ran in his blood. No one knew he ached like an amputee.

~

He sat, many weekend nights, at the window counter of a restaurant at the courthouse square with a milkshake and a hamburger growing warm and cold in front of him, watching the cars that stopped at the traffic light, watching his own reflection in the glass.

~

"It's your life," his father said. "Do what you like."

He knew his father could not mean it and said it out of a desire to sound fair or understanding (though, he later knew, there was no way he could have understood, given his small-town limits and the fact that there was nothing that could be understood about this urge to leave).

His mother, when he told her he was quitting college to go to California, had fretted with him, challenged him, and finally shook her head and looked to her husband, who paused (Paul could count two puffs on the pipe his father was smoking), then said, "We can't make you go back to school, but you'll have to remember . . ."

He no longer remembered what he had to remember. It was another of the terse lectures which Paul had long since learned to ignore and endure. What he did remember was the air of his father, nodding his points home in his character of father-knows-best.

"You've got one year of school under your belt," his father said at one point. "You might as well go ahead and finish." But three more years of resisting the pull and push of that loneliness and rage would have been more than he could bear.

So he went out into the world, which, at that moment and in that place, was full of possibility and dread.

WITHIN a month of the day of the photographs, Paul and Jenny began to live together in his loft apartment in a tall and ancient warehouse near the bay. There were dozens of others warrened in the place, and they came and went by way of an open freight elevator; the cables shimmered above them and the walls of the shaft slid by them inches away. He had the entire west wing of the third floor and had sectioned off portions near the windows for a kitchen, a bath, and a darkroom. The rest remained a dark half-acre of floor space. He had been there for years. She moved herself in among his piles of books and racks of negatives and hung her posters on the walls of the darkroom. She built extra shelves for her books and pushed his clothes aside in the closet to make room for her own. With her extra dresser and kitchen table, the place began to look like a secondhand furniture shop, but gradually, after a few weeks of adding curtains and shifting knickknacks on the shelves, it began to feel like a place where people lived.

She added to the place a smell of bread, cheap wine, and fresh-cut flowers.

Mornings, the fog worked the streets around them like a peddler. It checked each alley and side street and found no buyers, so it transformed itself and moved in among them as they dressed for work.

Catlike and impassive, it watched them stumble and yawn. It watched him watch her, saw him soak up every scrap of her. It watched him tie his shoes by touch so as to examine the muscles in her hands or, as she walked to the dresser, measure the rise and fall of her breasts. Buttoning his shirt, he watched her rub her head (as if it were aching or full of cottony thought) and walk, naked and erect, toward the shower. And when she shut the bathroom door behind her, he panned across the room, licking up the light that had held her.

Watching her in the fog-tricked light of those mornings, he sometimes let his fingers fall to the strap of his camera. Without even unbuckling the case, he mentally framed her moment by moment. He drew her in and out of focus so that in one moment she was sharp-edged and brittle as if she had been cut from tin, and in the next she had blurred into the background like a shadow or a patch of mist. He measured the lights on her and the shadows, even the small scabbards of shadow strapped to the muscles of her thighs.

But he never picked up the camera. He pulled on his shirt. He went to the kitchen for coffee.

~

In the middle of the night, muffled by the fog, they could hear, if they woke, strange sounds of laughter which climbed to them across the ladder of fog or drummed down to them through the walls.

Sometimes, instead, they heard music: random notes on a saxophone. Bent notes on a guitar. A voice.

Sometimes, along that telegraph of joist, brick, floorboard, and wire, they heard scraps of agony: Someone from above, around, or below them burst into a weeping or a raging full of threat, failed history, reminders of betrayals, guilts thrown down like knives, insults, names, violences, vilenesses. They might hear it in one sharp, short report, or they might hear it go on for hours or until someone called the police. They never spoke through those agony hours; after the shouting or the weeping stopped, she would turn into her sleep like someone going to work, shuddering through dreams so labored and awesome that he sat on the edge of her, hopeless and sleepless and washed through with frustration and all that familiar loneliness.

~

She made sure, at first, that the wine bottles found places to hide and that they let themselves out as soon as their business was finished. Some ended up as candleholders or vases, but most snuck out the back door like cheating lovers. He knew it. Her drinking had never bothered him. He knew no reason why she would want to hide it. He was wrapped up in his work, and the wine seemed to keep her happy. But within another month, for reasons he did not understand, she quit drinking, suddenly and altogether.

~

She left him alone with his work. She had her own, teaching in the day care center of a settlement house. He had his, in a warehouse near their own. In the afternoons, after work, he roamed the streets with his camera, sweeping up the last fragments of light, the last scraps of available image. Sometimes he went on the road, taking pictures of farmworkers, street people, demonstrations, waitresses.

At night he went to meetings, helped with the layout of magazines and community newspapers, or worked in the darkroom he had rigged up in a corner of the apartment.

She would watch him, often sitting in the dark, as she sipped slowly her cheap red wine. Later, after she quit, she watched as she sewed or made bread. She watched him even after he went behind the darkroom partition. She would watch him as he pinned up prints to dry. Or cropped photos for the magazines or worked at filing his prints and negatives.

Her side eye was always on him.

~

He came home late one night from a meeting and could not find her in the kitchen or the bedroom. "Hey, babe," he called. But he heard nothing. She was not in the darkroom, nor was she taking one of her long baths. It was not like her to be out this late, so he thought she might be upstairs visiting her friend who did the macramé things and sold them on Haight.

But something, a sound like the quiet shifting of feet, drew him out from the sectioned-off area in which they lived, out into the empty warehouse space. Great oak pillars bore the weight of each floor and made a kind of straight-row forest, a wooden cathedral. A scant, watery light fell into the warehouse space from a lamp near the elevator. He peered among the pillars and listened. Again, the quiet shifting of feet. Someone was moving in these rows, silent as a killer.

"Jenny," he called. His voice had gone hoarse. There was not a sound in reply. He could see only the rows of whitewashed pillars and the gray floors banded by black shadows of the pillars. He made himself small against a pillar for fear. His breath went shallow and silent. His ears tracked every scrap of sound. There was the scrape of a slipper, the creak of board against board, the whisper of another's breathing, the hushed, ancient sag of brick and beam.

"Jenny!" he called.

Then he saw her.

She was in her nightgown of flannel with the cotton frill at the collar. Her left hand brushed against a pillar. In the dim light shed by the doorway, he could see that her eyes had gone vacant, as if they had been turned to milk. Great dark pools had formed in the wells below her eyes. She walked slowly toward him as if she were walking under water.

"Jenny," he called hoarsely. She did not seem to hear him.

"Jenny," he called a little louder, though not loud.

"Jenny. Are you okay?"

"Jenny?"

She balled her hands into fists and began slowly to hammer at her temples, her brows, the roof of her head.

"Jenny?"

She teetered as if she were on the edge of a cliff. He was afraid he might call too loudly, afraid he might tip her over that edge.

"Jenny," he called again.

This time she seemed to hear. She stopped her hammering and brushed back her hair. "Oh!" She was startled. "It's you."

"Yeah, it's me. What were you doing?"

"I was just walking."

"But I've never seen you walk like this."

She had had this awful feeling, she told him, and all she knew to do was walk. He guided her back into the bedroom, and she fell into a fitful, murmuring sleep, the kind of sleep one might have at the edge of a bottomless blue hole.

~

She was on her way to becoming nothing. All that time with him, he was becoming more and more a person, with a role in life and a set of friends. But she was steadily becoming less and less. Which enraged him. He wanted her to be somebody. Wasn't that the whole point of life? To become the person you were meant to be? To build yourself up, make a mark on the world, have an impact. He did not care to make a name—most of the time he got no credit for his photographs in the magazines—who reads a cutline anyway? But he wanted to feel as if he had made a difference. He wanted to know that he had helped to change the world through his work. All around him, he saw people stretching themselves, striving, becoming, growing. But she seemed happy to shrink.

"Go out," he had told her, "get involved in something." He wanted her to take a course, join a group. *See things,* he told her. *Make friends.*

But she was steadily becoming less and less. She went to her job, she came home, and she watched him work. *Why,* she asked him, *does someone have to be something? Why does somebody have to be involved?* The argument ached in him like a set of bad teeth, and there seemed no end to her growing smaller until she shrank out of sight. He decided he wanted very much to leave. But for the longest time he would not leave. Nothing she could do would make him leave. Not even when he found out about Chuck. Not even after all the empty green bottles began again to line up in the apartment.

Instead, he dove deeper into his pictures. He made long trips into farmworker camps and trailer parks; he got to know postal clerks and bikers; apple pickers and the hardened children of the streets. And returning, he spent long darkroom hours refining his images. He dove deep into them like a fish into the sea.

~

"You hate me. Don't you."

He had just returned from a weekend on the road and had to work in the morning. He slung all his gear down from his aching shoulders and stared at her. She was there, in a canvasback chair looking out the window into the foggy night, saying, first thing, out of nowhere, related to nothing he could follow, *You hate me.*

"Why should I hate you?"

"I don't know why. I just know you do."

"You can't know something that's not true. I don't hate you. I love you."

"Bullshit."

"Bullshit nothing. I don't."

"You've always hated me. You know it."

"I don't hate you. I don't hate anybody."

"Bullshit."

"So why should I hate you?"

"I don't know why you do. You just do."

"I don't know what you're talking about."

"I'm talking about hate. It's like a fucking smell on you."

"Man, I don't . . ."

"Fuck your *Man, I don't.* I'm sick of you."

"What's going on with you?"

"There's nothing going on with me. There's something going on with you."

"Man, you're . . ."

"I'm what?"

"Nothing."

"No. Go ahead and say it."

"Nothing."

"Say it. Say it. I want to know how you really feel."

"I don't know what you're talking about."

"Say it."

"I already said. Nothing."

"Go ahead. You're too scared. You're too gutless to say what you really feel."

"Man, you're . . ."

"What?"

"Nothing."

"What?"

"This is crazy."

"So that's what you think? You think just because I want to know what you're thinking, I'm crazy."

"I didn't say you were crazy. I said . . ."

"You said this is crazy. So is that what you really think?"

"What the fuck are you talking about?"

"Here I am talking about what this relationship is all about and you think it's crazy."

"What are you trying to do?"

"I'm just trying to talk."

"You're trying to fuck with my head."

"I'm just trying to get us to talk."

"I come home and all of a sudden you've turned into . . ."

"What?"

"You're, like . . ."

"Say it. Say what you really think."

"You're a . . ."

"Go on. Say it."

Nothing.

"Say it!"

"Bitch!"

She curled in her chair and nodded to the foggy window.

~

Each fight went on for days. The first fight became the model for the fights that followed: Harsh stares. Smoldering words. Shuddering and tears. Bitterness poured out onto the table like piles of loot as he argued, cajoled, dismissed, explained, gripped the edges of tables and the handles of brooms, cursed, swore to change, refused to change, processed, studied, resolved to do more, resolved to do less, confronted, withdrew from the confrontation until finally he felt himself cave in. A part of him collapsed like a bridge whose abutments had eroded. He would shout *Fuck you,* slam the door, and, ignoring the elevator, stomp down the stairs to the street. He might smoke a joint in the park if he had remembered his stash. Or he might steam down to the docks and watch the water break against the pilings. He would walk or smoke until the entangled feelings lifted and he could feel safe to come back home.

And she would always be there. She would have swept up the broken dishes by then and restrung the curtains if it had gotten that bad, and she would be drinking black coffee and staring at the walls. And he would come in and say something like, *Look, I'm sorry I blew up* or *What can I do to convince you I love you?* The words would be no different from others he had used in the long battle. But now the words floated on a river of desperation.

She huffed, as if he had tried a stale joke, as if he had lied. He continued, *What can I do? What can I say?*

She would nod for a while without looking away from the wall; her eyes would have a smoky look to them which looked nothing at all like tears of anger but a kind of sadness that always left him shaking in his shoes.

Finally she relented, but only after she had seen him shoving the tears aside with his sleeves, only after she could hear the shaking in his voice. Only then did she turn to him and pull his sobbing head down onto her shoulder, onto her breast.

5

A SERIES OF black-and-white photographs:

A congregation of winos stands at a street corner against a gray background haze of buildings and streets. Without the harsh technicality of color, we do not see the broken veins in their faces, nor do we see the sores on their hands or arms nor the yellow and blood in their eyes. But we see the heaviness that has grown about those eyes. We see something of the weight of damage. We see the haggardness and ill fit of their clothing, as if they are collapsing within their coats. Nothing has been taken from their destruction. But we see, almost, what they might have been.

The first:

They stand in a circle, five of them. At the center, one holds out his palm. Another points; he appears to be counting coins. The others stand watch. From the serious and studied looks on their faces, they might be a group of Socratics, Talmudists, researchers at a university.

Another:

One has fallen. He is on his knees with a dazed and wounded look, his eyes aimed vaguely skyward. Two others hold his outstretched crucifix arms. Another tries to lift him from behind. The fifth leans into the frame of the photo from the left. He reaches out a hand.

Another:

The face of the one with the outstretched hand. He has a mustache, a light-colored shock of hair, and dense, shaggy brows in which light seems to coil. He stands in a darkened alley where the light softens. Less busy, the light here is free to fold itself around him, to examine him and nurse him. One eye, the one thrust closer to the camera, is swollen nearly shut. Darkness settles on the sore flesh around the socket like an ointment. Light clings to the surface of the shut eyelid and to the corner of his brow. He is grinning: a bad-tooth, sardonic grin. The good eye, drawn back, is nearly lost in the thicket of wrinkles and beard and brow. Half visible, the good eye watches the camera warily.

Another:

Occupying the right half of the photo, three of them, the one with the swollen eye, the one who had fallen, and one other. They stand in the full light of a broad street. They smile like politicians. The man with the damaged eye has reached out his hand toward a young Chicano in denim and leather and metal. The Chicano's friends, in the left of the frame, also stand near, smiling and watching the two at the center. Their hands, aiming for a high five, form a pyramid. Their eyes and smiles grace each other. All other eyes look toward the hands.

Another:

The man with the blackened eye stands facing a woman. His face, her back are to the camera. She has long, dark hair; a handbag is slung over her square shoulder. It is impossible to tell what she is doing, but the man is grinning at her—sheepishly, boyishly, openly, seductively—and his arms are stretched out open, palms upward in a gesture that denies responsibility, a gesture that teases, that welcomes and deflects.

The sun is on his face and the wind is in his lightened hair. In spite of the heaviness at his jowls and the damage at his eye, he carries himself with an out-in-the-weather grace and muscularity.

One last:

The man who had fallen. He is in a park shaded with trees. Their leaves soften the light on him. He sits at a park bench. The camera, standing at full height, looks down on him. He looks straight back up into the lens, directly into the eye of the photographer.

His elbows rest on his knees. Between his feet, on the concrete pavement, lies a dark pool of what looks to be vomit. His shoes are mottled with it. His jaw is slack, as if exhausted with retching.

There is no shame in the eye he raises to the camera. He studies you, watching, as intently as you study him. There is nothing in him that says: *Pity me.*

THERE came a strange moment when Paul knew that something had changed. He did not know what it was, but he sensed it. It was like winter as it settles in on a pond. The woods turn steadily more still. The branches blacken. The colors run south with the birds. And suddenly a thin glaze of ice crosses the water.

He could see the ice glaze across her. She became spookily serene. Nothing bothered her.

It was a relief, after all that heat and all those storms, so he did not question it. It was fine with him. It allowed him to concentrate on his work. It did not matter what meetings he attended or who he hung out with. He no longer had to have soul-baring talks about feelings he could not understand.

"I'm changing jobs," she told him one night when she came home from work.

He studied to see what sort of face was on her. But she was blank as a slate.

"So what's up?"

She sat opposite him at the kitchen table where he had been reading. She shrugged. "It just happened. It was, like, they needed somebody to work at the drop-in center with the alcoholics. So I said I'd do it."

"But you've been working in childcare for . . ."

"Years. I've been there for years. It's time."

With these words, her face suddenly took a shape. The muscles relaxed along her cheekbones. Her brows lifted. Her eyes widened past him. "They brought it up. It just seemed right. So I said I would do it."

"Well, I hope it's the right thing."

The light from the window fell around her like a mantle. She brushed back her hair with one hand and her face lit up with white, curtaining light. She smiled; she was washed in tranquility. She was radiant with mission.

She remained, after that, spookily serene. Nothing, in those days of her work at the mission, bothered her. She was glazed with calm.

At first he felt it was good for her. She loved it, he could tell. As much as she liked working with the little kids—and she was good at that—he could tell she had been waiting for something like this. After a week, he went down there after work and she introduced him around as if she were taking him to meet her family. *Ay, viejo,* she would call out. *Hey, old man.*

She loved their stories. She loved even their lies. And they had a lot of each. The old guys, some of them, claimed to be old-time Wobblies or that they had sailed after pirates in old China. The young ones had an entirely different set of stories. She soaked it all in and brought the stories home and repeated them all. He could tell it was nearly word for word. And he could tell she believed that these guys had something in them. They were all special to her. They all had a spark for her, a blessedness. She saw things in them no one else could see. She could get histories out of them no one else could get. He loved to watch her then, lit up and excited by it all.

So what could he say to her when she started to bring the old bag ladies home for the night, when she would make dinner for a gang of old railroad bums?

~

She got him down there to do a series of photos of them from the standpoint of seeing their strengths, of picking up on what lay within them. Her agency wanted some shots to help raise funds for the center, and eventually some of the photos went into a calendar and a booklet. He worked hard and felt good about what he made. He did not want to deny for a minute the desperation of their situation or the destruction they had inflicted upon themselves or any of that awful shabbiness. But he wanted to capture something that was fatally alive in them.

He wanted what was coming alive, even if they were dying.

~

He supposed he could have gotten jealous. There she was, surrounded by other men all day and all evening, excited about it. But he could not. Not then. Because she was so radiant, so full of everything.

He had begun to feel hope. Those were the times when they were the closest, when he felt the best about what they were doing together. All that crazy arguing had faded away. He felt lighter.

But it did not last.

~

When he came in from work one evening with his camera slung over his shoulder and a bag of groceries in his arms, he noticed a smell set loose in the house. A smell that had never been there before. A smell of old rags and sugar. A smell of crushed fruit. A heady, dense smell of fucking.

It stopped him. He was stunned with it. Nothing in the apartment had been disturbed. Not a stick of furniture, not a picture, not a book, not a thing he could see had been moved; there was nothing added and nothing taken away. And yet he had a queasy, afterquake feeling that everything had shaken, everything had altered, everything had shifted like plates along a fault line.

At first he did not see her. He looked quickly from one corner to another. He was not sure he wanted to see her, given what he had just smelled. The groceries grew heavy in his arms, but he did not want to move just yet.

He stood in the doorway, breathing in, deeply and slowly, studying the smell of fruit and funk that filled his nostrils. Already it was disappearing, as if it had pulled back under the covers, as if it had buried its head, as if it had gone into hiding.

In a moment, he was unsure the smell had even been there. He could only smell fresh bread, cut flowers, a simmering stew. The smell was by then so thoroughly gone he began to feel embarrassed with himself.

When he looked for her again, she was sitting on the couch (and hadn't that couch been empty a moment before?) with her legs curled under her, reading a magazine. He felt barely able to walk, unable to trust the surface of the floor.

He must have stood immobilized for some time, for eventually she said "Hi" with a smile and brief look up from her magazine.

He surprised himself when he said "Hi" back, surprised himself that he said it at all and that his voice was so improbably cheerful. But to say the word freed him up so that he crossed the loft floor, his boots thundering in the empty space. Even when he came back from the kitchen after depositing the groceries and laid his camera near the door of the darkroom, she still did not look up. She continued to read her magazine with a dim and distant smile.

He sat in the chair opposite her and looked at her. The evening light had fallen across her hair and shoulders. It heightened her small cheekbones and graced the down of her cheek. It draped her breasts and the folds of her skirt with the stony whiteness of marble. She was crossed with the shadow of the window frame. She wore a contented, fresh-bread smile. He felt his hands curl around an absent camera and tried to fix her, at that moment, in his mind.

He wondered, full of astonishment and fury: *She's got to know I'm bothered by something, but it's like she's sealed up in a bottle.* A glass door had been shut on him; she sat behind it in cold contentment. He wanted to ask her, *What did I smell? What was at the doorway?* But he was stopped by that image of glassy serenity which acknowledged neither guilt nor fear.

She finally lifted her eye from her magazine and asked him, "How was your day?"

"Fine," he said. His voice had turned hoarse and reluctant. "I had a good day."

~

He had the galleys for the calendar and, proud of his work, he wanted to show her.

But he could not find her at work. The center was full of old guys playing cards and telling lies at the tables and the young guys leaning against the walls or gazing out the windows. But no one there had seen her for hours. No one could tell him a thing.

So he left the center and went out into the street. It was odd for her to be gone at this time of the day, and he figured she could not have gone far, but he could not know for sure. He always felt a little concern for the way she walked these streets. "Quit worrying," she would say. "Every one of these guys knows me. I'm safer here than I'd be at Candlestick Park."

She could have been doing outreach; she could have gone out for a long lunch. They were pretty loose there. She could get away with a thing like that. So he ducked his head into every coffee shop, restaurant, bodega, taqueria, and sandwich shop in the neighborhood. Sometimes he saw the men he had photographed, whose images were now in his backpack nestled among the words and blocks of the calendar.

"Hey, Picture Man," they called. "What's happening?"

"Have you seen her?" he asked each of them. Bleary-eyed, with an end-of-the-month lassitude, they shrugged their shoulders and looked down toward the alley or away into the street. "No, buddy, I ain't seen her," one might say. Or, "She ain't been here today." But their voices were shifty and shaky, freighted with lie.

He searched that way for an hour or more, then went back to the center and shouldered his way in among the winos and castaways and sat among their smells of sweat and wine and tobacco to wait.

He fretted on a bench for maybe half an hour, drinking bad coffee and listening to talk that, for the first time, seemed demented and inflated with grand falsifications and self-pity. He felt as if each of them watched him secretly, as if each of them knew a joke that he did not know, as if each of them, so piteous, wasted, and shaggy, pitied and mocked him. He could not stand it.

"Tell her I'll be right back," he said.

But he did not come back. Instead he wandered the neighborhood for the rest of the afternoon. He was unwilling to sit again among the mockery. At closing time, he stood in a doorway across the street from the center. The director came down from the main office to lock up, a job that was usually hers.

Had he not felt the way he was feeling, he would have crossed the street and demanded to know, "Is she okay? Did something happen?" But he suspected what he would hear. And he did not want to hear it.

He continued to wander the streets until the honey-colored sundown light began to drop among the streets and buildings of the hillsides. It tipped each portico and lintel, each stone sill. Each brick, each scrap of paper, each curbstone was touched with it. Each pane of glass went golden; each held a small golden image of the buildings around.

He found her, finally, as the streets glowed with the last of the light.

She stood in a small, littered park, dark among the dark shapes of the trees and benches together with the one called Chuck. They leaned close together and laughed, he with a sly and conspiratorial bark of a laugh, she with a laughter of honey and husk.

The last light gathered on the red bruise of his eye and in the red nest of his hair and beard. The light collected around her in a nimbus and found the gold in her face and hands. It gathered in the space between them and even in the small space in which her black and his red hair mingled.

It turned the bottle that they passed between them into a living, honey-colored thing.

~

After three days on the street, she returned and they had a tearful and penitent reunion. She swore she would lay off the wine. She swore to do no more than an occasional joint. He swore to be more aware of her feelings and needs. He really wanted to be better toward her, in spite of the nagging sense that he wanted to be free of all this emotional complication.

But she had lost the job. She felt awful. It would have been wrong to cut her off then, at a time she was really down and really trying. So, in the next six months, there was treatment and failure, more penance and more reunions. Finally, shakily, she began to stay sober.

She got a new job shortly, working with children again. And again she began to get wrapped up in her work. She did well with children. A clutch of them would follow her down to the park like a bright and talkative flock of birds, all of them talking to her at once in three different languages and their eyes all lit up like Christmas. The sun silvered her starlight hair and needles of light shed from her as she whirled among them, telling silly jokes and singing silly children's songs.

She looked happy again, and full.

So, finally, he was finished.

He was finished with her and done with California. They had lived three years together, but he knew it was time for this to die. He had enough of complication and of living on the edge. He wanted no more emotional binges. He wanted heartland solidity. He wanted to breathe factory smoke and see bib overalls. If the revolution was to happen, it had to happen in the Midwest. He figured he could cut loose of her (and that he could play out all the farewells he had practiced), head back to the city nearest his home, find a way to make a living, and make his own way with his photographs. He could live without the little West Coast reputation he had made.

He talked it out with a friend and thought it out thoroughly. He knew he had to speak to her. But he wanted to make it as gentle for her as possible, so he had to think through the timing, what to say, the approach.

He did not want to do it on a weekend; she would not have work to distract her and she might get ripped and do something really crazy. He did not want to do it when she had to work the next day either. It would be unfair to catch her at work. Breakfast time would be all wrong. He started, half a dozen times, over supper, but it never seemed right.

So there was no right time to speak. He carried it around inside him for days, eating at him like the fox that ate the Spartan boy.

Finally he came home from work, thinking, *This is the night. I've got to do it tonight.*

But she must have known. Maybe she caught a hint from his friend. Maybe she smelled it. Maybe he said something in his sleep. Somehow she must have caught on, for she had a whole different attitude. She had gotten off work early and had spread the table. She had a strange sort of magazine smile on her face. When she pulled the bread out of the oven and set it out to cool, she looked as if she had stepped off the cover of a hippie version of *Ladies' Home Journal.* She had other things on the stovetop cooking. It was strange and unnerving, but he could stand the fox of his secret no longer.

"I have to talk to you," he said. He made her sit down and look at him. She folded her hands in front of her and faced him square as a box. She looked comically prim, in her apron and a rare bit of makeup, with the little smudge of flour on her cheek and the flakes of batter on her fingers. She made a couple of small moves with her shoulders; her breasts swelled slightly.

He choked on the words. He struggled, but finally he said, "I've been thinking about this for a long time, and I've just got to say it."

He had expected her to crumble at this point. But she looked calm, glossy, and serene. She moved her shoulders again, brushed a loose strand of hair back out of her eye, then folded her hands on the table in front of her again, just like a child in school.

"I want to go."

She nodded. No reaction. No storm. "Where do you want to go?" she asked.

She hadn't gotten the point. He wanted to say, *Anywhere away from you.* But those words would not come, nor any others that would tell what he wanted to say, none of what he had worked out with his friend, none of what he had rehearsed for himself as the fox gnawed him. Nothing.

She nodded, as if to repeat the question, still with that magazine smile: *Where do you want to go?*

"Back to where I come from." He barely got the words out.

"But I've never even seen it."

"Well . . ." This was the moment. If he were to tell her, it was now. He looked again at her vulnerable, homemaker eyes. She was still smiling. She was still waiting with her hands folded primly. And he thought of all she had been through in these past months, how deep a pit she had come out of, and he stopped. All the words he had rehearsed were wasted; he could not bring them out.

"Let's do it," she said. "I'm ready any time."

No, he thought. *You don't understand,* he thought. But after all these months, he was more practiced at disguising his thoughts than he was at revealing them.

So he began to turn his thinking around. Maybe, he thought, it was all for the best. He began to tell himself that what he was doing was a sacrifice, that he was giving up something of myself to make her happy and to keep her from falling off that edge. And there was the hope, sudden and irrational, that in a new place things would be better.

"Let's eat while we talk," she said, and she jumped up and laid the bread on the table.

He swallowed his lie like a host.

~

To get there, they crammed cameras, clothes, books, candlesticks, his entire file of negatives and prints, and even the curtains she had added to the windows, into the van he had always used for his road trips and headed east across the mountains. In two days of hard, day-night driving, they came to Colorado, where he assumed they would go see her family. They had visited once before; her family had welcomed him. He knew the way and had chosen a route that would take them close.

He assumed they would stop. He mentioned it and she never said no.

It was her turn to drive. When they got to the exit for her hometown, where the road would lead down to her parents' farm, he could see she was about to miss the turnoff, so he said, "Don't forget. This is where we pull off." For a moment he thought she had not heard. So he started to say it again. "Like, hey, pull over."

But her look stopped him. Her whole face had hardened. She gripped the wheel as if she wanted to choke it. Her leg stiffened on the gas pedal. The engine churned a little faster. She looked like a pilot flying through flak.

So he never said a word about it.

And neither did she.

~

They got lost in somewhere in mid-Nebraska. He decided to take what he thought would be a shortcut, but he must have missed a turn, for he could find no place in the map for the roads they wandered, lined with dusty wheat and tall green corn. When they drove through the fields of wheat, it was as if they floated on a gold-bearded sea. When they drove through the corn, it was as if the sea of corn had swamped them.

They saw what looked to be snug, comfortable white farmhouses at the ends of long gravel lanes cut into the vast plots of wheat and corn. Large, tight, black-sided barns, white silos, cribs, and outbuildings were reefs and islands that broke the monotony of grain.

But nothing that they saw offered a clue to their true way. Nothing that they saw matched their maps.

As they navigated the oceans of grain, the motor started a low, barely audible complaint, a bare whisper like a knife on a stone. One moment, the motor thrummed as usual, and in the next, above the smooth rumble was a thin, almost-silent rasp, an irritated whisper. The sound puzzled him at first, then troubled him, and after more miles, swept him with anxiety.

He looked over to her. She was staring out the window, deep into the rows of corn or into the sky beyond them. If she heard the complaint of the engine, she did not show it. For miles and hours, he saw nothing of her but the back of her head. For miles and hours, she did not turn or speak. He felt reproach: after all, he had chosen this road. He had insisted.

Ten more minutes, he thought. *If we don't come up to something in ten more minutes, I'll stop at a farmhouse and ask directions.*

But it was ten minutes and twenty minutes and half an hour and still he could not bring himself to pull over. The neat white farmhouses were too far down their narrow lanes, too far from his road. She continued to stare out into the green canyons of corn. He continued to worry over the husky complaint of the engine.

~

Finally they approached a gas station that anchored one corner of a crossroads. Across from the station was an abandoned restaurant, the windows caked with whitewash. They were surrounded by corn on all sides. A dark curtain of corn grew right up to the edges of the lot, and it was as if there were no other island in the sea of corn but this. They pulled up to the edge of the lot and stopped. He set the hand brake and left the motor running, for he wanted a mechanic to listen to the motor before he asked directions, got gas, and drove on.

When he looked at her, she was glaring straight forward into the corn.

"You don't want me on this trip, do you," she said.

This was not the time for an argument. He knew country people. Whoever was in the station would be watching. He wanted to do his business and get back on the road. But her eyes had darkened. Her face had a somber, determined cast. The sun glanced brightly off the waving green corn and from the gravel of the lot, but her face, in the shadow of the van roof, seemed to darken and grow distant. She had crossed her arms on her knees; her hands were balled into fists.

"Of course I do," he said. But he felt uneasy as he said it.

"You don't. You didn't from the start."

"From the start? From the start, I said . . ."

"It isn't what you said. You don't need to say a thing. I know you don't want me on this trip. You never wanted me to make this move."

"If I didn't, I would have said so."

She did not move or reply.

"I mean, we came all this way. Why would I go all this way if I didn't want you with me?"

The muscles around her mouth tensed slightly.

By now an attendant was standing in the door of the station. He pushed a ball cap back on his head and stared toward them with his eyes in a squint.

The sound of the engine was stronger now, more insistent. *Wish. Wish. Wish. Wish,* very quickly it sounded.

Wishwishwishwishwish

"Go on," she said. "Go talk to him."

~

A bearing in the water pump, the mechanic told him, and agreed to fix it. As they talked, at the front of the van, she pulled a bag from behind her seat and walked toward the station. He assumed she had gone in to change clothes or wash up. And he figured she would wait in the shade of a tree while they worked. But when he went back to the station to tell her about the damaged bearing, she was not in the car or under the nearby tree. Nor did she emerge from the restroom, nor did she answer his rap on the restroom door. He circled the station and the abandoned restaurant. He looked up the road and down and into the rows of corn.

It was as if she had been swallowed by the sea.

~

He spent the next two days searching for her. He filed a report with the county sheriff, stopped in all the little towns and general stores and restaurants in a radius around the station, and returned again and again to the crossroads in the sea of corn.

But she was gone, and with a guilt that gnawed at him like the *wishwishwish* of metal on metal, he drove toward his home state.

6

PHOTOGRAPHS:

A girl with dark hair stands over a slanted table, bent intently over some unseen project. Light falls to the table and splashes to her face and shoulders. On the wall behind her, out of focus, we see haphazard pictures and posters. She wears a loose flannel shirt with broad checks. A lock of hair falls across her forehead. A hairband holds the rest in place. She leans into her project; the muscles of her face are tensed, her sleeves pushed up to her elbows, elbows bent, fingers splayed on the table.

~

Same girl, same pose. Zoomed in close. She bites her lip. Her eyes narrow on the flat unseen thing on the table. Sweat, made visible by a splash of light, glistens on her upper lip, on her brow, and in the wells beneath her eyes.

Her brow is ribbed, like corduroy, like windrows in a field.

~

The same girl: Hanging photographic prints to dry: on a line, like laundry. She is at the left of the frame, and the line of prints extends to the right and to the left of her. We see the white backs of the prints, like a row of small, brittle bedsheets.

She leans to one side, sizing up the newest sheet as she hangs it. She squints with one eye. Her jaw is set, but not tense. She is not aware of the camera. She is all concentration: her whole body leans into her effort. Her whole body tenses to meet what her eye meets.

~

The same girl: Face, shoulders, unbanded lock of hair. Her face is turned, slightly and skeptically, to the left. But her eyes look forward and fearless into the eye of the camera.

Same lumberjack shirt. Same unfocused wall of photos and posters.

She smiles, slightly and sardonically.

She is not posing. She has created no mask. She looks directly at the camera as if it were a human eye, as if she expected the camera to talk.

ONCE more, Daniel Barnes pushed the weight from his chest. It was almost more than he could do. The muscles burned in his arms and shoulders. His teeth mashed together with the effort, and the back of his head pressed into the bench. He had heaved the bar just this far—halfway only—with inches to go before he could settle it into the rack. He pressed with everything he had, with the balls of his feet, the sinews of his neck, with his buttocks, his shoulders, and his belly. The nets of muscle in the small of his back meshed, hardened, and lifted off the bench. His eyes pushed against their sockets. His lungs were an iron bubble; he could not inhale; breath, escaping, seethed through his teeth. It was all he could do. But the bar moved so slowly, and the shaking in his hands and arms grew so wild, he was afraid he would drop it.

He did not drop it. Instead, with no final heave—he had nothing left to heave with—the bar moved slowly and shakily upward. Just enough! It was up; his arms were extended. He rocked back slightly to let the rack catch the bar, then let it settle into place.

Slowly, he rose off the bench and sat on the edge. He breathed heavy and slow and stared out the window at the white, sunless sky. The blood hammered in his temples. He picked up a towel from off the floor and wiped his face, neck, and arms with it. He looked down to examine his arms and ran his still-tremoring hands over them. The muscles bulged nicely and pressed out the tattoos on each arm. Blue veins stood up on his forearms and on the backs of his hands.

He looked back out the window. But for the bench, the scattered weights, the faded and flowery linoleum, a couch backed against one wall, and a television against another, the room was bare as the cell of a monk. A misty, diffuse morning light came in at the window and fell in a white blaze on the floor in front of him. In the foggy distance, he could see the gray towers of downtown. A pair of birds crossed the window.

He heard a whisper of slippers on the linoleum of the next room. From behind the door, his grandmother, in her voice somewhere between a rasp and a whisper, asked, "Are you all right in there?"

He had to breathe twice to catch enough breath to answer. "I'm all right, Granny."

"I worry about you," she said. "Slinging around them weights all by yourself."

"I'm okay, Granny."

"Well, you oughtn't be in there by yourself."

This was an old argument, and he chose not to respond.

He threw the towel into a corner. She scuffed away from the door and he waited until his breathing returned to normal and the last of the tremors left his hands. Finally he rose, stepped to the window, and looked out into the street. It was early; he liked to get up early. No one was out. Yet he stared out the window for some minutes.

He showered quickly and sat down to eat what his grandmother had prepared him. She sat in a chair in the corner near the kitchen door, with one arm propped against the kitchen sink, smoking an angry cigarette and watching him eat. She had long since given up trying to tell him what to do. But the old argument hung between them like a haze. Country music played quietly from a radio on the counter nearby, and she nodded in time as she watched him. She hit twice more on her cigarette and raised a wreath of smoke that made her squint, then coughed into her fist. The first cough led onto a chain of new coughs that left her gasping and exasperated.

"You okay, Granny?"

She grimaced to one side, but did not speak. *It's nothing,* her gesture seemed to say. *It's no big thing.*

"You got to take care of that, Granny."

She shrugged and drew freshly on the cigarette.

"You need to see a doctor."

She tapped her cigarette on the edge of the sink. This was another old argument, and she did not intend to enter it.

The boy shrugged this time, and continued to eat.

"You ain't seen Little J, have you?" his grandmother asked.

"Not since the other day."

She mashed out her cigarette and prepared to light another.

"What's up with Jonathan, Granny?"

"I was hoping you could tell me."

"I can't tell you nothing, Granny."

She pulled a lighter from her apron pocket. She had been a barmaid for years and still wore an apron every day. She struck on her lighter three times before it gave her a flame, then studiously applied it to her cigarette.

"So what's up, Granny?"

She squinted through the smoke again and looked steadily away from him.

He shrugged, then stabbed at his fried potatoes and painted them with egg.

"I been talking to his momma," she said.

"Why you want to talk to her?" He did not like his cousin's mother, and never had. His uncle had married all wrong.

"She tells me he's been staying up later and later. And school says he's skipping. And . . ."

"What's all that got to do with me?"

She tapped her cigarette. For the first time in several minutes, she looked straight at him.

"I just see him when I see him. He don't hang with me." He spiked two more pieces of potato, then mopped across his plate with a piece of toast. He ate a few more bites under her steady eye, then he stood.

"I'm going out, Granny."

She sat in her place and smoked slowly. She knew where he was going and she did not like it. But this was yet another old argument, and she knew she could not win it.

~

He crossed the courtyard and entered the passageway that led to the street. At this hour, the passage was dark as a tunnel. At the opening, he hesitated, still in the dark, to listen and watch for a moment. He stood death still, breathing quiet as a stone, and scanned both sides of the street. One man, maybe a third shift worker returning home, swung a lunch bucket down the sidewalk. He watched the man until he turned the corner, then watched a police cruiser coast past. Finally he stepped out.

He walked several blocks until he came to an alley where a man waited.

"What's up?" the man called.

"Wassup."

The man nodded, then lit a quick cigarette. He drew quickly on the cigarette and seemed almost to spit out the smoke. "Glad it's you, man," he said, "First, I thought it was some crackhead motherfucker wanting to jew me down on a rock. Some motherfucker . . ." He tapped the young man on the shoulder, then pointed to a spot marked by large, red, bubble lettering. "Standing over by that wall. Tries to tell me . . . I mean, I give him a straight-up ten. I give it to him, right? 'Cause I been knowing him. So I'm, like, here's a gift. Knowmsain?" He gestured, exasperated, with the cigarette.

"Then he wants to say, Naw, man, You only give me this little piece of shit. And I didn't have to give him nothing, but I did. So I says, Look, motherfucker, I ain't got time for this. Take your silly-ass rock and get out of my face. So then . . ." The man threw up his hands. "He tries to get all bad, says how he gonna kick my ass down to the river and back up again. And I'm thinking, Man, I just did you a favor. 'Cause I was in the joint with that motherfucker, and I don't just deal to just anybody. But now you wanna break bad with me like that? But I didn't say nothing. 'Cause I know how these crackheads are. Then he thinks he gonna put his hands on me, knowmsain? He grabs me on the coat and I said, That's it, man. I pushed him back in the alley and I shoved my pistol up his nose. And then he backs up real quick. Knowmsain? Talking like he didn't mean it and all like that."

"Don't mean it, don't say it," the young man said.

"That's what I told him. Don't let your mouth be saying what your ass can't back up. So he took his little rock and went on down the street. Talking how he's sorry and all that. Man, that's why I got out of street dealing. These crazy motherfuckers like that. You young boys can have all that."

He threw the cigarette down at his feet and stamped it out as if it had personally offended him. "And these little dope boys . . . They're just as bad. Motherfuckers getting on my nerves."

"So what you got for me?" The young man did not reckon it his business to know who had gotten on the man's nerves.

"What's your hurry?" The man drew back, then made ready to light another cigarette. "I got what you need. But first, I'm talking to you."

"So talk, man." He settled in to listen. He folded his arms against his chest and leaned against the wall.

The man eyed him as he struck his lighter and put the flame to the cigarette. "Like I said, there's these young boys down on Blair. Talking like they got they own thing going. Knowmsain?"

The young man nodded.

"But that ain't happening. We ain't gonna roll like that." He shrugged, spiked out his elbows, drew quickly on his cigarette, and spoke through the smoke he had inhaled. "It ain't gonna be like that. We got an agreement." He tapped his hand on the young man's shoulder and nodded. "Just like you and me; we got us an agreement."

The young man nodded. Their agreement was clear, and long settled.

"I'm gonna bust a cap on one of these young boys one of these times. I mean, you make an agreement, that's like . . . Knowmsain? You don't back out. It's an agreement. If you back out, it's like . . ."

He shrugged, and the young man nodded. The man smoked in silence for a moment and they both watched the wind push a paper cup down the gutter. Then the man looked up and asked, "So what's up with you, man?"

"Ain't nothing up with me."

"You got something on your mind."

"Ain't nothing on my mind."

"Naw, man. You ain't been on it lately. I can tell."

"Ain't nothing bothering me."

"How's your granny?"

The young man was silent for a moment. "She's all right."

"You need to take some time off, man?"

"Naw, man, I don't need time off."

"I can front you, I can front you."

"I don't need you to front me."

"'Cause we got us an agreement. I count on you. You count on me."

"I know, man. But it ain't like that."

The man shrugged. "Suit yourself." He shot the end of his cigarette out into the street and unfolded himself to light another. He smoked silently for a few moments, long enough to watch a bus pull up to exhale its passengers and inhale the new ones off the corner. He shook his head, then said, "It's a life, man. Everybody's got their little jobs. We got our own little job, too. But people don't look at it like that. Naw, man. They look at us like we're a bunch of rats. But it ain't like that. It's a job, man. You got to know your job and you got to do it right." He looked to the young man. "Ain't that right?"

The young man nodded.

"See, I like the way you do your job. You do it right. It ain't like these others."

"I ain't nothing, man."

"Oh, yes you are. I seen a lot of young dudes. You're different."

"I ain't nothing different, man."

"Naw, man. You don't bullshit around like these others. You straight up business. I like that."

"I ain't different, man."

"You know I keep my stash near here. Don't you?"

The young man did not answer.

"It's okay, man. I ain't laying nothing on you. But I can tell. You figured it out long time ago. So look, I'm gonna let you in on something. I'm gonna show you how to keep a stash so nobody can't find it."

"Naw, man. That's okay."

"See, I know you all right. Come on."

They talked several minutes more, the pale man gesturing and speaking through his smoke and the young man, still reluctant, nodding and following the man's gestures with his hooded eyes. Finally the man tapped the young man at the elbow, looked to the right and left, and motioned him to follow. The young man, with a bare movement of the eyes to right and left, followed him down the mouth of the alley.

They walked until they came to a cross alley, then turned and walked until they came to a doorway. Each looked to the right and left before the pale man snapped open a padlock on the door.

Behind them, the whole way, watching from behind a dumpster, from the shallow cave of a doorway, from a patch of shade on a wall, a young boy followed, stitched to them like shadow.

EACH of Paul's negatives, everything since that Berkeley day, lay within a plastic sheath; each sheath was stored in a three-ring binder. Each binder was labeled and shelved in alphabetical order. Nothing else in his life, Amy judged from the chaos in his studio, was organized in such a way. He had made sure each image was safely archived and each could be found. So why should the negatives of Jenny in the peacoat be missing? How could they have just gotten lost?

Paul would tell her nothing. "I don't know," he would say. "They got away somehow."

That made no sense. But that was all he would say.

~

She now had a key to the studio, so if he had to work late at the warehouse, he might leave her a note and she could do her work without seeing him at all. She might not see him for days. But she saw Jenny nearly every day, sometimes at her store, where she stopped for juice and chips. Or, more rarely, on the street.

"Hey, girl," she would call to her.

Amy would thrill at the attention. Eventually, she began to spend as much time with Jenny as she did in the studio. And she began to hear the woman's story.

~

They sat one afternoon at Jenny's kitchen table, which overlooked the street, talking comfortably through a cold, rainy Saturday afternoon. Jenny had, by now, told all her long story, from growing up on a Colorado farm, through her days in Berkeley and San Francisco, where she went to parties with the Grateful Dead and traveled with Paul to strikes and demonstrations. The closer her story came to this year, this table, this gray, rain-spotted window, the vaguer and more distracted her story became. But Amy felt she could listen to that voice of honey and gravel for days on end. Her own story, her own voice had no such fiber, no such flavor. Her own story was pale; it was thin as tea.

Jenny would stop in midstory at moments to look out the window at the steady, relentless winter rain, which, in this city, could go on for a relentless day and night. "Those were some wild times," she might say. Or, "I don't see how I lived through that one."

Finally Jenny started on a new cigarette and sighed, "You know, you help me a lot."

That surprised her. "Oh, come on."

"Seriously. Nobody else takes an interest in me. Nobody else has ever asked me about my life."

"Didn't Paul . . ."

"He took pictures. That's what he did. He didn't care what was underneath."

"But he's not, like, insensitive or anything."

Jenny drew thoughtfully on her cigarette and watched the smoke rise as she released it.

"I mean, he's never been, like . . ."

"Has he ever asked you one single thing about yourself?"

"Well . . ."

Jenny winched one eye down from the smoke. "Has he ever asked you what's your hobby or what's your favorite TV show or what you want to be or where you want to go to college or do you have a boyfriend or anything?"

"No, but . . ."

"But what?"

"But . . . I don't know."

"See?"

"See what?"

"He doesn't even know you."

"No. But that's not why I'm there. I'm just a helper."

Jenny snickered grimly. She turned to look out the window at the rain. The smoke of her cigarette curled up through her hair.

~

The next time Amy visited, Jenny called her to the kitchen table. Next to the saltshakers and the sugar bowl, she had placed a little pot of flowers, a handful of lurking posies.

"Some old man gave them to me at the store. I put them up there, but Hussein said they were in the way. So I brought them home."

"They're beautiful." Gaudy, half-wilted, purple-yellow flowers with their stems half-hidden in the cloudy water, they were, in fact, a relief from the gray string of days they were facing. Rain had streaked the windows and half-steamed them. Amy sniffed at the flowers and sat down. "It's odd to see them this time of year."

Jenny nodded and stirred her coffee. "Who knows where the old guy stole them from."

"Stole them?"

"Of course. Where else would he get them?"

"Bootleg flowers! Awesome!"

Jenny grinned. She showed her empty tooth and raised her hand to cover it, but could not quit grinning.

"Man, I can see it now. Police raid! Illicit flower dealers! They're not really pansies. They're poppies. They're not really poppies! They're opium! Draw the guns! Bust in the doors! Everybody with their hands up, no false moves! My mom'll be, like, Who was it that led my daughter astray?"

Jenny grinned and grinned, and tapped on the table with her fingers, and grinned and relaxed her grin slowly and looked out the window into the steady gray rain.

~

A week later, Amy sat with Jenny again at the window. As the day had grown late, the room had darkened. Bone-white light lay across the table and softened the white of the table and its various objects—coffee cups, ashtray, salt and pepper shakers, spoon, lighter, the smoke from her cigarette, the struggling pansies. It was as if the room were lit by candle. Jenny stared out into the rain. Her face was lightly washed in the sanctuary light from the window. Her features had relaxed and opened. She had taken on a strange, angelic sadness.

Amy was amazed. Jenny had totally transformed; in this light, she seemed flawless and smooth as marble. The ivory light had taken the spidery red veins from her cheeks; it had taken the scar from her forehead; it had taken the feathery wrinkles from behind her eyes and from the side of her mouth. It had smoothed the wrinkled folds of her neck and drew a smooth, stone-gray shadow down the hollow of her throat.

Jenny's right hand tapped slowly at her cigarette. The smoke rose in a pencil-thin column. Amy wanted to sit still and watch this image of Jenny transformed in the gray light from the window until the light diminished and was gone.

She's still beautiful, Amy thought. *Even after all she's been through, she's still so beautiful.* As beautiful and fragile as in those original photographs that had so excited her.

Suddenly, like a chill, the realization came over her that the negatives were somewhere in this apartment. Crazy as it was, there was logic to the idea. If Paul had not lost them or thrown them away, who else would have them? But the notion was stronger than logic. It was as if she could smell them in the space. She took a deep breath. The impish and persistent notion of gaining the negatives and making a set of prints pressed itself on her. She struggled with the notion—she did not want to lose this vestal image of Jenny in the failing gray light. But the thought of having the negatives, of holding them in her hands and studying each one, of throwing light through each of them onto paper, of pulling them up, all new, out of the bath, tugged her as if it were a mountain stream.

Jenny tapped once more against her ashtray, and Amy plunged. "Do you remember the pictures he took that day?"

Immediately, with no visible movement of any muscle, the crow-foot lines of Jenny's face returned. The veins crossed her cheeks like lines on a map. Amy thought, *I've done it now,* but she could not back out.

"See, I've got this idea. I'd like to make a print of them. I mean, not for his show or anything, but just, like, for myself."

Jenny looked toward her cigarettes, but did not move to take one.

"The problem is, he doesn't know where the negatives went." She paused. This was the hard part. "So I was wondering if, do you, like . . . Do you know?"

"What is it you want?" She picked up the cigarette in the ashtray, found it had died on her, and threw it down again. Her hand went to the pack of cigarettes.

"I want to make a set of prints . . ."

"And you think I've got the negatives." She tapped out a cigarette, struck three times with her lighter before she got a fire, then blew an arrow of smoke out into the kitchen.

"I mean I just . . ."

"What makes you think I've got the negatives? Did he tell you I had them?" Her voice was very sharp.

"No. No, he didn't. Like, no, he never even hinted at it. He acts like he doesn't even like those pictures. And the prints he has are all beat up, but the pictures are so beautiful, so . . ."

There was an awkward and awful moment of silence. Jenny squared herself to the window and smoked. She spoke without turning back.

"What makes you think I have them?"

"I don't. I mean . . . I was guessing. I thought, like, maybe you . . ."

"What is it with you and these pictures?"

Amy wanted to say again how wonderful she thought they were, how powerfully she had been affected by them. But she had said all that before.

"Honey, they're just pictures." Jenny paused; she reached her hand to the ashtray and tapped. In the gray light slanting in at the window, Jenny's face was shadowed and sad. Her face was turned to the window so that Amy could see her left side in profile. In the tensed muscles in the curve of her neck and the arc of her jaw there was a hint of sag. Gray light hung in the thin, almost invisible hairs of her cheek. Exhaustion and grief sagged in the lines behind her eye.

In the next moment, though Jenny had made no perceptible movement, there was a tightening down of her features. Jaw and neck were leather-tight. Her eyes had gone to flint.

"They're just pictures," she said again. She huffed lightly. "They're just pictures. They're no big deal. I'm no big deal. You should know that. It's like, you think I've got something for you. I've got nothing. Nothing." She waved the smoke away from her face. "I have no wisdom for you," she said. "I have nothing to show you. I've got nothing to teach you. Nothing. Nothing."

"I'm sorry," Amy said. "I didn't mean . . ." She was not sure what she did not mean.

Jenny continued to look out the window without speaking, drawing every few moments on her cigarette. Amy felt a familiar and uncomfortable sense of emptiness begin to grow in her. A chasm had opened between her and Jenny, and she could think of nothing to repair it.

"I better go," she said finally.

"It's okay, honey. I'm not mad."

"I know, but it's time for me to get with my mom."

"So come see me later."

"I will," she said. And she got up to go, but as she looked once more at the woman, it seemed that everything about her had changed. It was as if she had been pressed down by a weight; her features were compressed; her eyes had narrowed. Her neck had been driven down into her shoulders, and her shoulders had buckled like old timbers. Such a transformation in just a few moments!

"I will," she said. "I'll be back." But she left with a burden of guilt and confusion.

7

PHOTOGRAPHS:

A man and a woman, each of them middle-aged and hard-used. They stand, *American Gothic* style, in front of a farmhouse. To the right and rear, we see the barn; to the left and rear, a tractor and a neat row of fruit trees. The house, the barn, the trim orchard, the tractor, and even the couple themselves look solid and, not quite prosperous, but yes, solid. The couple stands arm in arm, shoulder by shoulder, but they appear awkward with one another. He has planted himself squarely but tentatively. He seems to rise on his heels, ready to step out of the frame and back to repairing the milker or stringing fence line. He smiles; he appears to be working at it. His hands are thick, awkward in this setting. One hand, on the arm through which the woman's arm is crooked, rests on the breast of his overalls; the other, with no such task, hangs tense and half-clenched at his side. The woman leans toward him; her hands fold themselves together like letters. There is tension in her shoulders, in her neck, in the way her hands, one placed through the elbow of the man, the other raised to meet it, fold together. Her skin is several tones darker than that of the man. Her eyes are wide and dark. She smiles, but her lips do not part; they purse together and are trim and purposeful. She wears a flowered dress with an apron tied over it. Her hair—which is her glory—sweeps upward and outward; its architecture supported by clips and barrettes. Her hair is black, so black the light of the yard sheds off it like silver.

~

Another:

The hands of a woman. A mound of batter in a bowl. The bowl and the batter are white. The bowl is a flecked, pocketed, absorbent white which soaks up something of the light that comes to it. The batter is shadowed at its sides so that it contrasts more sharply against the bowl; it is in a shape something like the cap of a mushroom. The woman's hands rest on the lips of the bowl. White patches of flour mark the backs of her hands and fleck her wrists and forearms. The white of the bowl, the batter, and the patches of flour darken her hands. The muscles of her forearms, wrists, and hands are clearly detailed; they stand out sharply against the white batter and the white bowl.

~

Another:

The hands of a man: He holds a large nursing bottle and cradles the head of a calf. The hand that holds the bottle is functional and strong. It envelops the bottle and holds it at an angle. The other hand, equally thick, is cupped slightly, as if, in its strength, it cannot fully open. The hand rests on the head of the calf—protectively, for he knows that if the milk stops flowing, instinct will tell the calf to buck upward to make it flow. The hand merely rests there; the fingers appear to stroke and calm the calf.

~

Another:

The woman and a younger woman: they stand before the same farmhouse; we see the same barn, orchard, and tractor. The woman has put off her apron; she wears a dark dress with a flower pattern. The younger woman wears patched and embroidered jeans and a heavy, woven cotton jacket. She has the same black hair with the same silver lights as the older woman, but her hair parts in the middle. It frames her face and her deep and suspicious eyes, then falls behind her shoulders. The two women face the camera. They smile tentatively. They embrace yet hold back. One set of arms crosses at their necks; one hand of each appears on the shoulder of the other. The other set of arms crosses at their waists and brings them close; each has a hand at the elbow of the other. And yet there is separation. Each leans back slightly; each is tense at the neck and shoulders. Their smiles seem awkward—not pasted on or artificial, but unsure, hesitant, ready to retreat.

~

Another:

A room that appears to be a kitchen. Cabinets line the background wall and the corner of a kitchen stove stands at one side. The man sits at the table in the center of the frame. Behind him and at his sides are women. He looks at none of them; he stares into the checks of the tablecloth; his eyes seem watery; they seem to have been cast in glass. He seems to be talking; his lips seem thicker than before. His head cants to one side. None of the women appear to listen. The oldest of the women leans back against the stove. Her arms are folded emphatically; she stares past him blankly toward the opposite wall. Behind the man, another woman. Behind her, another woman reaches up to place a dish within a cabinet door. In the other half of the frame, a third woman, who has the same stand-up hair and a similar dress as the older woman, stands talking to the woman in jeans and the woven coat. The woman in jeans has crossed her arms as well, but more nervously. She seems to look all places at once: to the one who speaks to her, toward the sitting man, toward the woman at the stove.

All three of the younger women have the same mix of dark hair and deep, suspicious eyes.

~

A final pair of photographs:

Down a long crop row, the man and the younger woman walk away from the camera and toward a distant, unknown point. Sunlight and dust mix in the air around them. Long rows of short, dark plants—possibly soybeans—run with them down toward that point. He is to the left, she to the right. He appears to limp and is canted to the left. To judge by the earlier pictures, he must be of equal height to her; but the give in his left leg seems to shrink him. She walks with her hands in her pockets and her head inclined as if listening to him as he tells a long story.

Again: same field, same long lines of new-grown plants running down to the same distant point. The man and the younger woman have walked much further down the line; they have become very small, very distant, like a pair of chattering crows.

JENNY Hilton was raised on a dry east-Colorado farm where, even though she was born to it, the flatness of the land amazed her. There was no way she could reconcile the strict levelness and distance of her home place with the soft rolling hills and rumpling coverlets of land she saw pictured in books and on the television. So she began early to wonder how her home place was left out of the amenities of land that she knew others possessed. Her home bordered on a river darkly lined with trees. Creeks and gullies fingered through the fields. Ditches lined the roads. But when she looked out around her, these were lost to her in the leveled arrowshaft flatness. Even the neighboring farmhouses and barns, the telephone poles, and the distant stands of trees planed out into the golden wheatfield levelness. It puzzled her; it perplexed her. Some days it terrified her.

Away from the house and the barn, she was a rabbit and the sun was a hawk. On the path out to the mailbox, she was a lone spot in her blue dress. A distant flight of birds made the only shadow. A car raised a hedge of dust a mile off. There was no protection. A rabbit had a ditch or a tunnel of grasses. A ground squirrel had the rocks. The coyotes had dens in the woods or their speed or their knowledge of culverts and furrows and fencerows. The birds had nests in the barn, along the fencerows, or under the eaves of the house. But she had nothing on that lane to hide her from the wide eye of the sun. She was naked as a new bird. She was a target for the enormity.

At a distance, too great for any shout or any other interruption, she could watch a hawk descend in a fatal diagonal, strike through the tall grasses, and rise with a small ground animal in its talons. The rabbit or quail or field mouse would dangle like baggage.

What was it I was afraid of? she wondered later. *Was it the distance only?*

~

One day she saw a man, dressed all in gray. He was walking the road toward the mountains with a duffel bag slung over his shoulder. You could walk endlessly toward those mountains, she knew, and never get near them. She watched him trudge past the mailbox and she wondered, *How could he keep walking to such a distant, unwalkable point?*

The man had a troubled red place over his eye. His gray, wide-brimmed hat was banded with a black rim of sweat. Her father got up from the tractor he was working on to watch him pass and watched him suspiciously all along the sun-plated road at the front of the property and all the way down the road to the property line. Then he watched him even longer, just as he sometimes watched the sky for a sign of bad weather. Finally, after the man was thumb-sized, small as a notion, her father went back to his tractor. Jenny watched the man even further. She watched him become a gray mote in the golden distance. She watched him until he disappeared in a little fold of earth near the creek. He did not come back up the other side.

~

What was I afraid of?

She knew that, most days, she played like the others, like her sisters, like the boys and girls they met down in the shady rock shelves of the creek. Most days, the sun browned her face and drew silver lights out of her black hair. "That's the Indian in you," her mother said. And she told her stories of her own half-breed childhood, of owls, of ponies, of lightning waters, of dreams that gave the dreamer her name. The Indian in her was a black-and-silver light that followed her in the fields as she chased the cattle with her dog or looked out at the golden bangling wheat or walked down the long green rows of corn, whose stiff leaves reached out like hands that could not catch her. She felt free those days.

But there were days she caught fear, just as some catch a cold. The fear entered her like a virus. Once it had infected her, she could only wait it out.

The first time she felt the fear, she had just begun first grade and the long daily walk out to the school bus stop. The morning held a silvering October mist, a morning light fragile as a crystal bell. The sun, in the red east, was troubled with cloud. Her sisters had already gone to the road. They stood out by the gate, shading their eyes with their hands, their light skirts billowing in the wind.

The fear came on her twenty feet into the lane. The fear was a coat thrown across her shoulders. It was a screen down before her eyes. It was a ringing in her ears; or sometimes, the words, *Don't move:* a thunderous whisper that said nothing at all but: *Don't move.* She did not move. She could not move. She was numb as ice.

Jenny!

Her sisters called her. They waved her toward them.

Don't move. Her sky was seething with threat. *Don't move.*

"Jenny, what is it?"

Her oldest sister was in front of her now. Her other sister checked the weeds with a long stick. "Ask her was it a snake?"

"Jenny, did you see a snake?"

Her father called up from the barn. "What's going on?"

"She seen a snake."

"You're gonna see worse than a snake if you ain't up there when that bus comes."

"It was a rattler."

"Get on up there."

"A big one."

"Git."

"Wasn't it, Jenny?"

She nodded her head in support. What else could she do? Her father reddened. He looked at her, then at the others, then picked up a flat stick.

"Rattlesnake, my ass," he said. He raised the stick like a saber. "If I don't see you head up that lane in just two seconds, I'm gonna make ever one of you wish it *was* a rattlesnake." He threw the stick down and stalked to the barn.

"It's all right, Jenny," her biggest sister said. "That old snake ain't nothing to be afraid of." Her other sister grabbed her by the hand and pulled her along the lane. Both sisters walked at her side, and as she listened to them talk about the nasty boys at school, about tricks played on the teachers, about trying out for cheerleader, Jenny began to feel better. The fear silently left her, just as a snake eases into the grass.

~

In the attic room where she and her sisters slept, she lay awake staring into the darkness and listening to the night sounds. The windowpanes made rigid blue lines on the ceiling above her. Under the low whisper of the wind she heard the growing sound of a truck. That would be Daddy's friends bringing him back home. She knew it when she heard the tires hit the gravel and the truck pulling up the long lane to the front of the house. She could hear the truck door slam and the goodbye shouts and laughter of her father and his friends as the truck pulled off.

Then she could hear the mingling of the low moaning wind and her father's song as he shambled to the door. The song was something slow and sad; his voice filled with meaning at the end of each line. But she could not make out the melody or the words. She heard him lower his song as he entered the house. Then her mother's short voice interrupted.

"That's enough."

Those were the only clear words she heard. The rest were mutters that reached her through the mute boards of the floor. They would not fight loud enough to wake the children. But she could tell, by the change in the breathing of her sisters, that they had awakened and that they, too, listened to the hushed angry words that rushed into the walls of the house.

~

Her mother had the eyes of a doe and the claws of a panther. Each morning she made a heavy, red-knuckle bread, and, with her fingers thick with dough, pushed back her hair with her wrist, the hair that was full of blacks and silvers like a Mexican saddle. She seethed with an incredible wounding and anger that were constantly rising in her like yeast and that constantly filled the kitchen with an odor of bread and iron.

~

A cousin's wedding:

They drove hours to get there. Again, there was the loud clasping of hands and cooing of aunts and relatives. Again, children flocked to the fields for games while the women loaded the banquet tables and the men gathered under the trees to tell stories and share secret flasks of whiskey. Again, the band spun out reels and polkas.

In the church, it was *Everybody quiet* and *Look at the bride* and the music and the young bride and the young groom at the flower-loaded altar and the preacher's black-robed words—was it just before or just after they made that awesome promise?—*until the dreadful day of doom when the secrets of all hearts shall be revealed.*

And later, during that long, tense, stony drive home, wide awake between her drowsing sisters, she thought she understood about the dreadful day of doom.

But what, she wanted to know, were the secrets of all hearts?

~

Her father seemed to live on the edge of a hope. That was what made him so angry, she knew. The anger was with him daily. Sober, at work or at the breakfast table, he could turn with a rattlesnake suddenness. And when he did, he could grow to a magical enormity. He might ask, snap, demand, as she played or watched him milk the cows, "What the hell are you doing?" And he would grow up bigger than the sky. The question would weigh on her with a suffocating heaviness as if she had been sat upon, as if she were the bent, darkened grasses that you lie upon on a hot day.

He never once hit her. His rage was more like a blanket that he dropped on her as he stood in the middle of a room, a blanket that made her hands heavy and that filled her eyes with darkness. Under that blanket, she could move, but she always moved with the fear of bumping into a wall or a lamp or the sharp corners of his rage.

"What the hell are you doing?" he asked. When she could stammer no reply, he steamed and she fixed her eyes on the nearest door and ran blind into the sunlight.

But her father's anger came from the killing of a hope. She always felt it, though she only put those words to it later, after she knew there were such words. For when he was drunk, it seemed the hope had swallowed him down whole and he could swim in it like an otter or lie down in its belly like a whiskey-soaked, laughing Jonah. When he was drunk, he was transformed; when he was drunk, he lifted up like a great black bird, dropped his buzzard-ugly anger, and flew.

What was he hoping for?

She never knew. She only knew it was hope flying that she saw in him drunk and hope killed that she saw in him sober. She watched him at a wedding or a party, dancing polkas like a young pony. Or waltzing in the slow dances (her mother never danced) with some cousin or aunt, like some soaring great-winged bird. Out in the parking lot, he would sing with one arm on the neck of some old buddy or one of his brothers. It would be some old-gang-of-mine song full of long, low notes. His smile, then, was so wide it nearly split him, as if he might unseam like an old coat. She would take time from the games she played with the other children to stand at the edge of his circle of friends, a solid wall of large backs and sweating shirts. And she would watch:

It seemed that at any moment he might burst open like a flower. She thought he might begin to ring like a bell. The way he staggered and smiled, she thought at any moment he might fly.

It thrilled her to see him break out of his hard-knuckle rage and scrape-knuckle labor to sing instead of scold. Even as she played tag or red rover with her cousins and neighbors, she watched him stumble and laugh among his friends. And as she watched, she felt easier, safer, free as grass. She played harder at her own games. When the blanket of his anger lifted, she could feel herself unbend. She could feel lights along her limbs.

But the way home was always dark. In the car, a frosted silence always dropped in between her parents. She and her sisters sat in the back seat, drowsy from long play, bored with the darkness of the misting fields. They sat fretful as lace, but afraid to argue, fearful of breaking the silence, fearful of the thawing argument and the noise (the whispers, curses, pounding on the steering wheel, muttering, and shouts) that would follow if their parents' argument flowered. They hated that ride.

She could not mole herself small enough nor find a place dark enough.

She always wondered, Why did her father's drunken excitements make her mother so hissingly bitter? Why did her father's ecstasies turn her mother so bitter? What did her mother see that she could not? Years later, she felt she almost had an answer. But as a child she had no answers, not in those nights, nor in the sands of the daylight hours.

Sometimes she saw herself and felt herself entirely within a shell. The shell was no thicker than a thumbnail. No harder either, but just as hard. The world (words, the people around her, the sun, things that hurt) bumped harmlessly against the shell. The shell wrapped her up when she was tired or fearful or when the silence in her house was like a heavy thunder or when her father had flung the sky full of rage.

It was almost like being stunned. She remembered the look on the face of a yearling calf that they had set aside to butcher, just after it had been struck by her father's hammer, just before it collapsed. It was a slack-faced look that meant that the pain, which a moment before had struck it like a bolt of lightning, had bounced back out and was traveling away at a terrific speed.

And as Jenny watched her own pain speed away, people would stop her and ask, *Are you all right?* Teachers would tap on her desk and ask, *Didn't you hear me? Are you all right?* She was filled then with a silent laughter. How could they know? It was all so laughable. She knew, but they could not know, that she was more all right at those times than at any other. How could they know? Their worry was laughable. Their worry was terrifying.

~

There was a time, just once, when fear flowed out of her like water out of a broken dam. A time, just once, when she was empty of fears and empty of thought, and filled with a rush of warm light.

At times, even now, she could remember it. She could bring back a piece of it, though not at will, and always with a massive sense of loss. It came back to her in certain moments, usually on winter afternoons, after the wine and its morning pain had cleared her, after that daylong rain of aching had soaked down into her bones and into a bad sack in her belly and what she had left was the bad taste and a fear in her belly the exact shape of an old rag doll. She might be looking out of a window that was dashed with rain or looking at the sunlight pattern in an old linoleum rug, and if she could just hold still enough for a moment, if she could keep the shifting pains from turning her eyes into stone, she might see it all pull together into its secret pattern, like the pieces in a kaleidoscope, that lattice of light, that stony rainbow.

What was it that made her feel that sudden surge of lights?

She had wandered with her sisters down to the creek. Her sisters played up the stream until their voices became as distant and wordless as the sound of birds. She was shorter-legged and smaller, so she had tired. She decided to rest on a broad, flat rock.

A cliff, a solid face of reddish stone, rose above her. Water stains streaked it like a track of tears. At the base, in the soft, red, rock-leached earth below it, a patch of sage grass grew, tall and powder-headed, thick and dusty as an old man's beard. She could see, along the top of the cliff, tufts of grass, overhanging branches, and the bare, tangled roots of trees. She knew, from many explorations, that a hundred yards on either side an easy shoulder gave her a path to the top. But to look at it from her creekside rock, the cliff seemed unclimbable, impossible. It rose fifty feet or more, and it was bare of anything like a handhold or a place to grab hold. There were just the flat rock face and the slid earth and the tear-track marks of the rain.

The high noon sun banked against the red face of the cliff. The light threw itself down onto her like a hot rain. She felt her forehead dampen; her hair was slick with sweat at her temples and across her forehead. There was a rattle of water in her ear, a slide and rock rattle sound that was clear as a shower of crystal. When she closed her eyes, she could still see the braided waters and she could see the flash of light. When she opened her eyes, she looked down at the water where it riffled over the rocks and crossed itself in a silver weave. Silver lights glinted in the leaves of the willows at the corners of her eyes. She began to ring with excitement.

She closed her eyes and a feeling took her like a wave. She felt herself lifted as by a flood and blinded with silver lights. She was thinking no particular thing, but she was aware that she was thinking no particular thing and that she no longer felt the rock underneath her, nor felt any pain, nor any of the chigger bites that had bothered her moments before, nor any fear (not of being late or her sisters talking or of ruining her clothes or even of dying like this). Instead, she felt a flowing out of her, as if she had become a tuft of creek grass and the waters flowed through her. She heard nothing but the rattle of the water in her ear. Within the rattle rang a set of chanting voices. The voices were not in song. They said no words, left no message, made no point. But they had a ring of silver.

She was cool, weightless, a slim silver fish hanging in the waters.

She had no idea how long she sat in that silver trance. She only knew that after a time she could not measure, she heard sistervoices calling to her through the high weeds, impatiently shouting her name.

She remembered later how the words finally tapped through to her and how much loss she felt when the silvering thrill left her. She could not ignore her sisters. They gathered around her like a team of nurses or an audience, full of questions, complaints, and commands.

What you been doing down here?

Did you get lost?

You're alla time getting lost.

We been looking for you an hour.

Are you all right?

Are you all right?

She looked around her in a daze, as if she had been suddenly awakened. There was a low feeling in her stomach, a feeling that she had lost something she was supposed to keep.

~

What she remembered of that first drink was harshness, frustration, and desire. She visited a friend from down the road, and that friend stole a quart of homemade from her father's cache behind the milk cooler. One mouthful: It set her tongue and throat aflame, and she pushed it away and left the barn. Her friend quickly hid it back. Jenny did not see where.

Moments later, as she stood in the sunlight waiting for her friend to come out of the barn, she had a fledgling urge for more of it. Something had been stirred in her and was cramping like a chick within its shell. Something had been loosened by that mouthful of white-hot liquor and was moving in her bones. She turned back to the darkness of the barn, but her friend was coming out.

"Let's go quick," her friend said. "Before Daddy catches us."

Jenny stood in the barn door, half in sunlight, half in shadow.

"Come on," her friend said. "Daddy'll kill us if he thinks we took his liquor."

Jenny stood, split by light and by shadow, immobilized with desire and with dread.

"Come on, Jenny."

"Jenny."

"Are you all right?"

"Jenny. Come on."

~

That night, when she came home, she was convinced that her mother watched her with a smoldering fury, that her sisters watched her with a kind of agony, as if they knew she was about to be struck by lightning. And her father did not watch her at all: he stayed late in the barn among the disassembled and cursed-at parts of his combine. She was convinced that he deliberately, to avoid her, ate his supper by lamplight, after she and her sisters had gone to bed.

~

Her mother's fury that night was like smoke: Jenny could almost smell it; she could almost see it billow up out of her. She knew that if she breathed too deeply, it could choke her, that she would suffocate under it. There was not a word spoken, not even a look, but as she lay down to sleep, she could smell her mother's fury, she could hear the crackle of the flame of it.

On most days, her mother's fury was a different thing. On most days, her mother's fury followed her like a shadow, like a haunt. It was not a fury directed at her. It was a fury expected of her. It was an urged-on fury that searched in Jenny for a mate.

"There's your father," her mother would say, "drunk again." And her eyes would storm across a room to her, furious that her daughter had no parallel sense of rage.

Jenny tried to find it in herself. She looked in all the closets and pantries of herself, but she found no rage, and little anger. What she found instead was fear.

~

Her sisters handled their mother's expectation of rage by making regular denunciations, for their mother's hearing, of their father and his habits.

"Daddy's drunk again," one might say. "Yuck."

Or, with a grimace and a shake of the head, "Daddy's been down to Uncle Roy's again, ain't he?"

There was something rehearsed and proper to their complaints. But their mother approved. It meant they had been enlisted.

Jenny was not enlisted.

"It's your father, drunk again," her mother would say. Then her mother would wait for her to respond, to shake her head somberly or to say, "I hope he don't pass out in the shed like he did last week."

Instead, Jenny would look out to the barn lot where her father was talking and laughing with a friend, and she would watch the lightened way he lifted his hands and slapped shoulders with his friend, and she felt her own lightening limbs shimmer with desire and expectation.

~

She did not take her next drink until she had gone off to college. She made it through her crazed high school years, which were tied up with miles of late-night roads over which she and her friends ran the ancient and hulking cars of their parents, and even managed to get through prom and graduation without another drink. The years of her mother's unrelenting disapproval had had such an effect that when she had the opportunity (at parties or from a case hidden in the trunk of one of those cars at the drive-in) she always told herself *not now.*

She knew the hovering fury she would have to face.

~

She was bused, each school day for twelve years, from the front gate of the farm through the small crossroads town with its feed mill and grocery store and the railroad gates that sometimes barred their way to the school where all twelve grades sat out the falls and winters and springs like seeds, aching for the summers.

She liked her teachers. They had been other places and told her of them. None of them expected a rage of her.

She emerged with a determination that she would see bigger and be bigger than what she could see from the fences of this farm and that she would avoid the roads taken by her sisters, who, one after the other, married high school boyfriends who had just gone into the service.

~

She did not take her next drink until well into her first college semester. She had picked a school in San Francisco, where she planned to major in English or sociology or anything else that had hope in it of lifting her out of ordinariness and dread. Suddenly, in the first month of college and with no warning, her life fell together. She was in a place where no one had known her before, so she could make herself new. She had gotten back her midterms and had good grades. She had an entire mountain range between her and the quarrels of her parents. She had a new feeling, as she walked the steep and foggy streets of the city, that she had been able to find a separate and viable self, one which no one could talk her out of. She could survive and prosper in a strange, complex, and massive place. She had friends who talked with her and who sought her out and who strolled out on Haight-Ashbury or Telegraph Avenue with her, who shopped and studied with her, who talked about the boys with her, but who could not stay with her through the awful hour of two in the morning when she would sometimes wake from a dead sleep as if someone had just clutched her at the shoulder and said *Don't move* (and, for a long and awful moment, she would not). They could not be with her through the moments when she felt herself ache for a release from the coils that knotted her belly.

To get through, she swallowed her fears as if she were swallowing pills. She charged into her classes and her projects and her times with friends with all the grimness of a soldier going into battle or of a father settling in to spank a child. For as long as she was shuffling books and index cards, as long as she was at her job in the library, as long as she was typing a paper or tutoring in the program for inner-city children, as long as she was planning an outing, she felt serene and untouched and admired. Gradually, after she had figured out the trick, the safe times increased. The times she felt gripped and endangered shrank back. As Thanksgiving neared (with its first visit back home) she felt she had earned a chance to experiment, to try out, to defy.

So one night, in an off-campus party, when the wine bottle came around to her, she held it for a moment in her hands. It was short, round, made of greenish glass, and dark as pond water. She held it for a moment as she might hold a kitten or the face of a lover. It felt warm, as if it were a living thing. Then she wiped the neck of it, put it to her lips, and began to drink. She pulled against it several times, long muscular pulls that reminded her, when she thought about it later, of the pull of a nursing calf and that lasted until the breath cried within her.

She was surprised at how familiar was the warmth along her throat and in her belly. It had all the warmth of a coming home.

She set the bottle down in her lap. She waited. Her friend who was next in line was nudging her to pass it on, but she waited. Nothing but the warmth had happened yet, so ignoring the others, and to their amazement, she lifted the bottle again and drank as if she had fallen asleep in it. She felt her friend nudge her again, but drank until she felt her lungs flare like those of a drowning woman. Only then did she pass it on.

She closed her eyes and waited a moment more. And then: She felt herself open like a flower. There was a new warmth in her hands and a warmth in the way the room caressed her. She knew that her friends were teasing her, that they were laughing at the silly new face she showed them. But she felt warmth in their teasing. It was as if they had been waiting for her to unbend, to loosen up, to enjoy. She remembered later that she spent the rest of the night laughing, that she danced and laughed and felt herself lifted out of her more weighted self as if she were a broad-wing bird.

So it did not bother her that they later had to carry her back to the dorm, that she vomited so hard it made her eyes hurt. It did not bother her that she spent the next day reeling under the hammers of her first hangover. Those parts fit neatly into a compartment of her memory set aside for those things which were minor and survivable. What mattered most was the feeling that, up to now, she had always lived her life as if something, some pearl of great price, had been stolen or lost.

Now, in a warm and blood-red rush, she had gotten it back.

WHEN Jenny first cut loose from Paul in that parking lot and plunged into the sea of Nebraska corn, it was as if she had snapped a lifeline. To cut loose from him was to choose to drown.

After that day, she continued to drown cross-country for years before she came to the city where he lived. She had not known that he lived there; she was drawn fatefully there, as if by plan. She had drowned many times over, and in many places in those years since she had left him behind, since she had cut, with what she thought was a final and masterful stroke, the cord that bound her to him.

Each time she drowned, she sank to a weedy, stagnant, black-mud bottom where she became comfortably one with the darkness, where time was clocklessly slow and microbial, where change was breakdown and recomposition. Others might see her in full light laughing or dancing or grinning large, but the truest and most hidden part of her had gone comfortably dim, slow, vegetal.

But she had not died in any of her drownings. She had not learned to drown that well. Each time she had bobbed up, all unwilling and gasping for air.

~

After she had cut loose from him and found herself alive and undrowned on the far side of the field of corn, she hitched a ride to the next big town and found, with eleven dollars in her pocket, enough cheap wine to drown herself for the next eleven days.

She knew that it was eleven days because they told her of it later.

Total strangers in a strange city had kept her alive.

~

In treatment, as she had emerged, bleary and aching, from the detox unit, they had told her, *Be true to your self. Respect your self. Love your self.* She had not even known she had a self. She had felt nothing where a self should be but an emptiness of self and a pit of fear. She had seen others who were replete with self, tormented with self, confident and satisfied of self, or even full of shame of self while she felt nothing she could call a self. She was an empty core. She was a hollow tree.

~

As she entered the sea of corn with the satchel thrown over her shoulder, she looked back. Paul and the mechanic sat side by side in the van, peering down into the belly of the engine. They were involved only in the engine. She was glad. She wanted no witness. She wanted only to dive deep into the corn and not be seen again. After she entered the corn, she did not look back again until she knew she could no longer see him. Nor could she be seen. She wanted to know that the leaves of corn had sealed her off from him. She wanted to know that she was enveloped in green and that there was no point at which he could reach her, that there was no way he could make that link again. Ever again.

She could as easily have stalked down the road and hitchhiked into the next little town. But it was as if the corn had called her and she had followed. As she sat in the car, suddenly all she could see and all she could hear was the corn which surrounded them like a solid green wall. Across the lot, Paul stood talking with the mechanic about the errant engine. She sat rigid and still, with her arms crossed on her knees and her hands formed into fists, but her eyes scanned the surrounding wall of corn. They had traveled down those walls as if they were the walls of the sea through which Moses crossed. She could sense, though she could not see it, the vastness of the sea of corn, and she felt a sudden urge to dive into it.

So when Paul came back to the van to check on her, she cut him off and told him, "Go on. Go on." She wanted free of him. She wanted no more argument. She had hit upon what felt at that moment to be a solution. She waited until he went for the mechanic. Then, once he and the mechanic had their heads deep in the jaws of the engine and the front, she rummaged through the back of the van, stuffing things into an overnight bag. It took her a few minutes, but she took only those few things she wanted. Then she stepped out and looked once around her at the station, the abandoned restaurant, the van, the two men working at the van, and at the thick, heavy-eared corn. She hitched the bundle to her shoulder, stood taller, and felt herself swell.

When the wind lifted, the leaves of the corn rattled like shells.

Later, in treatment, after the detox, they told her, *You almost died. When we found you, you were nearly dead.* She knew she was supposed to be frightened and that she was supposed to want to live. And she did. But she was not frightened at the thought of such a death. She felt there was something incomplete about her experience, that she was supposed to learn something from it and had missed the lesson.

It was something she had to learn and relearn and was still relearning on the day that girl came into the store with her jaw hanging down and her fist full of nickels and dimes.

The journey across the continent had begun so wonderfully. As they pulled out of San Francisco and drove east through the deserts and the mountains, the feeling of wholeness and intensity was still so powerful that she thought nothing could disturb it. She wanted nothing to disturb it, nothing at all. The big, wheeling sky, the shimmering deserts, the broad-boned shoulders of the mountains all told her that she was on the right path. They were traveling cross-country to meet a dream. Just like legends. The right path—that was what she suddenly knew she needed that day when he came to say he wanted to move. Something like a shaft of light went through her at that moment, and she knew it was the right thing to do and the right path to take. A wonderful sense that she was whole again and that she had a reason to be whole filled her. She had packed happily and happily rode the farmlands, deserts, and mountains.

From time to time as they drove, she turned from viewing the pines and postcard mountains to look at him—stern, intent on what was before him, his hair tied back out of his eyes with a bandana just like a pirate or a biker in a gang. The feathery creases at his temples twitched with concentration. His strong, thin hands—so strong and so thin that they reminded her of the talons of a hawk—gripped the top of the steering wheel like the talons of a hawk clutched on a windy branch. She felt newly secure, protected, and though she could not have named her purpose, full of purpose.

~

He had said, before they left, "You know we'll be traveling close to where your family lives. Look at the map." She looked. "We'll come right through there."

He waited for her to respond.

"It'll be a chance to see them, if you want."

She nodded, ever so slightly.

"Well, let's do it. I'd like to do it. I'd like to see them again." They had visited once before, a year ago.

She nodded again. "Oh yeah," she said, and did not even hear the catch in her own voice. She did not even hesitate to call.

On the phone, her mother sounded happy to hear from her and did not mention the years of neglect and distance. She did not ask once where all the years had gone or why she never wrote or what was she doing with her nice education.

"And we'll be happy to see your friend again," her mother had said. She had apparently thought about the right word to use.

Her father, she said, was doing well, but for the injury in his back and leg and well, you know how he gets sometimes.

Her sisters would come over with the kids. They would be happy to see her. They would all be so happy to see her.

~

The journey had started so wonderfully, but when they started down out of the mountains, she felt a lurch; it was as if she had been dropped. Something happened—she did not know what—so that her sense of safety and elation began to leak out of her like sand. It was a slow enough leak at first, and did not worry her. But she was concerned that the tear would widen, that the leak would leave her sagging, weak, and empty.

At the Colorado border, she said, "I'll drive." It was a way to feel powerful again, a way to put something in her hands and feel unthreatened.

"I'm okay," he said. "I'm doing fine."

"I'm ready," she said. "I'm ready to drive."

She knew, without looking, that his look was puzzled. But he pulled over to let her take the driver's seat.

He had pulled over where there was a wide place in the road. They each got out their opposite sides and slowly came across the front of the van. They each were aching from the long hours of sitting. They each moved slowly. A little copse of willows grew up around a culvert, then thinned out as it followed a stream down the edge of a pasture. Cattle stood still as bronzes. Locusts whirred like rattlesnakes. The sun was a golden hammer. As they passed each other at the front of the van, he stepped into her path. His right hand went to her waist and, as she pushed past him, brushed against her breasts. She knew that he wanted to go down to the cool of the willows to make love. But she wanted back in the safety of the van.

Once they had come free of the mountains, and of the foothills of the mountains, and the land began to level out, it was as if it all came back. She understood now the lurch in her stomach and her need to take the wheel.

They were on level, planed stretches of open ground, which were studded with pasturing cattle or plated with golden wheat.

Colorado was a threat. She wanted out. She did not want to watch her mother cry and pound out biscuits on the kitchen table. She did not want to watch her father limp thirsty to the barn at feeding time and limp back more lightly smelling of whiskey and hay. She did not want to match the normalcy of her sisters' lives with her own. She knew that her mother had been baking and planning. She knew that her sisters were ready, at the moment of a phone call, to pack the children into their husbands' pickup trucks and come over. She knew that Paul was watching her strangely as she passed the turnoff to her parents' house and knew that he would say nothing, ever, but would puzzle over her for years.

But she drove on. She drove on until she was so tired that she was running the van off the road and kicking up gravel. She drove until Colorado was far behind her and she was deep into the wheat and corn of Nebraska.

~

Once they crossed the border, she let him drive again until the rasp started from under the engine cowl and it began to erode her sense of trust in him. Until she became, finally, convinced of the enormity of his lie.

She had passed the road to her home and he had not said a word but "Here it is."

At first she was relieved. She did not want to explain a thing. Later, as the miles passed under their wheels, she began to wonder. *Why not? Why shouldn't he wonder? Why shouldn't he ask?*

Miles later, she looked over to him. She had not looked once in a hundred lost miles, and he was again intent on the road before him. Again, there was a feathering at the temple and still the hands strangled the top of the steering wheel. He was intent on the road as if she weren't there at all.

And suddenly, it was as clear as if he had spoken it: *He doesn't even want me here.*

The last sands of her security sifted from her belly. She felt foolish and useless. It was so obvious and had been so obvious and would have been obvious to anyone not so blinded and deluded as she had been.

So she determined that, at the first chance and at whatever cost, she was gone. She wanted to be as gone as if she had never been at all.

That was why she took the negatives.

8

A PHOTOGRAPH:

A woman at a desk. Obviously a professional woman. We see that in the smart jacket with the squared shoulders. We see it in the stylish cut of her hair and the collection of loose, bangly bracelets that cluster at her wrist. With the eraser of a pencil, she touches her forehead. With her eyes, she studies a text on the desk in front of her. With a finger, she appears to trace a line.

Her desk is laid out neatly. A little rack holds a stapler, a cup of pens and pencils, and a pad of small notepapers to one ready side. Behind her, on the walls, we see the corners of two framed prints.

Another:

She has taken a pencil in a tight, purposeful grip and has pressed it to the paper. The muscles in her hand and the flex in her brow and the manner in which she has braced her opposite elbow all suggest she is carving letters into stone. A cigarette waits in an ashtray; it raises a white pennant of smoke.

Another:

She has laid down the pencil and has taken up her cigarette between two fingers raised in a V. She leans on the opposite elbow; her eyes are lowered to the work in front of her. The smoke from her cigarette wreaths her hair.

Another:

She has broken off her concentration on the project in front of her and she looks up. She is in three-quarter profile. Her elbows are planted on the desk; her hands are folded together. The cigarette is fixed in the net of fingers. Smoke curls up from the cigarette in a path something like that of a river on a map. Her eyes are on the little river of smoke. It seems she reads it as a fisherman reads the water, as if it were a text, a scripture, an answer.

"YO, what's up?"

Amy looked around and saw Jonathan sitting on a stoop. A boy beside him scowled over a comic book. Jonathan gestured her to come over.

Amy gestured back. She had no time to stop just now, so Jonathan jumped up from his stoop, dodged across the street, and fell in to walk beside her.

She did not want to talk to him. She did not want to talk. She did not want to do anything at the moment. She did not want to be going to school. She did not want to lug a portfolio and book bag that each had grown heavy as stone. It was Monday. She still had homework she had neglected all weekend. Her mother had annoyed her with suspicious questions about how she was spending her time. She still felt depressed over her conversation with Jenny. She was overwhelmed and spent; she had no room left for Jonathan.

He tugged at her elbow. "What's up?" he asked again.

"Don't handle my coat."

"Come on, man. What's up?"

"Nothing's up. I'm walking to school. Which you should be doing yourself."

"I got time. I got plenty of time."

She gave him what she hoped was a skeptical look.

"Give me fifty cents for a pop."

"You shouldn't drink pop at this time of day. You shouldn't drink pop at all."

"Why not? You do. You probably did this morning already."

"Orange juice. Fresh, healthy orange juice."

"Yeah, right. So buy me a pop."

"You'll rot your teeth. You'll be twenty years old and your mouth will be all black and rotten."

"Come on, man."

She turned on him with a ferocity that she had not known was in her. She struggled with an impulse to slam him with her book bag. She wanted to hurt him, to see him damaged. "Quit it," she barked. "Just quit. I don't have any money and if I did I wouldn't give it to you. You're just a little beggar and a nag."

She saw him draw up. The strings of his shoulders tightened. His face whipped into a sneer. "Be like that," he said. He walked a few more paces with his face set straight ahead. "I knew you wasn't cool. I knew you wasn't nothing but a preppie punk."

He turned back in the direction of the boy on the stoop. He sat beside him and together they scanned the comic book.

~

School was nearly unendurable, but she endured it. *I want out of here,* she thought every hour. *Please let me out of here.* She wanted out of the boring routine and the petty rules. She wanted nothing to do with hall passes or lunchroom gossip.

Finally the last bell rang and she headed for the door. She covered the quick steps from the door to the curb, then paused. She had not thought of Jonathan all day. Now she contemplated going into the street and realized, suddenly, that with Jonathan turned against her, she was not as safe as she was just a day ago. School was boring and petty, but none of the damage that could come to her on the streets, and which came every day to people on the street, would come to her when she was in school. It was a strange, unsettling thought. Here were two separate and parallel worlds, separated by a narrow strip of asphalt. To cross the street from the shadow of her school was to step into alien territory. There was threat in the vacant lots and there was threat in the crowded corners. Anyone might come up and hurt her. Her only safety lay in being known. Suddenly, with this argument, she was a stranger. She stood staring and studying for a long time. It took an act of will to step off the curb and to cross to the side with the littered playground with the broken swings, where the alleys and the side streets split off and split off like the pockets of a lung. She walked the streets to the studio as if every brick hid a snake.

She tried to make herself bold. She told herself, *I'm not going to be ruled over by some little twit.*

But she knew she was wrong. She knew she could tease him and play the dozens with him. But she had done more than that. She had disrespected him; she had crossed a line.

So when she saw him sitting on the stoop of his house, she set her book bag and portfolio on the sidewalk and sat down beside him.

"What do *you* want?" He was tossing pennies at a can on the curb. With every fourth or fifth toss he missed and the penny rolled into the street.

"I didn't mean to dis you, man."

He nodded without moving his eyes from the can. "We're cool," he said.

"I mean, I wasn't really mad at you. I was mad about something else."

"I said, man. We're cool."

"So why are you, like, throwing your money away?"

"Forget you, man. Buy me a pop."

"You'll rot your teeth."

"You're crazy."

~

She worked her hour at the studio, then had to go meet her mother. She had a little time and she wanted, as usual, a snack. She was in the habit of stopping at Jenny's store for a pop and a bag of chips, but decided she had best skip it this time. She feared Jenny might not want to see her again.

Jonathan was at her side as soon as she left the door of the studio.

"Look at these, man." He showed her a stack of old postcards, yellowed and brittle, chipped at the corners. "Look at these old-time stamps."

"Where do you find these things?"

He shrugged and pocketed the cards. "So where you going now?"

"I'm going home."

"Straight up?"

"That's where I'm going."

"Yeah, right."

"That's where I always go."

"Now you're perpin'."

"I'm what?"

"You're telling a lie, man."

"You little twerp. What makes you think I'm lying?"

"'Cause I see you go straight from Paul's place to that little store where that lady works."

"So now you know everything I do?"

"And then you stay there and talk to her for like an hour."

"So?"

"So buy me a pop."

"I can't get rid of you and this pop thing."

"So just buy me one and you won't have to hear nothing more about it."

"Anything more," she corrected him.

"Right. Nothing more."

"So what if I don't have time?"

"Give me the money and I'll buy it myself."

"How do I know you won't buy drugs with it?"

"Come on, man. What do you take me for?"

"Cigarettes?"

He had to pause for a moment. "So, like I said. You buy it for me."

He pointed. They were in front of Jenny's store. She hesitated, looked once at the boy, and down the street, then stepped into the store. The little bell rang. Jenny was not behind her counter. A small flutter of fear ran through her. Hussein was at the other register, tapping numbers into a calculator. Nervous, she grabbed two cans from the cooler and snatched a bag of chips from the stand and brought them to him.

Where is she? she wanted to ask.

The owner did not look up from his calculator. He pointed down the counter to Jenny's usual station.

"Right here, babe," Jenny said from behind her register.

"I thought you were . . ."

"You think too much." She glanced at the two cans of pop and the bag of chips and rapidly hit the buttons of her cash register. She rang open the cash drawer, ripped off the receipt, and snapped open a paper bag. Amy dropped the coins into her palm and watched Jenny wordlessly count them into the cash drawer.

"So, look . . ."

"You gave me too much, babe." The woman handed her a stack of coins.

"Look, I'm sorry if it sounded like I was accusing . . ."

Jenny glanced over at Hussein, who was still tapping at his calculator and writing figures into columns. "It's okay," she said. "It's okay."

Amy persisted. "But it's like I really upset you and . . ."

"It's okay," the woman said again. "I'm okay."

"I really didn't want to hurt your feelings. I mean. I wouldn't want . . ."

The woman lifted a handbag onto the counter. "Here," she said. She brought out a manila envelope from the handbag. Its color had faded; the corners had gone fuzzy corners from wear and travel.

"Take this," she said.

"But I just wanted to say . . ."

"Take this," the woman said. She pressed the envelope into the girl's hands, along with the paper bag full of pop and chips. "Take this. I'm okay. Just take it."

The girl hesitated. She lifted the flap of the envelope.

"Go on," the woman said. "Take it home and look at it there." She tapped out a cigarette from a newly opened pack, nodded toward the door, and struck her lighter.

~

"What you get?" Jonathan asked at the door.

"I got you a pop."

"I mean, what's that she gave you?"

She shoved the package into her book bag and said nothing.

"It looks old."

"Eat some chips."

~

At home, in her room, after she was sure her mother was watching the eleven o'clock news, Amy opened the envelope.

The negatives: dozens of them, carefully stored in plastic slipcovers in rows the size of a letter page. She studied each in the light of her desk lamp, these images in which shadow blossoms into light and brightness is swallowed by dark, in which darkness is eaten and becomes clear as water, in which all brightness becomes clotted and dark, where only gray remains as it is. There again, in a world of reversed light, the girl in the wide straw hat, the smile and the ring of laughter, the mug of cheap wine, the hair like the wing of a raven (gone silver in this backward world), the child and the strange stumbling embrace, the violent pint bottle, dark as a pistol, thrust into her mouth.

She studied them for hours, one after another, until she had memorized each, until drowsiness took her like wine and she could no longer hold up her head. Then she slipped each negative back into its plastic cell, hid the packet under her bed, and slept.

A vicious, pelting rain obscured Ann Taylor's windshield and her view of the morning traffic.

"Amy," she said, squinting through the gray mist on the windshield and wiping it clear with a glove. "Honey, wipe your side of the windshield."

It was the third day since Ann had quit smoking. It was terrible such a rain had to come up today. It was terrible when she was already tense about starting work on a new contract with a new crew from out of town and a new team of always so unpredictable models.

She had cleared the patch of glass in front of her, but it was still streaked with condensation. The defroster was roaring, but it would be minutes before it would clear the rest of the glass. And Amy had yet to raise a hand. Her side of the glass was still full of fog. She was irritated. Such a simple request.

"Amy," she said again. "Just wipe the mist off the windshield, will you?"

Amy had been hard to wake this morning. She had grumbled herself down to breakfast, then stared into her cereal without a word. After breakfast, she had rolled her eyes and sighed and moped through the house and into the car. And now this.

"Why were you up so late last night?"

"I wasn't."

"I got up to go to the bathroom at three and your light was still on."

"That doesn't mean I stayed up late."

"Well, what does it mean?"

"I was studying."

"You were studying until three?"

"Why not?"

She could not win this argument, so she gave it up. But the stress of it only increased her yearning for nicotine. She had already begun to reach for a cigarette that wasn't there.

But before she could complete either of these movements, Amy had looked around, pulled off her hideous little baseball cap, the kind that all the boys and half the girls were wearing, and began to wipe the windshield with it.

Good, she thought. But the bit of argument still left her craving a smoke. Though no one could have known it to look at her, her breath now came lacy with tremors, her throat had gone dry as sand, and her hands, clamped on the steering wheel, were shaking.

~

Ann Taylor had tried three times before to quit smoking. Her doctor had already told her that the huskiness that smoking gave her, though it deepened her voice and made her feel more attractive, presaged more serious things. She knew all the reasons not to smoke.

But she failed each time she tried to quit, because without her cigarette in hand she found herself nearly mute. She could use her cigarette as a pointer; she could peer skeptically through its smoke; she could leave a contractor unsettled as she drew a new cigarette from the confines of its pack, set it alight, drew on it deeply, and spilled its contents across the face of an invoice. But without a cigarette in hand, she found that her words had no impact on others at all. They were like words spoken under water or behind glass. She felt helpless as a fly in a bottle.

~

She did not know just when she learned the power of those gestures. It was simply something she inhaled in New York City, along with her knowledge of clothes and her eye for good copy.

She had hit New York as a girl, after deciding, through much teenage reading of magazines, after much comparison of her own shape with the shapes she saw in those magazines, and after much encouragement from family and teachers, that she could make it as a model, that considering her looks and talents, it was a sensible, respectable thing to do.

And so, right out of high school (where she was popular but felt hopelessly bottled up and confined), having studied how to pull it off, and having made the right sort of New York contacts (including an aunt, considered somewhat, but not quite, crazy), she made her move. Though she now lived in the city of which her hometown was a suburb and traveled back to that gritty little suburb on a nearly weekly basis to see her still-living parents still living in the same old house (still neat and tightly painted and the yard still trim) and now found the town to be nothing more than ordinary and just a little slow, in her high school years and in the images that drove her to New York, the place had a painful grayness and a hopelessness that choked her like a smothering hand.

Her hometown lay in the floodplain of a small river that flowed into a larger river just a few miles down and where, together, they flowed past the city of which she could see the fringes. Because her town lay in the floodplain and because it centered on an asphalt plant (where her father and the fathers of most of her friends worked) and because the houses were small shacky things with small yards and gardens in the back, her town was not really what you could call a suburb, but rather a misplaced and abandoned small and gritty town. In the true suburbs, which had eaten up all the farmland around her town, the houses spread over full-acre lots and even the side streets were solidly paved and the sidewalks were not broken, buckled, and disintegrating. City and suburb: at night her gray little town lay between the lights of each.

She went to high school in the hill above her town, above the floodplain, within the real, true suburbs, where the houses were larger and the smells of asphalt and mud were blown away by the wind.

She had dates and was invited to parties and was nominated (but not elected) for homecoming queen. But it was never enough. She knew, even when they treated her right, even when they invited her to their parties and when their mothers said, "Such a pretty dress," even when she was taken out by the boys from the hill in their fathers' cars (which were not smoky and rattling and ragged at the fenders), that there was something wrong and deficient with her. There was always something wrong in the air around her. She and the others from her town, ruled by the river and the asphalt plant where her father worked and where the fathers of all her friends worked, were branded, as if they carried with them a mark upon their brows, as if they carried on themselves an odor of asphalt, a smell of mud. There was always a distance kept by the people from the hill that told her she still carried the smell of the small town, that she was still held by those choking hands.

~

Odd, she thought later, that she should go to breathe in a place where the air was so bad. Odd that she learned to breathe by learning to smoke.

But in late-sixties New York, she felt as if she had just broken free of a stranglehold and that she had left those choking hands behind her in the dumpy, boring, tree-lined streets with their chubby little box-shaped houses. All those people with dreams no bigger than next week's football game or those tacky little prom dresses (which they still sell, only shorter). Where a big night meant a spin to the drive-in movie. Where a big date meant that a boy going on to trade school for electronics wanted a chance to feel you up. Where the corners of the main drag were thick with boys whose minds were as narrow as their dicks were hard. Where making something of yourself meant (if you were lucky or your parents had worked real hard) going off to a college where you could learn to be a tidy little wife to a tidy little accountant after four years in the display window of a sorority.

She wanted out. She wanted free of those small-town hands.

She knew what she needed in order to get out: Boys could use the service or football. But if you were a girl and you didn't have money and you didn't have good grades, you had to make it on looks.

She did not mind a bit. She knew, from years of admiration and comment, that she had good looks. Ann had studied her move like a general. A week after graduation, she was living in Manhattan.

~

The aunt had made money enough to take the edge off her reputation for craziness, so she was allowed to make that move. The aunt had made her money working in some of those same magazines Ann had read and dreamed through at home, so she was in a position to set her up in the modeling trade. "Send her on up," the aunt had told her parents, who showed through their hesitation that they did not fully approve and that they feared the devouring city, but showed through their hesitation to refuse their sense of inferiority in relation to all that money (which was not much money at all but would seem like a lot to a factory family in a gritty suburb).

There was much worry and discussion and stroking of chins, but she knew she would win. She knew even then that money will always defeat people's notions of good sense. She was sure that money—her aunt's money and the money she stood to make on her own—would protect her, no matter what.

~

But neither her aunt's money, nor hers, nor any other money, could protect her from David.

She was making good money of her own by then. Her aunt had helped her with living space, contacts, advice, and example until she had become not a top model, but a solid and respected and money-making model, and she was, by then, three or four years into it, able to get out on her own and to set her own agenda.

Her aunt had set her a good example. In fact, she had been a wonder to her, for she had a control and mastery in her world—where doormen tipped their hats and called her Miss and where bright and expensive people turned half around to greet her each time she walked into a room—that was far from the grayish insecurity of the people of her hometown. It pleased her to know that her aunt had not been born to such mastery, that her aunt had shaken off the grit of that same small town and had polished herself smooth as bone, that her aunt had had to learn the same mastery she was now learning.

"Don't just be a dummy," her aunt told her. "They like you stupid when you're under the lights, but they won't want you on the dumb end of the camera forever. You'll be cold potatoes to them in a few years, so get it all up here." She pointed to her brow. "Get everything they'll let you take. And then take more." She nodded significantly and flashed her room-light smile. "And don't let them take *you.*"

So Ann observed, as closely as possible, the working of the camera crew. She reviewed prints, learned the mysteries of exposure, blush, tone, and cropping. She absorbed everything she could on how to do a layout, balance words and images, please a client.

Most of the time no one even knew she was learning. She sweated under the lights and held awkward and artificial positions in every sort of clothing for endless (but well-paid) hours, smiling during breaks a smile she had learned from her aunt and, during breaks, asking small questions and making mental notes. No one would have thought her any different from the models she saw as brainless and unambitious, content to stay in the hot lights and to remain twisted into those awkward, those artificial poses.

~

"Never let them know what you're thinking," her aunt had told her. "Never, *ever* let them know you're angry. And don't ever let them know if you want something. Even if you want it badly. Always keep them off their guard. Always keep them unsure. Always keep them wondering." There was a seriousness, almost a grimness behind the pleasant makeup as her aunt said those words. Her aunt, whose practiced smile lit up each room she entered, spoke those words as if they were prayers.

~

She learned the power that gestures with a cigarette could give her.

"It's just a six-day shoot," her agent told her. "It's a favor I owe this guy."

She had taken a cigarette slowly from her pack. She had then, as a gift, a hinged box faced with silver where she kept her cigarettes in neat rows.

"Look, I can get you five grand up front, and five more once the shoot is published. It's some quick, easy money."

She examined the cigarette as if it were a piece of fine jewelry; she moved it in the light as if it glittered, as if she thought it a treasure.

"I mean, the guy's never done me wrong yet . . ."

She looked him in the eye, then back at her cigarette.

". . . and he's stuck his neck out for me half a dozen times, so . . ."

She grimaced, lightly: just a twitch at the corner of her mouth, just the smallest hitch of her shoulder.

He threw up his hands. "Okay. Okay," he said. "I'll hit him up for fifteen thou . . ."

She brought the cigarette to her mouth and reached to the table for the lighter. He grabbed it first, flipped it open, and struck a flame. She hesitated a moment; her eye went briefly back to his, as if unsure she could even accept such a favor from him. Then she looked away and leaned toward him with the cigarette. She blew smoke down onto the desk between them.

"I haven't signed a thing," he said. "I haven't made a single promise."

~

What did David see when he saw me? she wondered now and again, at times when the thought of him crossed her. He must have seen her skill with the cigarette and the gestures. He must have seen the room-light smile that she had adopted from her aunt. He must have seen the way she turned heads without ever turning her own.

She was, by now, past the pain of losing him (or of throwing him down, which is what she did), but there were days when he rose back up and visited like a guest from out of town. He would stay close by but just out of sight for an hour, a morning, a whole day at a time, just as he did back in Manhattan. And if she did not think too much, if she kept him on the edges and almost, but not quite, out of sight, there would be a comfortable feel to such a day. She would carry a feeling of safety and gentleness, for that was what he gave her in those first days back in New York.

So far as she knew, he was the only one in New York who really knew her. (Except for her aunt, of course, who knew her, but acted as if she had always been from downtown, as if neither had ever smelled of asphalt or mud.) So far as she knew, he was the only one who had ever seen behind her elegant and carefully constructed self and seen the girl from the small gritty town. He was the only one to laugh at her, though the laughter did not feel like mockery but knowing. He let her feel that the small-town girl was safe with him. Those memories remained comfortable just so long as he remained no more than a hint, a shape at the edge of her vision.

But as soon as she let him come close, as soon as he entered her direct line of vision and she saw him, full-bodied and real, she caught herself, remembered what he really was, and threw him down again.

~

Their marriage, which began as an over-the-weekend impulse, lasted three years. He was on the road with his band for much of that time, so throwing him down mostly meant setting out his clothes (for that was all he ever kept there) in a half a dozen cardboard boxes in the hall.

She expected him to call her, to beg for a second chance. She expected at least an apologetic note. She expected a chance to vent, to tell him why, to hear him argue and promise, to say that the other women and the weeks on the road without a call were all in the past. She expected him to beg for a chance to change. But he left without a fight. He sent a friend around to collect the clothes.

~

He did not leave her much, but he left her with a daughter. Amy was two by that time, so Ann had had plenty of experience dealing with a small child by herself while he rehearsed or toured. Over the years, after he left for good, he sent the occasional check. And there were Christmas presents and birthday gifts—fairly consistently though usually sized wrong or off-age: a set of Legos when she was only four, a doll when she turned thirteen. But he never tried to call her; he never tried to visit. Ann had learned to handle her own abandonment but still could not believe he had so set his daughter adrift.

New York City was too much to handle alone with a small child. Her aunt had begun to look at her with eyes slightly glazed, as if, in marrying against her advice and in having this inconvenient child, Ann had somehow failed her. She had no one else who would help her but her folks back home, so she broke with the city which was so fast, so bright, so hard. When Amy was still small, she came back to live and work in the city of which her small hometown was a gritty suburb. But she did not leave behind what she had learned in Manhattan. She resolved she would never again let someone see behind her elegantly constructed walls. She would never again let anyone know what she was thinking or what she felt. She would never again be tricked into thinking she was safe.

~

Whenever her daughter got on her nerves (and some days, like this day, her nerves could get very bad), Ann never allowed herself to show a scrap of irritation. In general, this had worked, even a couple years ago when things had gone so badly. It had been a lot to learn and master in that period, a whole new phase of learning: a child, especially this child who seemed to be so much her father's child, could not be so easily managed by gestures. An adult would follow the surface of things. A child saw something else.

She loved her daughter. She was all she had. For years she had kept only a small circle of friends and regular contact with her family. She had let other men approach her, flirt with her, short-term date her, but they always gave up and she always let them. She wanted only to be safe. She wanted only to raise her daughter.

But lately something in her daughter was changed, and it was just like her to be so obnoxious about something simple like the windshield. This was nothing like the wild and angry behavior of two and three years ago, and she was glad of that. But why did she have to be so stubborn and so inconsiderate?

~

Ann and Amy rode in silence in the warming car. She tried to think: What did she need to do to make herself ready for a day working with the new crew and the new and unpredictable team of models? For she knew, already, that nothing would come together on time, nothing would be within budget, nothing would be as she had worked it out in advance.

She was still shaking, though no one would have known it. As a model, working in cold rooms and under hot lights, she had mastered the art of motionless shivering and the art of sweating without sweat. But the desire for not-just-nicotine but the whole experience of holding, lighting, drawing in, and expelling a long stream of smooth gray smoke had taken her over bone by bone. She could feel the tremors all through her fingers and into the palms of her hands.

Three days without even the thought of smoke and now this overwhelming urge for a fresh, smooth, trim cigarette. She wanted the busyness of opening the pack, tapping out the cigarette, and setting it alight. She wanted to feel the smoke roll across her tongue. So she practiced what they told her at the training: she breathed slowly and deeply. In a moment, the urge settled.

But still, the silence that had built up in the car felt oppressive. Though she could just dare a moment to glance away from the traffic, she turned to look at her daughter.

Amy was staring straight ahead, silent and self-absorbed. For a moment, Ann flashed with the same anger she had felt toward her just a few minutes ago. But in that moment anger vanished and the tremors in her palms were stilled. The morning light shot down through a gap in the canyon of the interstate, and she was struck by the image of her daughter's face:

Backlit by the sun coming across the freeway: her straight-ahead, silent, self-contained stare. She had just a moment to see it, and it was as if she had never seen it: the intention of the girl's eye, which did not appear to flinch in spite of the sun and the flash of traffic around her: the subtle flex in her brow, which, with a movement of a single muscle above that eye, had changed the entire cast of her face: the similar tension in the muscles around her mouth, making the lips rise slightly, pulling the chin up slightly, as if her face were an emblem of staunchness and determination. And such a fine-featured emblem: a wisp of hair had fallen across that eye. The girl seemed to have ignored that and all other things, including her mother's glance, as she concentrated on whatever thought pressed on her. The small hairs on her lip and the blacker hairs of her eyebrow were tipped with light. Even the small, barely perceptible creases in her brow and in her lower lip each caught its dressing of light and illuminated the concentrated elegance of her daughter's face.

Ann had to look back immediately to the highway. The traffic was heavy, and to look away like this for more than a moment was dangerous. But she held the image in mind a moment more as she maneuvered down the interstate; she studied this snapshot image as carefully in mind as she would a mockup or a studio shot: the wisp of hair, the intent blue eye, the raised and illuminated chin. She carried this image, this frozen second of contact, through the crush of the freeway, off the ramp, and onto the first of the downtown streets. She wondered, *Where did I get such a daughter?*

But by the time she could safely look again, the girl had turned her back to her and was staring out the window at the downtown street.

THAT turned shoulder had bothered Ann all morning long: In spite of what she had seen in the flash of a moment on the highway, there was still that gesture, that simple turned back. Such a subtle, ambiguous, and eloquent motion. It was so easily deniable. *I was just looking at the trees,* the girl could say. *The trees are pretty.* That gesture could mean anything. It could mean, *I am only watching the trees.* Or it could mean *I hate you; I deny you. I turn my back on you.* It bothered her so much that, once the shoot was on, and the needs and demands of the new and unpredictable models had been met, and each needy ego had been stroked and every necessary errand had been assigned to an appropriate go-for, every nerve in her system was chafed and split and aching for nicotine. Her head felt ready to crack; she could no longer think.

She turned to her assistant and said, "It looks as if we've pulled this thing off. I'm going home for a break." Home was a long way to go for a break, but with such a headache and with such a tension in her arms and hands, she could think of nowhere else to go. She figured she could come back down to pick up Amy from school when it was time. Or she could call the school and tell her to take the bus. She did not care just now. All her capacity for goal setting and logistics had been sucked right out of her.

God, how she wanted to wrap her hands around a pack of cigarettes. How she wanted to have her frayed nerves bathed in nicotine.

Just to leave the shoot and get out on the highway brought some relief. She made some calculations: It was shortly after lunch. Amy would have another three hours of school. She could take an aspirin, lie down, and rest. She had two hours or more before she needed to go back to work. Even if she rested for three hours, Amy would still be in her after-school study hall until five o'clock. She had plenty of time before she had to call.

At home she swallowed the aspirin, kicked off her shoes, and fell back flat on her back, dead asleep for the next two hours. Finally she woke, stretched, yawned, and caught herself reaching across the nightstand for a cigarette that was, dammit, not there. She checked the clock and decided she would call the school and see if Amy could get out early. She felt more rested; her headache had dimmed. She felt more forgiving of the turned back, her daughter's gesture of rejection. The school could page her; she could ask her if she wanted to come around to the shoot. She might enjoy that, with her recent interest in photography. Leaning her back against the headboard, she dialed the school and waited. When the secretary answered, she asked, "Could you page Amy Taylor for me?"

The secretary did not bother to put her on hold; she never did. For several minutes she heard the secretary's mumble, a voice chanting from an intercom, then a discussion closer to the phone, none of which was clear enough for her to understand. Finally the secretary picked up the phone to say, "She doesn't answer at the study hall."

"Well, could you give her a message to call me at home?"

"Yes, but . . ."

"Yes?"

"Well, I don't think we'll see her until tomorrow morning."

"What do you mean? She's with the . . ." Something was wrong here.

"Miss Henderson says she leaves directly from here to go to work study every day right after school. Have you tried there?"

She sat straight up in the bed. *Work study?*

"What are you talking about?" Her voice became brittle and commanding.

"Her work study in photography."

"I don't know what you're talking about."

A strangled silence followed. The secretary had clamped her palm over the speaker. A moment later, a voice that she recognized as that of the vice-principal came on to ask, "How can I help you?"

"You can find my daughter for me."

"I'm sorry?"

"She's supposed to be in study hall after school. And now I hear something about a work-study job. What is going on?"

"It's the same program you signed for in September."

"I signed nothing."

"In photography."

"If I wanted her to study with a photographer, I have three of them working for me. I don't need her to . . . Look, where is she?"

"I'm sure she's just fine. There's . . ."

"I know she's fine," she said. "I just want to know where she is. And I thought you people were supposed to know."

"Just a moment."

This time there was a click and the deadline silence of the hold button. She started to pace alongside her bed, as far as the phone cord would allow her. Had she been smoking, she would have filled such a nervous time with the motions of reaching for, tapping out, lighting, and inhaling on a cigarette. She pressed the phone between her shoulder and her ear and clenched and unclenched her fists as she paced. This wait was longer than the first. When the vice-principal came back on the line, she could sense in the woman's tone a desire to stay on top of this. She knew she had become, to this woman, a bothersome and hysterical parent. "I pulled the permission you signed from the file."

"The permission for what?"

"For the work study."

"I didn't sign anything."

"It says here, I grant permission for my minor child Amy Taylor to perform a work-study project with the Paul Lewis Studio. I understand my child is to complete sixty hours of . . ."

"Paul who?"

"Paul Lewis."

It had all come clear. She remembered their discussion. She spoke very precisely. "I signed nothing of the sort."

"But I have your signature."

"Listen to me. Listen. I signed nothing of the sort."

"Well, I'm . . ."

"What I signed, and what I paid for, was for her to be in the after-school study program."

"But . . ."

"So she wouldn't have to be wandering the streets until I got off work."

"Well, I understand, but you see we have to assume . . ."

"You assumed wrong. And I want to know what's going on."

"So do we. We'd like very much to get to the bottom of this."

She continued pacing the bedroom, frustrated that the phone cord kept her leashed within such a small range.

"So where is this place?"

"Just a moment." Again, the deadline silence. But only for a moment. "We don't have a location on this permission form. And Mr. Thompson has left the building. I could try to reach him and call you back." Thompson was the photography teacher who had set this up.

"Yes, do that."

"We're very sorry about this, but we saw the signature, so we assumed the work study had your knowledge and approval. We don't make work-study assignments unless we're sure they're legitimate. So . . ."

"Yes. Yes, I understand."

"So I'm certain this can be straightened out."

"Yes, I'm certain it can."

They each murmured apologies for this awful misunderstanding and agreed they would stay in touch until this could all be explained. And yes, the primary concern was for the welfare of the child. And yes, they would resolve this in a short time.

"We'll be in touch," said the vice-principal.

"Yes, we'll be in touch."

Her rage sifted out of her as she spoke, so that when they finally hung up, she felt oddly empty.

She probably thinks I'm an idiot. She probably thinks I don't know what I signed. She placed the phone back on the nightstand and fretted back to the kitchen. She had decided she needed a cup of coffee before she settled on what to do next.

It's not as if she's in danger, she thought. *If she's done this today, she's been doing it since the first week of September.* Two and a half months of deception. The girl had gotten good at it. *Why should I have even been surprised? It's just like her,* she thought. *It's just like her to lie and sneak around. That's just what she does. She can't stand to be told what to do. She can't stand to be told no.*

She remembered clearly now the conversation she and Amy had had over this strange photographer plan. She had assumed that Amy had forgotten all about it, that it was just another plan-of-the-week. There had been dozens, one after another, each one forgotten before the week was out. Amy brought it up just that once, and she had never brought it up again. Had Amy ever brought it up again? Why not? Had she really not signed the paper? Had she somehow forgotten?

That's crazy, she thought. Of course she had not signed.

She knew better than to wait for the school to call back with an address. Schools never work on any sensible schedule. While the coffeemaker did its work, she flipped through the phone book for the Paul Lewis Studio. White pages, yellow pages: Nothing. Of course not. She had not thought there would be, not an operation like that. She felt another flash of anger at the school. How crazy to set a girl like Amy up with such a fly-by-night operation? And then not even to talk it over with her! As if they were the parents!

She was not going to passively wait if she could help it. She poured her coffee and set out for Amy's room to see it she could find some clue there. She hated to go through her things like this; it was an invasion of her privacy. But this felt urgent. She felt violated, so she did not care so much about Amy's violation. She wanted that address.

She found nothing more useful than a pack of cigarettes and a lighter (and when did Amy start smoking?). She dropped these into her jacket pocket so she could confront the girl later and was about to give up looking when she decided to check the scuffed and faded manila envelope that she found in Amy's top drawer.

The envelope itself was creased, worn at the corners, and thin along the edges, an instant from falling apart. Inside, carefully stored in plastic sheaths, was a set of black-and-white negatives. But no address. Nothing to tell where her daughter had gone. She continued to rummage and search, but found nothing that would tell her a thing. So she sat down on the bed, sipped her coffee, and thought. The packet of negatives was the only thing which was out of line, the only thing she could not explain. So she picked up the packet again and carefully pulled out the strips. She took them to the alcove where she worked when she took work home, placed them on her light table, took out her magnifier, and examined them, one by one.

She knew how to read a negative, how to trade dark for light. In a string of images of silver and shadow, she saw a woman in a dark coat: smiling, unsmiling, standing, leaning, seated on a bench, embracing a child, thrusting a pint bottle into her teeth.

When she had finished, she put the negatives back into their ragged envelope and, thinking she would look at them again at work, put the envelope in her shoulder bag. Then, without a thought, without raising a single defense or rationalization, she drew her daughter's cigarettes and lighter from the pocket of her jacket. Trembling in every joint, she began to smoke.

9

PHOTOS:

A boy, small-boned and dark-eyed. He wears a quilted coat, torn at the elbow and split along the seam that holds the right sleeve onto the coat. His skin, in these black-and-white pictures, is ivory-pale. He has the small bones and large eyes of a squirrel and, like a squirrel, seems, even at rest, poised to leap. He stands in an open door, at the entrance to a hall. A bannister and wooden stairs rise behind him. The step on which he stands appears to be of solid stone, and it bears a worn depression across the middle, the mark of steady generational erosion of shoes and boots across it. The wooden frame around the open door is studded with mailboxes, four to each side, each one nailed or screwed into the frame, each with a name taped or painted on it. The spaces between and beside the mailboxes are chipped and scarred. There have been many mailboxes come and gone here; many initials carved into this wood; many layers of paint have been laid on, chipped off, layered over.

The boy, on his step, in this frame, seems impatient. We sense that the scowl is permanently etched into his nervous, squirrel-like brow, his mouth permanently pulled to one side and that he appears perpetually sardonic, forever tentative and skeptical. He scowls to one side. He raises the toe of his left foot.

~

Another:

Same boy in the same place, still impatiently shifted to one side. But now a woman stands close. She brushes his hair into place with her hand. He ducks his head slightly but does not seek to remove himself. He keeps an embarrassed eye on the camera.

The woman is dressed in a plaid winter coat that has a fleece-lined hood thrown back across her shoulders. The coat is open and we can see that she wears a white skirt and white shoes, as if in uniform, like a nurse or a waitress.

Like the boy, she is small. Small, and very thin.

~

Another:

Same boy, same woman, still in the same place: this time they have composed themselves in portrait manner. Each has straightened up and stands taller. The boy's head leans toward the woman's shoulder; his brow has relaxed somewhat; he seems unsure what he wants to make of himself. His toe is still raised.

The woman stands straight and gazes straight, almost boldly, at the camera. Yet there is something tentative and abstract, almost fragile, about her. In the radiant light rising from her cheekbones there is a hint of the girl about her. Yet she has been hammered and clipped by her years; we see the inch-long scar across her upper lip and the narrowing in her cheeks where a tooth is gone. The flesh around her eyes seems brittle, crackling like old china. We can see the black rim of eyeliner and the dim cloud of eye shadow she has been careful to spread across her lids; we see the corresponding shadow, like a reflection in a pool, of a darkening space below her eye. Her brows have been shaved and penciled until they seem flat and metallic as a hammered nail and as clearly artificial as the painted brows of a geisha.

Like those of the boy, her eyes seem both intent and distracted. Though she looks directly at the camera, her head turns, just slightly, as if she wished to turn away.

~

Yet another:

The boy, alone. He stands at the head of an alley. Behind him there are others, but they are not in focus and we can tell nothing of them. The convergent lines of brick in the walls of the buildings along the alley and in the bricks of the alley floor form a basket of light and shadow around the boy, as if he were in the center of a medallion.

He looks aside. Angry, sullen, his hands jammed into the pockets of his coat, he looks toward something, someone far down the street.

~

The last:

The boy: close up, we see the corner of his chin, but the focus is on the five objects in his open palm.

Three dark coins: an Indian head penny, a nickel with its buffalo nearly effaced, a quarter on which Liberty has been rubbed down to a shadow.

A skeleton key, flaky with rust.

A small crucifix, broken from a chain or rosary: Jesus is a little silver twig pinned at three points to his flat silver cross.

AMY knew she was in deep trouble. She knew it when she arrived at her mother's office a good ten minutes late and her mother said nothing at all. In fact, her mother said nothing at all through the whole trip down the elevator, into the parking garage, and all the way home. No *How was your day?* or *Did you finish your homework?* Nothing but a tense, thin-lipped silence all the way up the highway, and down the off-ramp, and into the side streets, up their driveway, and into the front door.

Her mother had stopped for Chinese without even asking what she wanted. As she trundled her pack and her portfolio to her room, she listened closely for slamming plates or cabinet doors. She heard nothing but swift, efficient movements as her mother set the table and dished rice and vegetables into microwaveable dishes.

She stayed in her room only a moment, only long enough to set her things down and to hang up her coat. But her mother had worked swiftly. The steaming food was laid out and the places set. Her mother was waiting in the living room, sitting at the couch. With an eye, her mother motioned her to sit.

"So what does he have you doing in this Paul Lewis Studio of his?"

She knew. Her mother had raised her right eyebrow.

She did not know how, but her mother had broken her lie.

A thin pennant of smoke raised itself from the edge of a soda can newly enlisted as an ashtray. *Omigod,* she thought. *She started back again.* She watched as her mother reached for the cigarette, inhaled deeply, then tapped the end against the lip of the soda can. The gesture was the same she had seen a hundred times, but this time there was something edgy and desperate to the movement. And there was a tremor, just the edgy hint of a tremor, to her hand. And instead of the usual smooth and model-like posture, her mother had stiffened in fury. Her mother was trying to contain it, but there was a beetle of wrath paced within each eye, and her hands were clenching and releasing.

Amy felt a swift flush of triumph. She had cracked her mother's composure. She was no longer smooth and powerful. She was like nothing in a magazine.

But her triumph failed quickly, for she had never known, from anyone, such a glaring, barely submerged, all-out rage.

Her first thought was to say, *I'm not doing anything wrong,* but that seemed so childish a thing to say. She could have said a lot of other things, but everything else she thought of seemed—not wrong, but something her mother would make into something wrong. She knew that in a such session, with her mother in such a mood, she needed to calculate her answers carefully. But she could never calculate carefully enough.

Her mother's eye went up again, just to let her know she noticed. As she raised her cigarette to her lips and drew on it deeply, her eyes turned to focus on the coal flaring at the tip. It was as if she had forgotten all about Amy for that moment. She watched as her mother's almost-invisible tremor died. She breathed deeply and her features gelled. She lowered her cigarette and turned up an icy, unreadable face.

"I asked," she said, "What do you do there?"

"I help out with the exhibit."

"What? You make coffee? You sweep the floor? What?"

"No. I do all sorts of stuff."

"I bet." She flicked her ash without even bothering to aim.

"Mom!" The wrong her mother was hinting at now was so wrong that she began to panic.

Her mother reached down to stuff out the cigarette in the lid of the pop can. She crushed the cigarette carefully and thoroughly before she dropped it through the hole. Then she raised her eye.

"It's not an unfair question, you know."

"I know, but . . ."

"I mean, you spend two hours each evening there with a man in his studio—I guess it's a studio since I've never seen it and I'm not even allowed to know you're going there . . ."

"Mom!"

". . . and I find out, without even trying, that you've forged my name on a permission slip."

"Mom . . ."

"I was so embarrassed I thought I would shrivel right up."

"Mom!" Amy was in tears by this time, and choking on them.

Her mother shifted her eye, reached for her pack, and tapped out a new cigarette. She dandled it in her fingers before she reached for her lighter. She said nothing, but waited for Amy to slow her sobbing and speak.

"I mean, it's not like I'm doing anything wrong."

Her mother leaned back against the couch. One hand held the unlit cigarette, the other stroked her hair. She nodded for her to continue.

"I mean, he's not like that."

"Not like what?"

"Some dirty old man type. I mean . . . I mean, it's not like I'm posing nude for him or something. I'm not *posing* for him at all. I'm *working.*"

This last seemed to make her mother wince, ever so slightly. Not enough to make her shift out of pose, but enough to create a small catch in the breath, a brief narrowing of the eyes. She remembered her mother's career as a New York model and realized she had said a thing which could not easily be unsaid. She dropped her eyes and raised them to see that her mother had recovered. She lit the new cigarette, drew on it deeply, and blew out a long splinter of smoke before she turned and asked, "Well, what is he like, then?"

She fumbled for something to say. "He's just . . . I don't know. He's just really into his photography. And he's really into these people. They're like, all these poor people and farm workers and stuff. And it's his first real show after all these years of not being recognized."

"Yes. Yes, I know. You've told me all about that." She tapped her ash into the can, then shifted back to her original question. "So what is it you're actually doing."

She shrugged. "I help him get photos ready for this show. And he teaches me stuff along the way." She knew it would not sound like much when she said it.

"What does he teach you?"

"Like, what it means when you crop a picture a certain way. Or if you crop it another. I mean, you have to really think about what you're leaving in and what you're cutting out. A small cut can change the whole impact of the photo. You can shift the whole balance of the . . ."

Why am I even telling her all of this? she thought. She realized, with a shock of embarrassment, that her mother had more years in this business of cropping and editing than she had been alive, that her mother made such decisions nearly every day, that it was her business to do so, though she had never once tried to learn a thing from her. It had never before occurred to her that her mother might have something to teach worth knowing.

Her mother acknowledged as much with a small, ironic lifting of a scimitar eyebrow, but said nothing.

The thought confused her, for she was not sure, knowing this, that she could learn the same thing, even so technical a matter, from her mother. Or that what she could learn from her mother was the same at all as what she was learning at the shop. She became aware of a vague and emerging uneasiness, as if the ground of this conversation had just shifted.

"Yes," her mother said. ". . . cropping." She nodded. *Go on,* the nod said. But her look was distant now, and she drew deeply on her cigarette.

JONATHAN stood watching from a hidden place. It was a bright, cold day, full of sudden turns of wind, and he shivered at some moments; at others he paced, stamped, and blew into his hands for warmth. He could have been warmer had he been out in the midmorning sun, but he watched instead from the hidden place he had selected. He could have been warmer had he been in school, but he had other business to attend to. He had paced, stamped, and blown for nearly an hour, watching steadily from his dark, hidden spot into the bright, busy street. If he had not had such a strong sense of the business he was about, he would have been distracted and bored. But he was alive to every movement on the street. After a great deal more pacing, a great deal more stamping, and a great deal more blowing into his cold hands, Jonathan saw his cousin emerge from the alley into the bright, lancing sunlight of the street.

Jonathan pulled back into the shadow of the dumpster. His cousin pulled up the collar of his coat, looped the speakers of his headphones over his ears, and stuffed his hands into his coat pockets. Behind him the man in the black old-fashion jacket emerged from the alley, spitting out smoke and muttering as the wind caught him.

In a moment, the two separated with a tap at the elbow and a nod. Jonathan's cousin toward his corner, the black-coat man toward his low-slung coffin-colored car.

"Sweet," Jonathan said. "Man, that's a sweet car," to no one near. In fact, there was no one near at all. Hardly anyone ever used the alley. The buildings that lined it were empty. Frayed, blackened plywood covered most of the windows. The doors were nearly all nailed shut. Graying moss grew among the bricks. It was a good place to hide, and he had been hiding here all day, since just after first bell at school.

He had really planned to go to school today, since he was just this close to a truancy charge and he had promised his mother, I will, I will. But half a block from school, he had seen the boys from up on Blair, and they all said, *Wassup, Little J, Come here* and they rapped with him. *Wassup with that raggedy coat, man.*

"My mom's gonna get me one her next check."

"Forget that, man, we can hook you up right now. You know? You don't want to go around looking like a buster. We can hook you up."

They told him what they wanted him to do. He could hear first bell ring and he could see all the other kids line up in the playground, but he was standing with the boys from Blair, chilling like one of the fellas, and it was, like, I got something better to do now.

Jonathan's cousin quickly took up a post beside a utility pole, but the man in the black coat hustled the half-block to his black, catlike car. Jonathan admired the black leather and sharp cut of the man's coat even if it was old-fashioned, and he admired the black sheen and the claw-colored ornaments of the car as the man got in, hit the ashtray, and turned the key. The car started with a rumble—not at all loud or sharp, but with a low, steady, thunderish rumble, powerful enough that Jonathan felt the rumble in his chest. He liked the sound, and his chest and fingers thrummed along as the man released the brake and set the car in gear. The tires barked and the car pulled off.

Once his cousin had gone to his corner and the man and his car had disappeared into the maze of traffic, Jonathan backed further into his alley and out of the wind. He zipped down the front of his coat, pulled it open, reached into an inner pocket, and pulled out a crumpled pack of cigarettes.

There were just half a dozen left. He had started with a whole pack just this morning and now he was nearly to the last. It was the first time he had a whole pack to himself to smoke. I got to slow it down, he told himself. The boys from Blair had given him the pack and five dollars and told him, *Go get you something at the store.*

He called to a red-eyed wino, "Hey. Old man."

"I ain't that old, little man. I just been used hard." The man had a gray, stubbly beard and long gray hair pulled back in a tail that curved up, then down like the handle on a pitcher.

"Yo. Buy me a pack of cigarettes in that store."

"How old do you think I am?" He pressed down the coils in his beard and cocked his head. His red eyes were moist and there was a winy smell around him.

"You're old enough to buy me a pack of cigarettes."

"Naw. I ain't old enough for that."

"Come on, man. You go in there all the time."

"Milk. I get milk."

"Come on, old man."

"I ain't as old as you think."

"I can give you a dollar besides."

"Two dollars."

"Two."

"I think the years just caught up to me."

Jonathan gave him the money the Blair boys had given him and waited. He knew the wino might cheat him once he was in the store with all that wine, so he loaded up his pockets with rocks. But the wino played him straight and brought him his pack of cigarettes.

"Now I got you the cigarettes, why don't you let me fire one of them up?" said the wino.

"I already gave you two dollars."

"That was my service fee. The cigarette is my tip."

They went back into the alley, out of the wind, to light up. Jonathan was a little scared to go back into the alley with the old man, but he still had his pockets full of rocks, so he went. In the alley, he drew the pack out of his jacket pocket, hammered it several times on the heel of his hand, pulled loose the cellophane, and folded back and tore off one corner of the foil. Then he tapped two cigarettes loose from the pack. Jonathan had a lighter from home. They leaned their heads together and cupped their hands to make a little tent from the wind, and Jonathan, enjoying his little power, struck the lighter and lit them both from the same flame.

~

Johnathan could not roam the street because of the police. And he could not go home—his mother would kill him for sure. And all his friends were in school. It was way too late to be going to school—he would have to go straight to the principal's office for a late slip and probably get a detention. And he could not go back to the boys from Blair until he at least tried to bring them what they wanted, and he could not do that until he was sure he could pull it off. The alley, with its hive of abandoned buildings, was the only place he could hide. He played kickball against himself up and down the alley floor. He peeked out at the street to see the traffic of businessmen, old people, and whores. Whenever he became bored, or hungry, or cold, he smoked one of the cigarettes. Whenever he became really bored, he left his post for a time to explore the buildings that opened onto the alley. He explored each one, cellar to attic, and, though each of them had been raided for its copper and other salable treasure, he found his own small plunder: a claw hammer head with no handle, a book of stories from the Bible, and a pair of blackened coins. He placed each in the pockets of his jacket and continued to search. In the attic of the last building, he found nothing at all but the gray planks of the floor and the naked, rough-cut joists and beaverboard of the under-roof. Porthole windows at each end of the attic let in a dusty light that showed him, cut into the ceiling, a square hatch leading out to the roof. He undid the latches, pushed the hatch aside, and climbed out by the little dark ladder built into the hatchway.

He settled himself uneasily onto the roof. It was sheet metal, slathered over with tar. It had a low, rolling slant, just enough to make him feel precarious and dizzy. The hatch was just three feet from the edge.

There was the street, a hundred feet below, with nothing at all but the box gutter to protect him if he rolled. There was the big, open, enormously blue sky with white bursts of cloud rushing under the wind. There were the square gray office towers of downtown, watching with big shoulders and hands on hips.

There, on the street below him, were his cousin and the black-coat man.

~

Back in the alley, Jonathan saw his cousin and the man with the coffin-colored car come together, talk briefly, and enter into the alley. He waited some minutes until they emerged, separated, and disappeared. He waited some minutes more until he was sure they were gone. Then he left his place in the wind-sheltered alley, crossed into the wind of the street, and, with a look to each side, entered their alley, turned at the cross alley, and found the building. He moved a garbage can under the fire escape, reached up to grab the bottom rung, and swung himself up. He climbed in through a window only he knew and climbed through passages only he knew until he reached a room full of large, metallic, white shapes.

It took him only a few minutes of search, and then he had what he had waited for all that long day.

WHEN Roger Nolan steered onto Broad Street, his way was blocked for a moment by a tall, awkwardly slender, woman-looking jaywalker. He braked to let her pass and turned to his passenger.

"Is that a he or a she?"

The young man with him shrugged. "I ain't gonna try to say." He was himself a tall, awkwardly slender Black youth of around fifteen years. He wore a thick coat done in the colors and stitched with the logo of a professional football team. He wore a knit cap with the same logo pulled down nearly to the level of his eyes. He capped one hand over each knee and stared past the jaywalker as if that person were of no interest or concern to him. "It could be either one," he said.

The jaywalker continued her slow strut across Broad Street and slowly turned her gaze across the two of them. Her eyes were marked by a bright splash of mascara; dark lines extended her brows to the corners of her face; her mouth and cheeks were rouged and painted with such precision and abstraction that she took on the eternal and impassive look of a painting in an ancient tomb.

"Ain't that a motherfucking piece of . . ." Roger stared the jaywalker back in her eye and shook his head. A muscle twitched briefly in his cheek; his eyes narrowed. The muscles in his temple and jaw tensed under his pale skin. If the young man had looked over to him at that moment, he would have thought him ready to explode into violence. But he did not look. The jaywalker passed and Roger's face relaxed. He set the car back into gear. "Man, I could jump on that if I knew it was for real." He looked to his passenger and grinned.

The young man, in spite of an effort to remain somber and aloof, grinned nervously in response. Roger noted this relaxation of the young man's tension. He figured the young man was still in the habit of deferring to an elder and grinned again. "We gonna set you up," he said. "You hang with me, you can buy all the real pussy you can handle." He continued down the street in the direction of the bus station. It was the noon hour. The sidewalks were full of people, the street full of cars. Half a block down, Roger had to stop again for jaywalkers, this time a young man in blond dreadlocks and a young woman pierced with rings at her nose and lip.

"What is this shit?" Roger said. "Ain't there no normal people running these streets these days? It's all mixed up." He shook his head again. "It didn't used to be like that."

He looked; the boy nodded, and Roger went on. "I mean, used to be, everybody more or less kept to their own territory. The Whites was all down here. The Blacks was up the hill on Blair. Italians was down near the river. But now it's like, everybody's everywhere. Knowmsain?" As they inched along through the noonday traffic, they could see turbans, ballcaps, mohawks, skullies, short-brimmed fedoras, the white sailboat hats of the police, the paper forage cap of a boy headed for a fast-food job, the little, flat, brimless caps of Muslim men and the shawls of their women, and the even smaller knit caps worn by the Jews.

"But I don't care. I'm for everybody. It don't make me no difference. People is all the same to me, Black, White, Brown, whatever. It's all the same. Knowmsain? You scratch one, you scratch another. They all bleed the same. Now look . . ." He pointed, and the young man beside him looked. "You see these yuppies over there?" It was a group of men in ties at the door of a café. "And you see these young brothers over here." He shifted to the other side of the street where a group of young Black men stood watching the traffic. "They all just want the same thing." The young man rolled his eyes briefly upward, then back down.

"And do you know what that is?"

The young man did not know.

"They all want a little bit of the . . ." He gestured, looking for the word. "A little bit of the money. Or a bit of the action. Or some leg. Or a place in the suburbs. Or some sort of . . . whatever. They all just want a little something out of life, is all. Knowmsain?"

The young man nodded. "I can hear you," he said.

"Life got to give you something or it ain't really life."

The young man nodded.

"So that's why I don't understand. Everybody really just wants the same thing and they think they got to get over on everybody else to get it. And really, it's about backing each other up. I mean, I don't really want nothing different than you do. Knowmsain? I mean, you got your gold and all that shit. Me, I don't care nothing for that, no offense. To me, it's just a waste of money. But I got my own stuff, which you probably think, What's this bullshit? But it's really all the same. It just looks different. So we don't need to be going at each other's throats. We need to be working together. And that's what goes fucking wrong. People don't want to work together. People don't want to stick up for each other. I mean, look at those fuckin people in Bosnia. Neighbor killing neighbor. People standing around saying, Ain't it awful? Ain't it awful? If it's so motherfucking awful, get your ass up and do something. But nobody wants to do nothing 'less it's their own little set. But it can't be like that. Loyalty, man. Loyalty is the most beautiful thing in this motherfucking earth. Without loyalty, we got nothing. Knowmsain?"

The young man nodded again. His hands were still on his knees and he still stared straight forward, but he nodded solemnly. He understood.

"And all these motherfuckers out here saying, I got your back. I got your back. I want to see it. Show me; don't just talk about it. 'Cause see, these young guys think they seen some stuff. They talk like they had it so tough. I ain't talking about you, knowmsain? But these other boys. They ain't seen nothing. Nothing like what I seen. Hard times, man. Hard times growing up. Hard times in Nam. Hard times in the joint. Ain't none of these boys seen hard times yet."

The young man snickered at the thought.

"Hard times is nothing to eat but cornflakes at the end of the month," Roger Nolan continued. "Hard times is stuffing cardboard in the bottom of your shoes. Hard times is getting your ass whipped every time you raise your head. I seen some hard times. Anybody mess with me, I can show them some serious hard times. But it don't have to be like that."

He was stopped at yet another light, so he took a moment to pull out a cigarette and set it burning. He drew on the cigarette and tapped the wheel as he waited for the light to change.

"Like in Nam, man. You're too young to remember, but it wasn't about no Black or White or Red or Brown, it was us and the gooks, man. We stuck up for each other. I had me one partner, he was a Black dude, man. And it didn't matter. We hung together, smoked weed together, drank a little hooch. I was a skinny little motherfucker back then. He said, when we get back, I'll bring you home and let my mama feed you. Dude saved my life, three times. Three times. And I did the same for him. That's loyalty. And I'd do it again. I'd lay down my life for him right here and now if I had to."

The young man had continued to stare at his knees. But now he turned. He asked, "What happened to him?"

"They whacked him, man. Just like Bubba in *Forrest Gump,* man. They whacked him."

~

They turned off Broad and steered onto a side street. Roger made several other turns before he got to the place where he wanted to stop, for he intended to confuse the young man, who was from the other side of the neighborhood and did not know these streets.

"I'm gonna leave you here a minute," Roger said. He pulled the parking brake, opened the door, and tapped the ash off his cigarette.

The young man was already out of the car and making ready to head down the sidewalk with him.

"You wait here by the car. I'll be right back."

The young man's face gave no hint of disturbance, but his eyes flashed with apprehension.

"You'll be all right," Roger told him. "Won't nobody mess with you; they know you're with me."

The young man cut his eyes to the side, leaned back against a fender, folded his arms, and scowled. He clearly did not like this place with its small storefronts, empty lots, cracked sidewalks, and its sound of static and country music.

Roger stopped. He did not like this attitude. "Don't take it personal, man. I wouldn't let my own mother see where I hold my product."

~

Roger Nolan took several more turns before he turned down the alley. He looked quickly to right and left, then caught his breath, just a moment, as he nearly always did. To enter this nest of alleys, he was submerged in silence and gray light as if he had taken a plunge into deep water. The sounds of the street—the sirens and engines and arguments—were muted. Here in the alley it was quiet, dark, and abandoned. Here he heard nothing but the low, fluttering call of the pigeons. The looming gray buildings blocked the sun so that everything was cast in a fish-tank gray. Nothing moved.

He began to walk slowly and to sip at the air with breaths so silent and slow that his chest barely moved. His skin prickled all down his arms and across the back of his skull.

For each time he entered the alley, it was as if he had returned to the village.

~

He was raised in a building close by, just a few shadows away, on the next street over, where as a boy, in a past ruled by men in leather coats, he roamed the streets by day and by night weathered such father-storms of alcoholic rage that when a governmental wind blew down his street, he let it blow him out of his blue jeans and black T-shirt and into a steaming jungle with a pack on his back, boots on his feet, a helmet on his head, and an M-16 in his hands, standing alone at the edge of a smoking village.

~

In the dream he dreamed most frequently, in the one that invaded his thoughts most often, he stood again with his pack, his boots, and his weapon, a lone young soldier separated from his unit. Again and again, he entered the eerily silent village with its gray, smoking buildings. Again and again, he heard only the flute-like call of the birds. Again and again, he found only the same five pale corpses. Again, there was the moment that seized him like a talon: a movement to the right, a sound, a wing-like flutter of black. His breath caught in his throat like a bird in a trap. He turned, he swung the M-16 into position and fired. In five bursts, he emptied his heavy weapon into a dying and agonized shadow.

~

No one ever saw him in this struggle. No one watching would have ever known. But there was a brief moment at the head of the alley when there was just the smallest catch in his stride, when he wanted to turn and run, when a wave of fear ran down the back of his neck and into his arms and legs.

Quickly, he shook himself, took another deep breath, and looked around him. He was not in the village; he was in a complex of alleys behind a certain street in his home city. He heard the sounds of buses, sirens, radios, voices. All that, and the muted call of pigeons. He looked forward to this moment each time: the moment of mastery: five feet into the alley, he shook himself, took a deep breath, and moved down the center of the alley. His fears took flight like a flock of birds. He breathed smoothly as an engine. If he had spoken, there would be no catch or rattle in his voice. He was not in the village. These graying buildings were no smoking collection of huts and colonial stations.

~

He still did not know what was in the shadow that he fired on that day in the village. He had not stopped to look. He ran out of the village, and continued to run, in spite of the weight of pack and weapon, until he fell, exhausted, along the empty road.

But he heard the cry: thin, song-like, unidentifiable, a dirge, a yell, an animal complaint that rose up, circled his head, and slowly crackled into silence.

~

Having mastered the village, Roger moved quickly down the alley and quickly to the corner, where he turned down another alley. Fifty paces down the next alley, he came to a doorway framed in wood and set into a small recess in the wall. Quickly—he did not want to leave the nervous young man too long in the street—he pulled a key from his pocket and snapped open a padlock set high in the corner of the frame. He pushed open the door and stopped to admire the daylight darkness of the room. It was an animal darkness, cat-fur black, palpable and breathing. Not a bead of light entered from the boarded windows. He felt his ears twitch and search the silence, but there was not a sound. In a moment his eyes adjusted and he saw emerge the white shapes of perhaps a dozen stoves, washers, and refrigerators that loomed in the darkness like boulders or like a pod of silent whales. He did not bother with the light switch on the wall. Instead, he stooped and felt along the wall next to the door. He found the flashlight he had placed there, snapped it on, and split the darkness with a yellowish saber of light.

Had he needed, he could have felt his way to the place. But he liked to be sure there was no one else. So he panned the light from corner to corner of the room, then stepped to the far corner and pressed with his toe on a floorboard so that the opposite end lifted. He picked up the board by the raised end and set it against one of the washers. Then, kneeling, he pointed the flashlight into the empty space.

Where he should have seen a neat row of cellophane packets filled with butter-colored pebbles of cocaine, there was nothing at all. In the space between the joists, he saw nothing but dust; he felt nothing but the web of a spider.

He stood, suddenly. *Wait a minute,* he thought. He recounted his actions over the past two days and recalled them all clearly. There was no way. He had placed the packets there and he had not moved them. So maybe he had the wrong board? But there was no other board. He had cut the board out himself, and there was no other. He pressed his foot in a dozen places, hoping he was wrong. But nothing gave. That was the one.

He knelt again, to search with his fingers one more time. *There were seven,* he thought. *Seven goddam packets.* Each one done up neatly in a sealed plastic bag. And each one gone. He felt around for a crack through which they could have fallen, but he had built the compartment tight. There was nowhere they could have gone.

Looking skyward in the dark, he began to curse. *That backstabbing motherfucker. That punk. That ignorant piece of nothing that still ain't learned to wipe the snot off his nose. That . . .* He cursed silently at first. No wonder, he thought, the boy was so cold to him when he had treated him so warm. No wonder he was so silent, so shut up in the shell of his coat and cap. *Motherfucker's been setting me up all along,* he thought. *I been treating him like family and he's been fixing to set me up.*

Still kneeling, he drew up with the utter outrage of it, and with a wordless and extended curse, threw the flashlight against the metal flank of a dryer. It rang the metal like a bell and shattered.

And left him kneeling in rage and darkness.

~

"Wassup, man," the young man asked. "What took you so long?"

"We got a little problem," he answered. The dope boy was still glancing side to side at this unfamiliar place.

"Wassup?"

"Come on, man." Roger unlocked the passenger door and motioned the young man to get in.

"Wassup?" The young man did not move. He was looking at Roger, puzzled and reluctant.

"Come on, motherfucker. First you act like you don't want to be here. Now you act like you don't want to leave. Get in, I said." He even opened the car door for him. "We're just having a little technical difficulty. A supply chain problem."

The young man folded his arms across his chest. "You got my shit?" He had squared himself to the sidewalk and was set to stand firm.

"Now there you go, calling it shit again. We're talking product, merchandise, salable goods. Stuff, even. But not shit. Yeah, man. I got what you want. I just got to go to another place to get it."

"But you said you had your shit right here."

"Yeah, well, I was wrong. So get in and we gonna go where your shit is."

He pointed again to the door and started around the car. But the young man pulled back his sleeve to show off his big gold watch. "Man, I ain't got time to be bullshitting around while you figure out where you keep your shit."

The man slammed the car door and was on the young man like a panther. He pushed him to the wall; he pressed him against the bricks with his left hand. His right hand hid itself under his coat. "Don't ever," he hissed, "talk like that to me again." The young man struggled briefly, but the man held him tight. "I ain't one of your butterheads. I ain't gonna take any shit you give me. Knowmsain?"

The young man nodded. Just the briefest of nods.

"Now. Understand. I got an automatic pistol under this coat. A Glock 9. I don't even need to aim it. It'll hit you with enough horsepower to kick your head to the end of next week. Make your momma one real sad lady. And I ain't afraid to use it. I'll use it in a heartbeat. Prison don't scare me and the chair don't either. Or any motherfucker that crosses me. Including you and all your brothers up on that corner."

He relaxed his grip. He knew he could. "Understand. I ain't got time to fuck around. I ain't got time for disrespect. So we are gonna get in this car and take care of our business." He released the young man, pulled his hand from his jacket, and looked around. He knew a dozen or more people from the street were watching, but none who would show it.

"So. Understand. I run into a little problem. But it ain't got nothing to do with you. We had a little altercation, but now it's over. Knowmsain?"

The young man knew.

"Are we good?"

The young man nodded. They bumped fists and the man pulled up a pack from his shirt and offered one to the young man.

"I'm a little tense," he admitted. "Knowmsain?"

The young man made a conciliatory gesture and nodded.

"It ain't about you," the man continued. He drew deeply on his cigarette and fired the smoke out into the street.

"It's about some other motherfucker needs killing."

"HE'S out to pop you, man."

The tall, awkwardly slender Black youth nodded gravely. He was staring out into the street with eyes that appeared to be nearly closed. He wore a heavy down coat against the cold and a thick knit skull cap pulled down nearly to the level of his eyes. His hands were warming in the pockets of his coat,

Daniel did not speak. He, too, stared out to the street with half-lidded, watchful eyes. He, too, kept his head tilted back slightly and his hands in the pockets of his coat. The two together seemed to fold into the bricks of the machine shop wall and to disappear.

"Straight up, man."

Daniel's silence was like a shrug.

"He said it, straight up, man."

Daniel slightly shrugged again.

"He's like, I'm a gonna drop that young motherfucker like a bad habit. He's like, He ain't gonna know what hit him."

"He's got no reason to wanna drop me."

"Man, he said it."

"I ain't done nothing to him."

"He sure thinks so."

"I ain't done nothing to him."

"Man, he said it."

"I don't owe him nothing."

"I'm just telling you what he said, man."

"I paid him for everthing he ever gave me. I didn't ask him to front me nothing."

"It ain't about that, man. Somebody jacked his stash."

"Anything I owe him, I pay it."

"He thinks you ripped him off, man."

"I didn't do nothing."

"He thinks you got in his little room back in the alley and stole his shit."

"Man . . ."

"He come out of that building where he keeps all his stoves and refrigerators and shit, and he come all jumping bad with me till I made him back off, and he's like, Sorry, man, it ain't about you. I say, Man, don't put your hands up to me like that. He's like, Sorry, man, it's some other motherfucker. You know how he says, motherfucker this, motherfucker that."

"I didn't take his shit."

"He's like, I trusted some young motherfucker I should have never trusted."

"I didn't do it, man."

"And I knew he was talking about you, man."

"I didn't take nothing from him."

"He's like, Young dude was like family and all."

Daniel's silence smoldered.

"That's why I knew he was talking about you."

"Man, I don't have no key to get in there."

"Some motherfucker must have broke in."

"I didn't take nothing from him. I pay for what I get."

"He says didn't nobody else know how to find where he had his shit."

"Man, I make my money on the street. What I want to steal his shit for?"

"He's like, I'm gonna blow the motherfucker away like a rabbit in the woods."

"Motherfucker ain't no family to me."

"He's like, I got the gun to do it."

"Motherfucker thinks he's family. He ain't *even* family to me."

"Glock 9, man. That's what he got."

"He ain't nothing to me at all."

"He took me around to some other place and got me my shit, all the time he's like, I ain't *never* gonna let no motherfucker beat me again."

"He wants to think he's family. But he ain't nothing to me."

~

Daniel stood in his place against the wall of the abandoned machine shop, watching the street with brows pulled close and dark and eyes drawn narrow as slits, so narrow it seemed they had been winced shut.

Let him talk, he thought. *He got his piece, I got a piece of my own.* The weight of his weapon pulled comfortably at his coat, like a small child pulling at the hem of it.

He wants to talk all bad, let him talk. He had his own business to watch out for. If the man wanted to think he stole from him, let him think it. If the man wanted to try him, let him come on. He was ready. He had always been ready. Trusting no one, he had prepared himself for years, mind and body, for just such a turn as this.

"He done already killed some dudes," the tall young man had reminded him. "He was in Nam, and in the joint. Man, he killed dudes in both them places."

"He says he did."

"Man, I know some dude. He says, Don't nobody get that teardrop in their eye 'less they do somebody in the joint."

The slender young man had begun to talk more than Daniel wanted to listen.

"He's like, Motherfucker turn on me, I take him out like the garbage. I'm gonna hunt the motherfucker down like a rat."

~

Once the slender young man had gone, Daniel stood alone on the street, looking out through narrowed eyes and seeing, without appearing to see, everything that moved, from the lights of the Broad Street restaurants to the bus station with its running neon dog. He was not afraid. Any little fear that emerged, he swallowed down quickly, digested it, and converted it into strength in his limbs, resolution in his mind, and sharpness in every sense.

The only sign that anything like a fear had ever crossed him was in the steely wincing of his eyes.

He had swallowed down fear and made it strength, so he went about his business in peace. He gave an extra rock to the man in tatters. He fronted a piece to the downtown salesman who promised to catch him up when he got paid. He let the pasty-faced man with his cart pass by without comment and he let the train of shattered winos pass without curses.

And when he saw the preppy girl from the art school, still in her black crow-like clothes, stalking the street with a camera slung from her neck, he was moved by a strange, protective curiosity to leave his post and to follow her.

10

A SERIES OF photographs:

A young man stands against a wall; he faces the camera. The wall is a solid gray mass of concrete. But when we look more closely, we see it is chipped, water-stained, and flaking. The wall reaches to the top of the frame and to the right and the left of the frame, and it is as if the wall carries a great mass of weight; it appears, somehow, pressed down and shadowed. Words and symbols have been spray-painted onto the wall. Of these, we see fragments:

LIN AVE BOYZ

Spi

Tec-9

ONYA IS A

The body of the young man blocks some of these words. Others trail off to the edges of the picture.

The young man is made bulky by a heavy, thick coat marked with the logo of a football team. And he is made dark by the thick-knit toboggan cap pulled down close to his eyes. His hands are in the pockets of his coat and his shoulders square up close around his ears. His eyes look out warily from under the knit brow of his cap.

He looks straight at the camera, square and intense. His face—with his jaw thrust forward, mouth tightly closed, and brow hidden beneath his cap—is solid, unreadable, a wall.

~

Same young man, same wall. Close-up: Same intent and confronting eyes. The focus is so sharp and the light lances in so intently that we nearly see the fragments in each iris. A crack in the concrete travels up crookedly from above his left ear as if it were a stroke of dark lightning. We see flecks of what seem to be lichen; we see small dark pits where the concrete bubbled and hardened.

In the face of the young man, closer now, we see faint wisps of beard on his lip and chin. But this is the same hard-set jaw; these are the same tensed lips. He has made his face into a mask of immobility. His eyes are paradigms of blackness; they take in intently but they let nothing out. He smirks, ever so subtly. So subtly that if we look again, the smirk is gone. The face, solid as stone, blank and imperturbable, says, *You will not read me.*

~

The same young man in the same bulky jacket. The camera has moved far back. In a distance now, the young man is a small portion of what the camera finds. He stands near the right border of the picture, in front of the wall we have seen before. Shaky and bold, the spray-paint markings fill the spaces above and around him. We now see that the wall is a portion of a bridge abutment or a highway ramp. We see the young man looking (and we look with him) from where he stands at the foot of the wall down along the long arcing line of the viaduct and into the mists of the city.

~

The young man again, standing with a Black youth of about the same age. The two young men stand at the head of an alley. Behind them, the alley darkens until we see a hint of light where it opens again. The two young men stand side by side, facing the camera, right hands raised and clasped. Each wears the same stone-hard and impenetrable countenance. Each set of eyes is alive and defiant.

~

An empty room, clean and bare. A couch to the left, a television and stereo to the right. Between, the bare floors. At the center and rear of the room, a window with a simple shade drawn down over it. Light emerges from the edges of the shade: a rectangular aura that spills light onto the bare boards of the floor.

~

The young man again, sitting on a couch, a bare wall behind and above him: He has shed the bulky jacket. He has pulled off the cap, showing his close-cropped hair. But he is no less unreadable, no less a wall. Light from a window splashes the left side of his face. Shadow covers the right. It is as if we see the light and dark of the moon. Or as if he wears a painted mask.

~

One last photograph: Same young man. His eyes look downward, toward a pistol cupped in his hands. The pistol is sleek and dark and he holds it gently, as one might hold a pet. Again, the light comes in at the left and dresses his hands with light at the one side and shadow on the other; light dresses one side of the pistol with a soft metallic sheen and leaves the other side empty and black.

A panel in the side of the pistol is drawn and he studies the works. His lips are pursed as if he speaks to it.

AMY would never, ever have taken his picture, much less shot up nearly a roll of film on him, had he not been so persistent, so unmenacing in his persistence, and so impervious to all her scorn. She would never have taken his picture if he had not insisted, almost as a matter of right, that she shoot him, if she had not been, finally, curious to see what might be under the mask he had put up. It was so obviously a mask, and yet it was expressive of *something.* Maybe he had not consciously chosen the mask; maybe it was something had grown up with him from his youngest years. But it was so much like other masks she had seen that he seemed nearly archeological, as if he could have been mounted on a wall like a shield.

She would not have photographed him at all had he not stepped up to protect her, though she had not wanted and did not believe she needed his protection. But he had put himself within a few sheltering paces, as a guardian angel, a granite, unwanted presence.

When her mother had broken her plans and shattered her secret life in the studio and the streets, she was filled with a defiant grief that took her out of her seat in third-bell math and led her out the door of the school with her camera over her shoulder. She wanted to capture the scenes she felt sure now to lose: the storefronts, the man of the bluegrass records, the Rag Man, and each of the seven winos. And though it was almost a sacrilege, considering the photographs that Paul had taken so many years ago, she wanted Jenny at her counter in the store, Jenny on the street, Jenny in the slant gray light of her kitchen window. She could have waited, she knew. Eventually her mother would forget and relent and she would be free again. But she was filled with a desire to possess the streets now, without permission, to act without and against all rules of her mother and her school.

Once she passed the iron fence of the school, she wandered into the streets, turning corner after corner until she turned into a narrow lane with a grocery at one corner, a vacant lot, a string of shops, a row of curtained windows. She stood in the lane as she might in the middle of a wood. It was as if she had left the road and the town and had taken a trail, then a path, then the pathless forest floor to a spot where she could find herself uncovered by human law, threatened and free. She looked around her at the brick forest of storefronts and the stoops and blinded upstairs windows and recalled that this was the first time she had been out on these streets during midday, midweek hours. She was seeing things that she had never been allowed to see. And she was amazed at what she saw from just that one spot on the sidewalk. Old people sat out on balconies. A group of teenage boys and teenage girls—skipping their school just as she was hers—walked in a knot toward the park. The owner of a used furniture store swept his walk, looking up and down the street between each sweep. A man with a stick and a five-gallon bucket full of water and sponges washed down a storefront window as she waited. She felt even more lawless and even more defiantly at home where she stood.

As she wandered, she took photographs: The window display of the church with its Bible and faded plastic roses. The balding man of the scratchy bluegrass records, smiling down from his window, framed between a pair of coffee cans that each held a spindled tomato plant. And, as she perched on the bumper of a pickup truck to raise herself, the long, straight length of Broad Street, where parking meters, curbs, and the rows of parked cars stretched into the distance in lines which appeared to converge, as in an illustration of perspective, while the shifting collection of signboards and passing people cluttered the walls of the shot.

She found one of the seven winos and talked him into standing still long enough to frame him for a shot. She was pleased with the way she staged him: the frail and randy man at the head of a set of stone steps that were worn and depressed with a century of climbing, leaning into a doorway with carved, viny facings. *Yes,* she thought. *An awesome shot.* The steps worn with climbing, the stone vines, and the grizzled and wine-shattered man: she had them all in the frame of her camera. But just as she had lined it all up, she felt a distraction from the side. She took her shot, but more quickly than she had planned. She made ready to take another, but the distraction was still there. She took her eye away from the viewfinder for just a moment and saw, leaning back against a fence with his arms folded and his head cocked back, watching her intently without reserve or embarrassment, the dealer that she saw every morning on Broad Street.

His stare and his arrogant stance disturbed her and she snapped another too-quick shot of the old man. She knew that, in shooting so fast and so startled, she had broken all the rules she had been taught and that her picture—so carefully staged—would be a blur. "Let me try just one more," she said to the wino. She cranked her film forward, raised the camera again, and started to refocus. But the old man's face now filled the viewfinder. He had come down the steps and in another two seconds was at her side smelling of sweat, tobacco, and cheap wine. With his hand on her elbow, he whispered something wine-hoarse, leering, and thick of tongue, directly, and with an odor of cheap wine, into her ear.

She jerked her arm, but the old man's frail-seeming fingers pinched tighter at her elbow.

"Say, missy," the old man whispered, his voice hoarse and cloudy with wine. She pulled again to get loose.

"Let me go," she shouted. If she had to she would have jabbed him in the eye. She would have slugged him with her camera bag; she would have scratched like a cat. She tingled with heat and rage. She coiled her body like a spring.

But in the instant before she could move, the Dealer shouted, "Let her alone, you scraggle-headed motherfucker."

The old wino hesitated, turned his head in the direction of the Dealer, dropped her arm, and dodged. But she had already begun her swing. She hugged her camera close with one hand and with the other and, with all the force she could call up, lashed her camera bag across the empty space. She would have torn his hand loose with the swing. Then she would have shoved him away. Then she would have cursed him like a washerwoman. But when her arm cut the empty air, the old man was already out of reach, already scrambling up the stony stairs, tossing back hoarse, mumbled, toothless curses over his shoulder.

"Yeah, and yo momma," shouted the Dealer toward his back. "Yo momma and her momma too, you feeble-minded, skinny-ass, chicken-hawking, weak-brain, soggy-head pervert."

The old man mumbled a moment at the door.

"Winehead," the Dealer spat. "Mad Dog–sucking motherfucker." The man waved down the words and disappeared behind the door, but the Dealer continued to curse the old man professionally, impersonally, loudly, and without heat. It was a cold and perfect fury that did not for a moment break the stony imperturbability of his face.

He paused, and she demanded, "Why did you do that?" She was furious at the old man. But she was even more angry with the Dealer for stepping in. "Why?"

He shrugged, and looked away as if she had said nothing at all.

She shouldered her camera bag. "I just want you to know, I did not ask you for any help."

"So was you gonna let that red-nose, big-ear winehead motherfucker feel you up?"

"Of course not."

"So how was you gonna stop him?"

"Just because I'm a girl . . ."

"He's a stinking, old, wine-smelling, big-ear motherfucker." He looked up to the doorway where the old man had disappeared. "Perverted, shrunk-up, pickle-brain . . ."

"Why do you have to talk like that?"

"Like what?"

"Like all those names. Mad Dog sucker and all that."

"'Cause he is."

"He's just a sick old man."

"Sick old man was set to do you if he could."

"But what's it to you?"

"I can't stand the motherfucker."

"So?"

"All day sucking down wine like that."

"So?"

"And then he's gonna mess with you like he's gonna take you upstairs to his pissy old house."

"So what's it to you?"

"So you gonna do that?"

"No! But what's it to you?"

"It ain't nothing to me. Nothing ain't nothing to me."

"Good. I didn't ask you for help. You can leave me alone."

"Be alone as you wanna be. I got nothing to do with it."

His arrogance stoked her anger again. "You just think you're so bad."

He spat, with perfect accuracy, onto a flattened plastic bottle in the gutter. He was still leaning against the fence, arms folded, eyes cast toward the street. The bulky jacket hid the contours of his body, and the knit cap was pulled down across his brows and ears so that he was hidden almost as completely as a knight in armor. Around him were the rusty fence, the lot full of stone and litter, the cracked sidewalks, and a scattering of scrapped papers and crushed cans and broken bottles. The Dealer, with his bright and perfect starter jacket and matching cap and his impossibly bright shoes, was the only bright and unbroken thing in the entire block.

She wanted to reach for the camera that still hung loose on its strap. She held back. But he had seen the motion and the direction of her eye.

"Yeah, I'm bad," he said. "I'm too bad to burn. And you know it too. You want to take my picture, but you're scared."

"Why would I be scared?"

"You don't want your friends to know you got that close to somebody like me."

"I don't care what my friends think." She did not, but she did not want to debate it either. Not with him.

"You take all these pictures of freaks and smelly old winos so you can show how good your yuppie self is. But you don't take pictures of anybody strong."

"What?"

"That's right. You don't want to do nothing about nobody that ain't all broke down."

"You got a lot of nerve, talking to me," she fired at him. "You've got no business talking to me. You talk about me taking pictures like it's something bad and there you are selling drugs to sick people."

He gestured—so what?—with his right hand. "I don't sell it. Dope fiends buy it."

She shook her head. "And then you bully sick old men . . ."

He waved dismissively.

". . . And who knows what else you've done. Besides trying to get that little boy to . . ."

"To do what?"

She was not sure she should answer. Had she set Jonathan up?

"To do what?"

"To sell drugs for you."

"Don't nobody sell nothing for me."

She looked dubiously back at him.

"Is that what he told you?" He stood straight up with the words, suddenly, with a surprised and wounded look on his face. It was as if a sculptor had cracked the stone. "That little wet-nose motherfucker is talking some shit." His eyes became large and wide. His hands swung in wide, theatrical gestures: the left was extended and open, the right, cupped toward his heart. The light of the sun filled him up. In his brilliant clothes, he was radiant against the gray and broken streets around him.

Without thinking, she raised the camera, framed him, brought him into focus, and shot.

~

Hours later, she left the Dealer near the bridge where he had shown her what seemed like an acre of graffiti and went to look for Jenny, for she wanted her picture as well. Now that she had the old negatives, she could print them off some time later, but she wanted to have her own shot, her own record.

When she got to the store, Hussein was standing behind the counter, tapping figures into his calculator as if he had never left off.

"Is she here?"

"Not in two days," he said without looking up. The fingers of his left hand marked his place on a column of figures; the fingers of his right rested on the keys.

"Is she . . . ?"

"Not a word in two whole days. I don't know a thing."

"She didn't call?"

"I don't know nothing," he said. He held up two fingers. "Two whole days. Nothing at all." He looked back to the column of figures and tapped, very hard, on the calculator.

She left, feeling as if she had been asked to leave.

A bead of worry formed within her, but she decided, *Jenny must be sick.* That could be the only thing. A bad cold, she thought, or the flu. She carried that scrap of hope the several blocks to Jenny's apartment.

Jonathan was sitting gateways across the doorway to the building. His back was against one side of the doorframe and his feet against the other. "Wassup?" he called.

"Nice coat," she told him. It was a bright new coat, puffy with down.

He glanced down at a sleeve, as if he had just noticed, then moved his feet to make room for her.

"You're pretty bold, aren't you?" He was in full view of any passing police car or truant officer.

"I'm sick, man. I can't go to school."

"Yeah, you look real sick."

"Aw, man." He pressed his temples as if he had a sudden spasm of pain. Then he looked up. "So why ain't you in school?"

"I'm on a special art project."

He raised an eyebrow, possibly in admiration at the ease with which she came up with such a lie.

"Anyway," she said. "That's not what I want to talk about."

He pressed his temples again.

She set down her camera bag and sat on the stoop. "I want to know why you tried to start selling drugs."

He raised his head and screwed up his face in shock and amazement. She cut the air in front of her with her hand. "Don't play me," she said.

"What? You think I would . . . Aw, man!"

"Daniel told me."

"So what's he tell you?"

"He tells me that you've come around asking to be his—what do you call it?—runner."

He covered his mouth with his hand and raised three fingers in a gesture of derision.

"And he wouldn't let you."

"So?"

"And do you know why?"

Silence.

"You're setting yourself up."

"So?"

"So it's a dead end."

"So? He's in it."

"So I don't want to, like, read about you in the papers. TEN-YEAR-OLD KID KILLED IN DRIVE-BY."

"Eleven."

"Whatever. I just don't want to see you go down."

"I ain't going down." He had shifted his features so entirely that he seemed nearly another person. His face was in a stony scowl and his eyes narrow. His hands made an exaggerated and theatrical sweep. "I'm a G," he said. "I'm a gangster. I'm too quick for them."

"Nobody's quicker than a bullet."

"What do you know about it?"

"I read the papers. I watch the news."

His hand had covered his mouth again. He raised the derisive fingers. "The news ain't nothing."

"And I know what happens."

"You just know what the papers say. You don't know what's real."

"I know dealing is a ticket to a short life."

"Oh well." The fingers again. "Life's short."

He leaned back against the doorframe. To his left, the street cascaded with light; to the right, the hall held such a darkness that, had she taken that picture, the darkness would have called away portions of his face. No darkroom trick could have brought them out.

"She ain't there," Jonathan told her as she stepped over him into the hall. "She's gone, man."

"Where did she go?"

"She been gone two, three days, man"

"What do you mean, gone? Did she leave town?"

He raised his hands and shrugged.

"And you haven't seen her?"

"I didn't say that."

"So she's gone, but you've seen her. Where?"

"You don't wanna know, man."

"Of course I want to know."

"No man, you don't wanna know."

"I could kill you sometimes."

"I seen her at the bus station."

"The bus station? What's the matter with the bus station?"

"Nothing. But she didn't look too good, man."

"Was she leaving town?"

"How do I know?"

She started up the stairs, just in case he was wrong. She did not recall that the stairs were so dark, or that the banister, which she relied upon to guide her, had such a tacky, gummed-on feel, or that the smell of the stairs was so ancient and was such a mix of dust and stale urine. She had not realized she would be so grateful at the first turning for the porthole window with the four clouded, pie-cut panes that let fall four columns of empty, gray, pie-cut light.

She followed the gray light to the top of the stairs, found Jenny's apartment, and pushed the door open.

The light, in spite of the high, open windows only partially shaded by her curtains, was the same empty gray light that fell in columns into the hall. But here the gray light dispersed into the room like smoke. She stepped in and looked around her. Nothing had been disturbed. Her futon was still neatly laid out, the clothes were still stacked or hung in the open closet, her bookshelf still held its half dozen books. In the kitchen, the pantry still held its few plates and cooking tools; the table, a pot of wilting flowers, a coffee cup, half empty.

~

Jonathan was gone when Amy came back down the stairs. School was nearly out; it was time to go back. To follow her plan, she had to slip back into the building in time for home room bell, collect her books and portfolio, and walk back to her mother's office. Following that plan, she drifted down the several blocks toward school. She left the narrow side streets, crossed Broad with its galleries and cafes, walked two more blocks to where she saw her school in a crazy new way, as someone who looked at the building as *a* school, not *her* school. The building was massive and stony in a way she had never understood: square and heavy, powerfully shouldered and narrow in the windows. And though she knew that inside the school students were learning lessons, drawing, singing, charting dance steps, and making prints, to the new eye she brought to it as one who saw *a* school and not *her* school, it was empty and foreign and dark.

She knew she had to move, to slip back in the print-shop door that she had left propped open, but the street had become a river to her, deep and wide and difficult to cross. She stood on the sidewalk opposite her school for a very long time, silent and still as a stick of driftwood. The entire high school enterprise—the class pictures, yearbook placement, the ritual and anachronism of cap and gown, felt impossible heavy. She could not imagine the effort of crossing the street to dress her mind into her high school self. It seemed a burden she could not bear to lift.

When she turned to go, she did not know where she would go. But as she walked the narrow streets, the air was singing with light. In minutes, as school let out across the neighborhood, she found herself, amid shouts of release and challenge, in the middle of a sea of children.

HERE came that little scrap of a boy, just tearing up the sidewalk, blazing up the afternoon in a crisp coat of orange and green.

Damn, Roger Nolan thought. *That motherfucker's gone and bought this boy a coat.*

The boy had a book bag slung over one shoulder and he strode with a wild, mad-hatter look in his eye. Quickly, before the boy could jet past him, Roger stepped into his path, slipped his arm over the boy's shoulder, and swung him into the alley.

"Wassup, little man?" He was careful to put no pressure on the boy's shoulder. He did not want to scare him. But he did not remove his arm. He thought, *My money wasn't good enough to buy him a coat, damn if my money didn't buy him a coat anyway.* "I said, what's up?"

"I'm coming home from school."

"And what's our hurry?"

"I don't know."

"'Cause it look to me like you high-balling it *to* school so you can *look* like you been at school. Knowmsain?"

"Naw, man. I can't skip."

"You can't skip, but you the only little dude on the street. So how you get out of school and don't nobody else get out?"

"I'm the first one. Everybody else is coming."

"Now look. I went to your same school when I was young and it's over that way, and your house is over that way." He knew where the boy lived.

"But I can't skip. I got probation and I got . . ."

"I know, little man. I know all about you and juvenile court. Now. Tell me something real quick: Your cousin buy you that coat?"

"What coat?"

"The one you're wearing, little man." He plucked at the coat's bright sleeve.

"This coat?"

"It looks good on you, little man."

The boy shrugged.

"Who bought it for you?"

"I bought it for myself."

"So, you got a job? You collecting cans? Wassup?"

"My allowance. I get it by . . ."

The boy began to press against the arm across his shoulder. "I got to go, man."

Roger released the boy's shoulder and with the other hand pushed the boy flat to the wall. "You don't need to be in no hurry, little man. We got to talk."

The boy nodded, but the look in his eye was that of a trapped rabbit and he pressed steadily against Nolan's hand.

"I thought maybe your cousin bought you that coat. He got all that good money. What's a coat like that run? Hundred dollars or so? That's a lot of allowance."

The boy nodded again, then looked out to the street. His eyes had gone very bright; his pupils had gone wide as dinner plates, black and shining as water in a well. "I got to get home," he said. His voice had gone hoarse. "My mom, like, told me to come straight home."

"You gonna get home," he said. "There ain't no problem. I just want to talk a minute. Your mom ain't gonna mind if you talk to me. I done her some favors through the years. You ask her."

The boy nodded. His eyes grew wider yet; they seemed to spread to the sides of his face.

"Your momma knows me. Your cousin knows me too. He been knowing me a long, long time. I know him. I know his daddy. I know all your family, little man. He a pretty sharp young man, this cousin of yours. He's good to his granny. He's good to you. He likes to look out for his people. That's one thing I like about him. He don't just think about himself all the time. Knowmsain? So listen up. There's a reason I want to know this." The boy tried to squirm away sideways, but Roger pressed him again to the wall. "Did he buy you that coat?"

"I bought it myself. I did. My mom . . ."

One more lie. Straight down the road it was nothing but lies. Rage seized Roger again, all up and down his arms. And though he made no move, the boy sensed the swelling rage and, once more, fearful, pressed against the hand that held him.

"I got to go, man. I'm gonna be late. My mom'll be, like . . ."

Roger pressed the boy back to the wall. "Look, little motherfucker. I'm talking to you."

The little side-stretch mouth twitched to the left, toward the street. His wide black eye followed it.

"Don't worry about what's out on the street, little man. You got to worry about me right now. Knowmsain?"

The boy twitched again, his whole face this time, then tried to squirm loose. He may have spoken; he may have been unable to speak, for there was a caught rabbit in his throat. Again, he pushed against the hand that pressed him back.

The man's rage gathered in his chest and poured down along his arms. Without a thought, he gathered the near shoulder of the bright coat into one hand and folded the other hand like a vise around the boy's small jaw.

"Listen to me, little motherfucker."

The boy nodded, as best he could.

"I don't plan to hurt you. But you better not fuck with me. Knowmsain?"

The man could feel the boy's breath across the hairs of the back of his hand. He pressed again so that the boy's eyes widened further.

He could crush this boy's face like a nut. He could grind him into the wall. Every fiber in him yearned to smash, pound, pulverize, hurt. He yearned to smack respect into that little twisted face. He drew a breath.

And stopped. He released the boy's face and shoulder, brushed out the wrinkles in the coat and tousled the boy's hair in a gentling, consoling manner. The boy, not ready to trust, did not move.

Roger Nolan dusted his hands.

"I get it, little man. This ain't even about you."

The boy did not respond.

"I get it, you don't want to rat your cousin out." He looked to the boy to see what he could read of him, but his face was still crazed and wary.

"I reckon I went off the hook for a minute," Roger said. "I got something on my mind."

"I got to go," the boy said hoarsely.

"That's good, little man. You go on now. We all right?"

"Yeah, we all right. We cool."

"'Cause you always been all right by me."

"I got to go."

"Yeah, you go, little man. You go." He clapped the boy on the shoulder of the crisp, blazing coat and held out his right palm in the gimme-five gesture. He waited as the boy looked down, mistrustful, then slapped his palm with a nervous hand.

"You tell your momma I said hey," he told the boy.

The boy shifted his backpack and nodded. Quick as a lizard, he darted into the broad, blazing street. The man watched the boy teeter down the street, into the next block and around the corner. As he watched, he pulled a packet of cigarettes from a pocket of his coat, hammered the pack again and again into his palm, then stripped off the cellophane and a corner of foil, tapped out a cigarette, lit it, and continued to stare after the boy until he disappeared around a corner.

II

PHOTOGRAPHS:

A narrow, covered walkway between two brick buildings. At eye level, a row of black mailboxes is fastened to the right wall. The mortar lines and the lines of convergence where the brick walls meet the sidewalk take the eye back to a courtyard. We see the vertical lines of a board fence that borders the courtyard, and we see the random black lines of the branches of a wintering tree.

~

The mailboxes. Each is fastened to a block of wood which is itself attached to the brick wall. The paint on the brick wall is chipped; small islands of brick show beneath the paint. The mailboxes are marked one through four in white paint applied with a thin brush. A name is scotch-taped to each of the mailboxes just below the slot for mail. The first name is printed in crude block letters, the second in cursive tendrils. The third has been scissored from an envelope and taped to the box. The name on the fourth is weathered too faint to read.

~

Same narrow walkway: a person in a heavy black coat walks into the courtyard. On the walker's back is a pack of the sort a schoolgirl might carry. We see her in the moment she turns the corner and, in a blur, will disappear.

INFURIATING, Ann Taylor thought. *Forty-five minutes and not a word. Not a call. Nothing.*

She had called the school, of course, half an hour ago when she realized Amy had not come to the lobby to wait as she was supposed to do. And of course, everyone at the school was gone, the principal, the after-school people, everybody. All she got was the recorder with its annoying secretarial voice. She had called down to the security guard at the front desk of her building, and no, the guard had not seen her. There was nothing she could do now but wait. Waiting was not something she did willingly or well.

It had been a busy day, and she had gotten wrapped up in her project. So she had not gone to the lobby to check if Amy was in. And of course, it was no one's job to tell her, so when, finally, at five o'clock, she had gone to the lobby to tell Amy she just had to wrap things up and she would be just five minutes, she was surprised not to find her. She had been so cooperative the day before and the day before that, setting up camp in the lobby with her homework and her sketchbook.

But she was not camped out tonight, and though it had been no one's job to tell her, she shot Rebecca the receptionist an evil look. Rebecca had her own children to pick up from day care and she was neatening her desk and picking up her things. But no, she hadn't seen Amy. And why? Was she supposed to meet her here?

It was no use explaining.

"I'm sure she'll be here soon," Rebecca said. She smiled and sprinted for the elevator.

Then, in ones and twos and threes, everybody else in the office had left as well. *Good night. Good night,* they all called, as if nothing in the world was wrong. And for them, maybe nothing was. "Good night," she had told them as they strolled out at just five past five. "See you in the morning," they all said. They all had their reasons for leaving, and they left.

But she was stuck here waiting in the office, with no idea where her daughter was or how to find her. She knew, now, exactly what Amy had done. She had gone back to that photographer's studio—in spite of everything she had been told—in flat violation of her rules. It was not only a direct flouting of her consequences and the limits set down for her, it was hugely insensitive. *I would like,* she thought, *to get out of here at a decent hour.* It was hard enough to beat the traffic when she left right at five o'clock, and she could see in her mind the bumper-to-bumper sludge that awaited her.

She could wait for Amy to show up or she could go look for her out on the streets. Or she could just go on home. It would serve the girl right, she supposed, to have to find her own way home. But that seemed so irresponsible, even dangerous.

Maybe, she thought, *there is some good explanation.* She suspected not, else she would have called. She really ought to have called. The more she thought about it, the more upset she became. After all, there were those horrible stories. Abductions, rapes, anything could happen.

For the first time that day she felt the urge for a cigarette. Her hands trembled. She ached to see the air in front of her split by smoke. Her whole body cried for the lance of nicotine.

She regained control by pushing back from her desk and taking several deep breaths. She was determined to quit this time for sure, so she breathed very slowly for several breaths, and immediately felt better. The breaths were clean and calming. *This is a problem,* she thought. *I solve problems for a living. This can be solved.*

She started by using the tools she had at hand. She called the house and left a stern message on the recorder in case Amy had gone straight home. Then she called as many of Amy's friends as she knew and left word with each parent she could reach that Amy was to call her *immediately* at work if she arrived there. She had only a vague idea where the photographer's studio was, but she had contacts who could help her track him down. The gallery where his exhibit was scheduled was closed for the night, and the people who would know of him were probably stuck in the traffic she had not been able to beat. She had to wait for any possible help along those lines.

There was no sense starving herself while she waited, so she took the elevator and gave the security guard a note which read,

AMY—

Stay right in this lobby

until I get back.

—MOM

Short and curt. She hoped it would let her daughter know she was in trouble. Just in case Amy slipped past the not-always-attentive security guard, she taped a similar note to her office door.

She ate in the new vegetarian place across the street, where the waitresses were strange creatures with rings in their noses and irritating hair. But it was close to the office and relatively fast. She took a window seat so she could watch for Amy if she came by. Amy did not, of course, and when she had finished eating, the note at the security desk and the one on her door were still in place.

"No, ma'am, I haven't seen her," said the security guard with his country accent. *Why is he still here?* she thought. *Doesn't he ever go home?*

She did not really want to know, but, as if he had heard her wondering, he volunteered, "I'm working a double shift tonight, so I'll keep my eye open for her."

To mask her irritation, she continued to breathe slowly and deeply. No one watching would have known, but her hands began invisibly to tremble. There was no one in the lobby but that guard, no one at all in the elevator, and no one, for once, in the office to know whether she shook or whether she cried or whether she tore at her hair.

But refusing to shake was an old and persistent habit. She was not going to give in to emotion or panic or even the ache for a cigarette. Breathing deep, breathing slow, she pulled herself together. "Thank you," she said, with just a hint of tremor in her voice. "Thank you," she said again, to show herself she had stifled that hint.

From Rebecca's station, she made a few more phone calls. *No, we haven't seen her. We understand. I know you must be worried to death. We'll call you if she stops in.*

She still could not reach the gallery director or any of the arts people who might know the whereabouts of the studio. She imagined some longish dinner party keeping them all where she could not find them, a party to which she had not been invited.

She did not want to go back to her own office. She wanted to be right at the door when Amy came in. But there was nothing up front to do, so she went back to see what she could work on. A stack of projects waited on her desk, with plenty of work in them, enough for a whole night if she had to wait that long. There was her shoulder bag as well, full of work she had planned to take home, along with that ancient packet of negatives sticking its frazzled corner up into the air. The sight of it made her boil, so she grabbed up the stack from her desk, left the room, and placed herself at Rebecca's station. But the station was too busy and distracting, and instead of working she fiddled with paper clips and the Rebecca's family photographs in their little cute ceramic frames. She felt empty and achy all over again and constantly distracted by the large picture window to her right with its wide view of the city.

She started, finally, to examine a stack of layouts, an ad campaign for a new line of computer software. But the light in the office was strangely tinted; she could not focus. She looked up to that hated window that overlooked the wild blocks to the north. In the western corner of the window, the sun was dropping and the sky was growing red. *I'll pull the curtain,* she thought. *I'll do better under the lights.* But when she stepped to the window the cluttered vastness of the scene stopped her: block after block through the basin and up into the hills around. The sky was patched and fired with cloud. The dusty brick walls of the neighborhood buildings were cast in red by the falling sun and crossed by great black checkerboard blocks of shadow. Slowly, the great patterns broke down and she began to notice details—movements of cars and trucks, the crossings and recrossings of people on the sidewalks, children in the playground.

She stood and watched for a long time. Slowly the streets darkened and the buildings began to melt away. Streetlamps and lights in the apartments flared one by one. The whole scene seemed to mumble with change like a sleeper with her dream.

These were the blocks where her daughter was lost. She studied the crossing patterns of building, street, and alley. She breathed slowly and deeply, slowly and deeply.

~

After another hour, she finally reached the gallery director on the phone.

"Oh, your daughter's been working for him. How nice."

"Yes, so do you—"

"I suppose she's learning a great deal."

"But—"

"He has such vision."

"Yes, but—"

"And he's such a perfectionist about—"

"So, do you—"

"—about his prints, you'd think—"

"—do you have his address? Or a phone number?"

"Well, you know, I have all that sort of thing at the office. I try not to carry my job home with me, but you know . . ."

Ann heard a rattle of jewelry and makeup cases.

"I thought I had it right in this handbag, but . . . Hold on," she said suddenly. "I think I know where it might be."

The phone clattered onto a tabletop. Ann tapped a pencil on Rebecca's desk, watched by the smiling faces of Rebecca's infuriatingly normal children.

"I'm sorry," the gallery woman said when she finally returned. "All I have here is his old apartment. He lives in his studio now, and I don't have that address here."

"Oh no." She had not meant to let her disappointment show.

"But I understand it's just a few blocks from the old place. It's not far at all."

And what am I supposed to do with that? she thought. She took down the old address, thanked the woman from the gallery, and hung up.

~

The police had been no help at all.

"And how long has she been gone?"

"Well, I don't know, because I don't know when she left school, but she's three hours late to meet me."

"And has she done this sort of thing before?"

"Well, she's done things, but she's never left me hanging like this."

"Does she have a boyfriend?"

"No, she doesn't. What does that have to do with it?"

"Well, you never know. She might be out with a boy."

"I told you, I believe she's at a photography studio."

"And you don't know where? What street? What part of the neighborhood?"

"If I did, I'd be there now."

"Well, ma'am . . ."

"Yes . . ." He seemed to be trying to drift out of the conversation.

"If she doesn't come home by morning . . ."

"By morning!"

"If she doesn't come home by morning, you can file a runaway charge down at Juvenile Hall."

"A charge? I have to file a charge on my own daughter?"

"So we can pick her up."

"Well why can't you pick her up now?"

"Because we have no warrant."

"Well, then I'll file one now."

"But she hasn't been gone twenty-four hours."

Twenty-four hours! There was no telling what could happen in twenty-four hours. No way to know what might happen to her in those dark and intricate streets.

~

She had called again to each of her daughter's friends, each contact who might know that photographer. The police, after her third call, agreed to watch for her as they cruised. She had been up and down the elevator a half dozen times. She had called the house more times than she could count. There was nothing else she could think of to do.

Finally she set out to search. She left her note on the office door and another with the security guard at his post, then walked into the parking garage. Nearly everyone else was long gone, and her car was parked three levels down. She was not at all reassured by the video cameras at the end of each row. The garage was silent as a crouched cat. The clicking of her heels echoed back at her, amplified and redoubled until the sound was like the firing of a string of pistols.

She found her car and steered it out of the belly of the building and onto the street. Two blocks up, she crossed the parkway and entered the neighborhood. Involuntarily, she gasped as if she had fallen down a slope. Within minutes, after the first pair of turns, she could see no more of the bright towers of downtown. The stunted, brickish buildings around her loomed. They closed in on her like a fist.

~

She had only the photographer's old address, which she found after a half dozen wrong turns and a string of guiding curses. The building was three stories tall and, in this light, depressingly gray. Gargoyles faced her from the cornices and from the right and left corners of the doorway. Light shone from behind some of the blinds, and, when she rolled down her window, she heard the sounds of excited voices, rap music, and television commercials.

But none of this told her where the photographer had gone or where her daughter might be. She knew only that his shop was somewhere within a few blocks of this spot. She decided she would use the building as a base to search from, and, with her windows rolled and the doors locked, she began to circuit the blocks around it, looking out from the bubble of her windows for something that looked like a studio.

There were stores and carryouts and shops of every kind, and even a string of artist's studios with windows full of sketches and mangled bits of artistic iron, but no photography studio. And no one was even around for her to ask.

So she came back to the first building and stared at it and stared up and down the street and even got up out of the car to study where to go next or what to do,

I should go home and wait, she thought. *That's what I might as well do.* She was filling again with frustration and fury when she heard the thin voice of a boy.

"Is it one of them that talks to ya?"

He was a skinny boy with a twisted mouth, wearing a bright jacket thrown back over his shoulders. He stood in the middle of the street and looked her car over from bumper to bumper.

"I'm sorry," she said, "I didn't quite understand."

"Does this one got a talking alarm, says, like YOU'RE TOO CLOSE." His voice took on a clipped, digital tone. "GET BACK. YOU'RE TOO CLOSE." He waved his arms and jumped back like someone surprised by an alarm. The bright jacket, still new and stiff, crackled.

"Oh no," she said. Her car did not speak. It only made a noise.

"Yeah, but it's a Beemer."

"Pardon?"

"It's a BMW, a Beemer."

"But it's older. Ten years old."

"Cool."

She hoped he might leave then. He was small, but there might be others. Instead, he asked, "Are you, like, looking for something?"

"As a matter of fact, yes. How did you know?"

"I can tell. I can tell about people."

She nodded and started to get back in the car.

"So whatcha looking for? I bet I know where it is."

"Oh, I don't think . . ."

"I mean . . ." He looked aside, and dropped his voice a tone. "Are you looking for some stuff?"

"I'm sorry?"

"'Cause I can hook you up."

"I don't know what . . ."

He studied her a moment, nodded his head as if he had come to a conclusion, then waved his hand. "Never mind," he said.

"I'm looking for a photographer's studio."

"Paul's?"

"You know him?"

He raised his eyebrows. "I got ya," he said. He nodded down the street. "Come on." He started down the street in a strange, rocking walk that involved stuffing both hands in the pockets of his jacket and rolling his shoulders. He rolled a few paces, turned, and saw that she had not followed. "Don't worry, man," he said. "It's, like, just a little ways."

He saw her further hesitation. "Ain't nothing gonna happen. You with me."

This is insane, she thought. *I may never be heard from again.* The boy started down the street again. "Oh, wait," she said. She wanted the packet of negatives, to give them back to that photographer. So she ducked in the car door, pulled out her shoulder bag, and locked the door.

The alarm chirped softly.

"That's cool. Somebody messes with it, it's gonna start, like *AAP, AAP, AAP, AAP.* It'll mess them up, man."

She hitched the bag onto her shoulder and they walked, not just a little ways, but three blocks, then four. She grew steadily more apprehensive.

"Look," she said, "I appreciate your help, but . . ."

"Hey, it's cool. We almost there."

"But you said . . ."

"I bet you're into old stuff."

"Pardon?"

"You collect old stuff, like . . ."

"Antiques?"

"I'm into old stuff, man. Anything old. Books, old money, bottles. I got lots of old bottles. Anything."

"I see."

They turned another corner and onto a block she had cruised three times without seeing a thing. "That's it," he said. He nodded toward a narrow storefront with a wide, uncurtained window. Light spilled into the store front from an inner room. Several photographs looked out from the window. *This is it,* she thought. *Why didn't I see it before?*

She turned to thank the boy, but he had already spun around and was headed back down the middle of the street.

"Later," he called.

Before she knocked, she watched a moment as the boy rocked down the dark street in his bright crackling jacket.

PAUL Lewis was in the darkroom when he heard the rap at the door. He shouted, "Just a minute" and waited for the timer to run down. But again he heard the rap at the door, a dozen quick-hammered raps in succession. The timer rang and he transferred the print to the developer—another dozen raps—then to the bath—a quick, sharp half dozen—a pause as he pinned up the print to dry followed by eight quick, urgent, sharply driven raps on the glass.

"I'm coming," he called. "Hold on a minute." It was nearly ten o'clock at night, and though people knocked at all hours at the glass door of his shop, he was startled this time by the figure crossed by the lights from the streetlamp down the block and the lamp in the back corner on his desk. At such an hour, he could expect to see one of the neighborhood junkies trying to sell him a cassette player for five dollars, or a cop, or one of his contacts among the activist groups who used his photos. He liked talking with the winos, fast-food workers, prostitutes, and children who stopped in and who let him take their pictures, but this was no one he knew. He stood a moment, drying his hands on a towel. At first, with a flicker of anxiety, he thought it might be Jenny, this woman had such a ghostly appearance in the dim crossing lights. But this person was taller, and thin, well dressed, and not at all the battered and randomly dressed figure he expected Jenny to be by now.

Instead of Jenny, or anyone else he knew, within the frame of the doorway (and under his own reflection, which lay over her image like a double exposure), he saw a woman, a stranger, her right fist still pressing against the glass, her face averted to study the walls of the studio. She was dressed in fashionable, professional clothing—a long patterned skirt, a white blouse open at the neck, a dark jacket with padded shoulders, spangly, glittering earrings, her hair held back by a pair of clips. She had stopped knocking and was now looking, not at him nor even necessarily for him, but toward the wall where he had hung the pictures he had already framed, where he had pinned blowups of other prints, where his student, whom he had not seen for two days, had stuck up the poster for his exhibit.

She was in her forties; at first he suspected she was homeless and looking for help. Fierce and distracted, she had, if you ignored the professional clothing, the chiseled, classic features of an Okie woman from the thirties. Her eyes were worried, sidecast, and distant; there was muscle etched clearly in the arm up against the glass; there was a hunter-like intensity in her brows.

She looked like the sort of person he expected to see at his opening. But not here, not in the neighborhood, not at such an hour.

He threw the towel toward a table and started toward the door. He thought, *She may have broken down; she may need help.*

But her look was invasive, investigative, so much like an avenger or a conscience that he stopped again for a moment.

"Come on in," he called. "It's not locked."

She looked doubtfully at the latch, pushed open the door, took one step into the room, then stopped. She leaned forward slightly and continued to study the room. She seemed startled when he said to her, "Is there something I can help you with?"

She looked at him sharply, so sharply that he felt wounded and stepped back. He said, more loudly, "Are you looking for something?"

She looked puzzled, but she said, after a moment, "Yes, I am." The fierceness seemed to go out of her for the moment.

Still wary, he asked her, “How can I help you?”

She nodded, stepped past him, and looked toward the door of the back room.

This was rude. He said, “Excuse me?”

She appeared to gather back some of the fierceness, then said, “I’m Amy’s mother.”

That made sense. He nodded. “Well, glad to meet you.” He was not glad. A new knot of anxiety formed in his belly. “How’s she doing?”

The woman looked around the room from her new angle before she answered. “I was hoping you could tell me.”

“Tell you what?”

“Where is she?”

“I have no idea. Is she okay?”

“Was she here today?”

“No, I haven’t . . .”

“Is she here now?”

“No, she’s not. Is she all right?”

“When was she here last?”

“Like I tried to say, it’s been two days.”

“She’s not here now?”

“No. I said, I haven’t . . .”

“So where is she?”

“I don’t have a clue.”

“You better not be lying to me.” Her voice took a higher, angrier pitch. She clenched and unclenched her hands. She took a deep, slow breath. “Because, if you’re hiding her . . .”

“Look, I’m not stupid . . .”

The woman looked past him to the back room.

“You can go back there and check if you want. I have nothing to hide.”

The woman made no move, but she stared toward the back room for a full minute. She breathed steadily and slow. Finally she asked, “Why didn’t you call to check on her?”

“I’ve been busy myself. I work a day job. There’s a lot of work to do here. I figured she must be grounded or . . .”

“Yes, she’s grounded.”

He shrugged. “If that’s what you have to do . . .”

The fierceness gathered within her again. “She lied to me.”

"About . . ."

"About coming here."

He braced himself for trouble and waited.

"She was not allowed to come here."

"She had your signed permission. It ran through the school."

She shook her head.

"I saw the paper. I talked to her teacher."

She shook her head again.

"Are you saying she forged it?"

She raised an eyebrow, but the fierceness did not leave her.

"Well, I'm sorry, but I was going on what they told me at the school . . ." Under the hawklike gaze of the woman, he felt more and more entrapped. He had a vision of scandal and ruin. "She's a good kid," he said, "and she's done good work. I don't think she'd want to do anything wrong . . . I just figured . . ."

"So why did she lie?"

He shrugged.

"What was so important here that she had to lie to me, her teacher, and probably you, and even forge my signature on a permission slip, just to do your dirty work?"

His defenses flared.

"Look, it's late. I only take insults during business hours."

She did not blink nor shift her fierce demeanor. He went on. "It was all photography. I can show you exactly what she worked on. She printed that whole stack. She matted that photo right there. She's good at what she does. She didn't sweep the floor once."

The woman looked aside.

"It was straight-up professional on my end. I needed help and she was there to provide it. I taught her how to do the work and she did it. She might have lied to you to set this up, but she did nothing wrong here."

She turned to face him. She had moved to where the light from the street and the light from his back room made a pattern of conflicting lights across her face, breaking it into a bright side and a dark side, squares in light and squares in shadow. She raised a hand.

"Look," she said. "I need to find her. And I can't waste a lot of time with you. But I need to know something. I need to know . . . I want to know . . . What would she get here? What did she get from you that was worth all that lying and sneaking around?"

He was stumped. "Look, I don't know what causes anybody to do anything, so I . . ."

"Cut the crap." She turned and faced him directly. "There's a reason she comes here. And I want to know it."

"So ask her."

She steamed. "I have."

"And what does she say?"

"She says she wants to learn photography."

"So why can't you go with that?"

The fierceness flared up again. "Because there's something more."

He shrugged. "Look," he said. "I've got a lot of work to do."

"I want to see the pictures."

"Which pictures?"

"From these negatives." She pulled her bag from her shoulder, set it on the light table, and shuffled through it with a puzzled look. "They were just . . ." She looked toward the door. "That little . . ."

"There's a lot of pictures here." He waved his hand toward the stacks of prints and the pictures on the wall.

"Where are the pictures of the woman?"

He peered at her: "What woman?"

"The woman in the black coat."

"Black coat?"

"The one she told me about. The one that's in those negatives."

"What negatives?"

"The ones she brought home. I had them here a minute ago."

"If they're the ones I think, I haven't seen them in years."

"Well, you can see them right now." She dug again into the large clunky bag. "I had them right here . . ." She looked puzzled. "I thought . . ." She looked out toward the door of the shop.

"What's the matter?"

"They were right here."

"Look, it's . . ."

"I just had them. I put them in this bag."

"It's okay."

"I put them in here just so I could be rid of them. And now they're gone."

"It's okay."

She looked again in the bag. "This is so embarrassing."

"I said it's okay. I've lived thirty years without them."

". . . That little boy . . ."

"What little boy?"

"There was a boy who took me here."

"Did he give you a name?"

She made a motion; for just a moment her hands seemed to tremble and for just a moment she wrung them to keep them still. "No," she said after a deep breath. "It doesn't matter. I'm sorry. I don't have much time and I know you don't either." She clenched her fists and pulled herself straighter. "I have to find her. I don't know where she is. But first," she asked, "could you do just one thing?"

"If I can."

"Could I see those pictures?"

"Of the woman?"

"The pictures of that woman."

Reluctantly, he went to the filing cabinet, pulled out a batch of prints, and laid them in her hands. He watched her carefully scan them, as carefully as her daughter had, though without the adolescent riffs of enthusiasm. One by one, she pondered each shot, and when she was finished she handed the stack to him with a look that took him head to toe.

"And where is this person?"

"I have no idea."

"Are you sure?"

"Amy thinks she lives near here somewhere."

In fact, since Amy had told him she saw Jenny on the street and at a carryout, he had been on watch for her. He never saw her, but he watched over his shoulder as he walked back and forth to work or to the store—not her store, but a store past her store. Half a dozen times he thought he heard her gravelly laugh. Half a dozen times he thought he heard her call his name. And when he thought he heard that laugh, when he thought he heard her bark out his name, he was riven with anxiety. In spite of himself, he looked around as he might if he thought she were a sniper.

Half a dozen times, he had thought, *This is petty.* He had thought, *This is old stuff. This is a waste of time, walking around like I've got something to hide.* So he tried to walk the same streets in all the same hours as he normally would, having excluded her from consciousness, having decided, because this was old and petty stuff, that it made no difference to him whether he saw her or not.

The woman looked over each of the old prints of Jenny in her black coat, studied the room once more, and swept her hawklike eyes over him one more time. After she let the fierceness arise and subside in her eyes once more, she said, "Thank you. I'm sorry I bothered you so late. I hope I didn't keep you from your work."

He nodded as she hitched her bag onto her shoulder and stepped out into the street.

He studied the empty frame of the door for several moments, then hurried to the sidewalk, protectively, to see her to her car. Apparently he had studied too long, for when he got to the street there was no sign of her. There was not a particle of wind nor a breath of sound. There was no motion to the swinging sign over the storefront church, nor to the dark heads of the thistles in the vacant lot, nor to the discarded racing forms and pop cans in the gutters. The dark shapes within the used-furniture store appeared to have settled like a herd of dark, sleeping animals. Just as settled were the chairs of the barbershop and the tanks in the welder's yard. Everything was still: the open dark mouth of the alley where the winos usually gathered, the dryers in the beauty shop, the peeling and battered doors of the warehouse were all still. Even the nighthawks had deserted their sweep of the streetlamps.

Then he knew this was to be a long, dark night. A night in which he could find no rest, in which sleep was impossible, in which he roamed his shop uselessly pacing and fretting, confronted with all the faces in his files and on his walls, voiceless faces full of accusation and reproach. He could not think of a single wrong thing he had done, yet he felt twisted up with wrong and reproach in his belly, in his hands, in his thighs. He knew that he could forget going to work in the morning, that he could forget getting any work done in the shop, that he would be, for this long, dark night, useless and irrational.

He turned heavily back to his darkroom. The towel he had tossed lay in the doorway. He bent to pick it up and, as he did, the heavy spot in his belly, in which he felt most closely the center of his nameless remorse, heaved itself up and made itself felt all down his arms. He turned back toward the door and flung the towel with all the force he could find, toward the frame in which he had first seen the woman's fierce and piercing face.

The towel shot out from his hand, then, in midflight, unballed itself, caught the air, and floated uselessly to the middle of the floor. He felt a violent urge in all his limbs: He wanted to shatter something, to have one thing onto which to pour all the violence that moved along his arms.

But there was nothing, he knew, that could contain all this violence. He knew that, if he once started, he would destroy everything he had made in thirty years.

The fierce woman was gone, but his own dark image still lay on the glass, staring back at him from the blue hole of the street.

WHEN Ann Taylor got home from searching, she still bristled with an uncomfortable energy. There was still no word from Amy. She checked her messages and found nothing on her machine. There was nothing more, at this hour, she could do. She paced the kitchen, filing dishes and rearranging utensils in the drawers until she thought, *This is crazy; I've got to work tomorrow. I've got to get some sleep.*

By habit, as she went to her room, Ann stopped at Amy's door. Nothing there had been disturbed.

In her own room, Ann switched on one small lamp on her dressing table and paced across her floor for several turns before she told herself, *Settle down.* It was after one o'clock. Her nerves were keening for nicotine. But she was determined to get some rest. She sat down at her dressing table to remove her earrings, her makeup, and the clips in her hair.

She was used to mirrors and makeup. It had been her profession for some years to use makeup and mirrors to create a new face for each occasion. But just now the little that she wore bothered her as much as if it were a plastic mask. Quickly, using only the creams and tissues at her table, she removed the trim lines of her mascara, the faint blush from her cheeks, and the lipstick which seemed now so garish. When she had finished, she stared into the mirror at the naked face she met there. It was a thing she had not done in a very long time, to look steadily at her own features without building up or tearing down the face she wore to work, to parties, to dinner. It was her same face, with the same runway cheekbones and oval eyes. Of course, she had lost that adolescent roundness, that doe-like softness that had put her into those ads for shampoo and tissues long ago. But that was to be expected. She did not want a soft, malleable face to present to the world, one that any photographer could make into anything he wanted. She needed her sharper, edgier look to do what she did, because for years she had had to cut her way through the world as if she were flint.

She had not seen the flint in her features before, but she could see it now. She could see it in the tightness around her mouth, and in the seams at the edges of her eyes. It was as if she had turned into some elemental thing, a lump of earth, a stone.

It was as if she were looking at her own naked bones.

FOR several hours, Paul stalked back and forth through his studio as if he were a stranger, studying the pictures and posters on the walls, the prints hanging in the darkroom, and the dark, silent shapes of his equipment, feeling no connection at all to the collected images nor to the people who had given them up to him. It was as if someone else had done this work. Someone else had made those visits to the migrant camps. Someone else had shot these factory scenes. Someone else had snapped these grim lines of police, these secretaries, these arrogant and vulnerable teenagers. These pictures in their frames, ready to mount the gallery walls like a silent, gray army, were his entire testament. And yet, for now, they shrugged their gray shoulders and told him nothing.

The battered stack of Jenny's photos still lay on his desk. These alone, of all the work in his shop, now spoke to him. He picked up the cracked and wrinkled prints and read them over and over again until he had newly memorized each grain of light and each shadow until it was again palpable, present, warm as breath.

It was as if he could hear her voice again amid the complaint of grandmothers in their doorways and the groan of engines up the steep streets. It was as if he could feel under his feet and in the muscles of his legs the sharp angles and hardness of the walkways and alleys where he had first photographed her. It was as if he could inhale again the smell of fog and rotting vegetables in the streets and could smell again her odor of sea salt, bread, and cheap wine.

He ached in a way he had not known was possible. He felt the absence of her in a way he had never felt her presence. He was aware of the darks of her now more than he had ever known her lights.

When he had done with looking at her pictures, Paul could neither work nor sleep, nor could he move more than a few feet away from the stacks of matted prints ready for the gallery. And so he found himself studying again each face, each cluster of wine-drinking men, each woman wiping down a table or lifting a sheet, each striker walking a cold morning picket line, each child playing ball in a stone-bound alley. Now, instead of the detached and stony indifference he had felt before, his memories and connections were immediate, engaged. He felt himself studied in return, as if each person had crossed the white borders of the photograph and stepped silently into the room to watch him.

Watched and examined in a room crowded with memory and remorse, he stood, finally, shakily, as if he had been tried and found guilty. What he admitted to himself next was like taking a leap into the Blue Hole he remembered from his youth.

He looked again at her dozen or so photographs and again it was as if her breath were at his neck, sweet, damp, full of wine and fog. And he realized, suddenly, how much, illogically and beyond all resentment, he still wanted her. He could imagine, having watched what happened to women on the streets, what damage had been to done her over these last years, but still he wanted her. It was a simple notion, but it so surprised him that he felt shaky on his feet. He had always treated her badly, but he wanted her and he had never known it to tell her.

~

But Jenny, lost as she was, was not the one who needed to be found. He came out of the filing area like one waking from a sleep and realized that, if Amy was gone, then Jenny might have some knowledge of her whereabouts. On that hope, and on the hope that he might find her, he left the studio.

He did not expect to find the girl at such an hour, as late as it was. He did not expect to find her at all, but he was willing to do something crazy to shake off the crazy feelings of desire and remorse which shook him. Walking, even walking as shakily as he had begun to walk, gave him comfort.

It was a dark, clouded, moonless night, the like of which, in the country, in the absence of streetlamps, leaves the walker blind as a mole. In spite of the light from the streetlamps, the security lights in the windows of the stores, and the glare of late-night televisions, he felt his way down each block as if it were a dim-lit tunnel, guided less by light than by the smell of each doorway and each patch of sidewalk, by the night sounds, and by the air, which formed itself around each corner, each parking meter, each granite stoop. The scent of humus and flower rose from the front of the vegetable stand; the used-tire shop sent up an odor of Akron; the fish bar surrendered a smell of haddock and burnt oil. Sirens rose up from the hills above him. He heard the scuffle of rats in a cardboard carton. A radio wailed. He heard what might have been a person weeping or a person cursing, and he heard what he thought for a moment, with a thrill of expectation and terror, was a woman's granite laughter.

He was in a narrow side street. He stepped out to see better where the laughter came from and stood in the center of the street, turning around to face all the dark faces of the buildings around him.

The laughter came and went; it left behind an utter blue-hole silence. There was nothing alight but a single lamp burning in a window high above him.

~

Exhausted with dawn and grief, Paul decided to make one more round before he trudged back toward his studio. The rising sun was hidden by the brick walls around him, but he welcomed the milky light that made its way to him. He figured he would go back to the shop, sleep an hour, and head back out to search again. He would skip work if he had to.

He walked up the center of a silent and narrow street just a few blocks from home. Not a soul was out. The slowly waking sounds of the city were all around him, but nothing stirred or breathed down this street but himself alone. The light pecked at every pebble of the asphalt, every bubble in the brick, every grain in the concrete.

A woman entered from a cross street thirty yards ahead, stepped down from the curb, walked to the center of the intersection, then stopped and turned toward him. She stared at him a moment before she quickly moved on.

A pack was slung across her shoulder, and from each arm hung a bundle of luggage.

JENNY laughed when she looked down from her window and saw him in the street. She did not know why. She knew it was not to mock him, for she had no right to mock anyone at all. But here he was, on her street at four in the morning, at the very last moment she could have seen him before she carried her bags down to the bus station. It was so strange and sudden and yet somehow fitting that she should see him stalking in the street, looking to the left and the right at each of the windows and doors that were tight and dark as coffin lids. It was clear he was in search of something, and she of all people could not mock a searcher.

But the laughter bubbled up from deep inside her; it escaped in one quick burst in spite of her effort to hold it back.

She stepped away from the window so that he would not see her. She pressed back a second burst of laughter, then calmed herself gradually until a heavy sadness replaced the laughter and the corners of her eyes began to fill with tears.

He was gone when she went back to the window. She did not know what had brought her to the window at just that moment, but she no longer questioned such things. She went back to her packing, which, given how little she owned and how little she planned to take, would take only a few minutes more. Then it would be time to walk to the station.

~

For two days she had wandered the streets and for two nights she had haunted the bus station, the alleys, the foyers of public buildings, and the willow brakes near the river. It was cold, and none of these places offered comfort, or friendly faces, or warmth for very long. But it was not yet the worst of winter, and she knew she could handle the weather out of doors and alone. For she was in search, just as was Paul and she knew not who else.

~

Thirty years. She had lived this way for thirty years, owning no more than a nun would own, moving from city to city, restless at each stopping place, and each city etched with memories of painful drownings and rescues.

These last few times she had tried, really tried not to drown in the wine again. But the last of her drownings, on these very streets, had been her worst. She had dropped to a place she wanted never to visit again. She had done things on those streets she would pity anyone to have done. And yet she had come back up. When that young girl Amy showed up at the store and said that she knew the pictures and that she had recognized her in the street from the pictures, a wave of shame had washed over her so heavy that it had nearly knocked her down.

~

The first person she had come to know in this city was that little boy. The boy with his questions and his hands in everything. On the day she moved in, having just moved into town on a rumor and a whim, he had followed her down the street, reminding her of a squirrel—nervous, big-eyed, teeth protruding, full of little barks and twitches. He had seen her come onto the street with her suitcase and her shopping bag, and he had said, "So you moving in here?"

She was. She had found a place by rumor and whim.

"Why you got that old suitcase? My mom, she got suitcases like that but she uses them for old sheets and stuff. You got old sheets and stuff in yours?"

He followed her to the apartment door and did not wait to be asked in.

"So you moving in here? On the second floor? That's cool 'cause we live down the hall and we got a cat but Mrs. Alinsky don't know it 'cause it ain't allowed."

He went to the window and looked out to the street. "This is a cool street. 'Cept for the wineheads, 'cause they all a time telling stupid jokes. There's wineheads here but ain't no crackheads. 'Cept for my mom, but she ain't on it no more."

Jenny set her bags down, smelled the must and mildew, and threw open the windows to air out the room.

"So what's that thing?" She was laying out her sleeping mat. "Don't you have no furniture? Man, we got a kitchen table and some chairs and beds and a TV and a beanbag chair and a crib and a frigerator." She had only the refrigerator and stove which came with the apartment. The bare floors of her room were dressed with white light. Later she would collect a dresser, a table, and a pair of chairs. To start, she used the kitchen sink as a makeshift desk. She hung a few things on hangers in the closet. There was a shelf above the sink, and there she put a box of crackers, some peanut butter, a can of coffee, three plastic plates, a saucepan, and a skillet. That night she would buy some vegetables and rice at the little market on the corner, and she would collect spices and utensils at little shops and secondhand stores. She would make friends with the man who ran the Asian food shop two blocks down and they would trade San Francisco stories. She would later make bread in the apartment stove. She would put flowers in a mason jar and place them on the window ledge, where light would come down through the petals.

"What's that?" the boy would ask that first day as she hung up or shelved each item. "My sister's got one of these," he said, holding up a potato masher.

"Please don't get into my things."

He dropped the masher back into the suitcase and picked up the battered manila envelope. "What's in here?"

"Those are my personal papers. Leave them alone."

"What's these?" He pulled a strip of negatives to the light.

"Those are personal." She moved to take them back.

He stepped to the window ahead of her and held them to the light. "They look like ghosts."

"That's because they're negatives," she said. When he obviously didn't get it, she added, "It's like a regular picture, but the lights and the darks are opposite of each other."

He squinted through the negatives until she took them from his hands, then he squinted at her answer as she put the packet on the closet shelf along with her various papers, books from the last treatment center, records from her last couple of jobs, some letters from home, and a set of postcards to send to friends. Later, once she got a dresser, she moved the papers to the top drawer. And it was among them she kept the packet of negatives.

~

She lived in the apartment for months, ignorant of Paul's presence just a few blocks away. Through the little boy, she met Hussein, the owner of the little store, who liked that she was good with numbers and could talk salty with the customers, so she worked there, part-time at first, then more and more, until she was behind that counter night and day.

It filled her time and kept her arguing and playing the dozens with the boy and his friends, and arguing and listening to the lies of the hustlers, and arguing and listening to the complaints of the old men and women who came to cash their checks and buy their coffee and bread. And then there were the students on their way to school, cops on break, downtown workers, and the winos.

She resented the winos. She resented each brightly colored bottle of wine she sold them. She told herself it did not bother her to work there every day with the prominent and colorful bottles of wine behind her. She was done with that, she had decided. She had only to look into the faces of the men and women who bought them, some broken, some just now breaking,

She had achieved a sort of stasis. She felt that as long as she moved along the path from the shop to her room, and deviated only as far as her few needs might take her, as long as she kept her contact minimal when she was not safely behind the counter at the store, she might be safe. She could not be pulled under again.

But the day came when she wobbled, and then fell. She felt no particular crisis, no sense of tension or undue exasperation. She simply decided, suddenly, she was jealous of even the shabbiest of winos, who, in spite of their damage, in spite of the visible loss that screamed out of them, smiled as they bought the brightly colored bottles and smiled as they shuffled out the door, and she knew, without even needing to see them, that they smiled and laughed as they broke the seal.

So one day she took down the largest and brightest of the bottles, paid cash for it, locked up the store an hour early, and took the bottle to her room as if it were a lover.

~

She fell to the streets with all the fury and loss by which the angels must have fallen. It was then she drowned the hardest she had ever drowned. She barely remembered half of it and did not want to remember what she remembered. She drank her way into the alleys and streets. From the streets, she ended up in a shelter. From the shelter, they sent her, shivering and pleading for her mother, to the detox center. There, they dressed her in a shapeless gown and fed her Valium for three straight shuddering days. While she was still stretched and spent, they put her into the unit with the others, where she sat through the same lectures and meetings she had ached through before, hoping to understand it all this time. But in all that drowning, she still had not learned what she needed to learn.

Hussein had saved her the job and she had settled back into her stasis where she might have drowned again, but that she was swept by that wave of shame the day the girl stumbled in with her fistful of change and announced, "I've seen your pictures."

~

No, she told herself, not again. But she felt herself failing once more and she realized it was time to be rid of the negatives. It was the only way to escape the shame. She had kept them in their frayed manila envelope for all these years, the one thing she had kept track of in spite of all the jails and evictions and detoxifications and treatment centers and the horrible and untellably shameful times on the street. As she had lost all else, she was somehow able to keep these.

Once, in Detroit, she had thought she lost them for good. An old woman she had seen in the neighborhood stopped her on the street. "When they set out your things, everything else got stolen or ruined in the rain. But I saved you this." And she handed her the manila envelope. She seemed fated to keep that packet.

But when the girl came around to the store and announced that Paul was near, she knew it was time to let those negatives go. It was time to dispense with all the emblems of her former self. She had not wanted to do it. At first she had held on and held on, but now these last tokens of her ghosted self were gone.

~

Jenny woke in the early morning in the grayest of gray light and went immediately to the window as if someone had called her name. There was no one in the misting street but that little boy in a green-and-orange jacket that blazed out of the dimness like a tongue of fire. *Does he ever sleep?* she wondered. *Does no one ever bring him in?*

The boy looked watchfully around, almost as if he had heard her thoughts, and moved around the corner out of sight.

Then the street was empty, but for the mist.

She dressed for work in the dark, pulling out and putting on her clothes by habit and touch. But she felt empty and lost, as if in giving away the negatives she had given up a child, and that child was as lost as the child she had just seen on the street.

Dressed now, she stood to gather her things for work. But so empty and so lost, she could not think: Her earrings: where were they? That little container of rouge: it was right here. And the book—she was on page 212 already—is it by the futon? She looked around her for a moment to locate these things, any of these things, then stopped. It was as if she heard a voice saying, *Don't move,* and for several moments she did not.

When she finally did move again, it was to get money and her warmest coat. She knew her task now: she had come to this, the final bare-bonesing of self. She would abandon, not just the negatives, but all the illusions and accumulations of identity she had filled herself up with. The job. Her little kit of makeup. Her shelf of books. Letters from friends. Pride. Her six pairs of earrings. Even this girl. It had been lovely, and a comfort, to have someone listen to her as that young girl listened to her stories. But that, too, was one of the illusions of self she intended to lose. And the stories: she would have no more stories.

And language: for in the two days she had now wandered and watched, she had gone mute as an animal. Now she watched the streets and park lawns with snakish eyes, smelling and tasting the world as it drifted by her on the wind.

~

What, she wondered, *is the secret of all hearts? What is the secret to be revealed at the dreadful day of doom?* That dreadful day of doom when the secrets of all hearts will be revealed.

She was at the riverbank, near the abutment of a bridge, hidden between the concrete foot of the bridge and a brake of willows rooted in the silt. The lighted city was behind her. Another city lay across the river, and the silver lights of each—the near city and the far city—were caught in the ripples and seams of the black water.

She smelled dead fish and burning wood and—where was this from?—an odor of asphalt. Beyond the willows, some fifty feet away, a group of men sat talking around a driftwood fire that snapped and shot up sparks and smoke. The men did not see her, but she could see them and she could hear snatches of words. Something about wine and something about money and something about a drowned man washed up right here at this bank. No, no, the others argued, it was at the next bridge down. She listened to them argue the drowned man up and down the river for a long time. Every now and then, one would throw another tire or a twisted piece of driftwood onto the fire, then clap his hands and rub them in the heat.

Finally, one by one, they wrapped themselves in their coats or bindles and slept. A raccoon shuffled in the willow leaves and cars still rattled the expansion plates of the bridge floor, but there was no more talk of wine and drowned men.

She had been so long now in the penitential cold that she felt no bite from it, even without the fire the men shared. That fire, which had settled, still lent a red and looming light to the underbridge girders and to the bare canes of the willows. Anyone watching could have seen the red glow touch her face as well.

She was alive in every cell.

The shoreline itself was some thirty yards down a short embankment caked with silt. She stalked silently down through the willow canes, past the sleeping men and their stack of driftwood and tires. She placed herself in clear view of the river, sat in the soft cake of silt, and waited.

A barge churned past, throbbing steadily like a heart and throwing its running lights over the black water. The wake behind it was a lattice of disrupted, crisscrossing waters that broke the city lights into fragments. She gazed as the wake settled and the fragments formed themselves into their former patterns. Suddenly, with no movement on her part, without even a breath, she felt herself lifted as if by a great bird. There was, suddenly, no fear, no shame, no failing body; there was only the shifting, watery latticework of silver lights.

The barge churned around the bend and disappeared. The wake settled, and the city lights on the water began to run again in smooth downriver lines.

It was over quickly, but she was supremely, utterly happy. She shivered now, and she felt wolfishly hungry, but she was enormously happy, for she had risen to such a point without the wings of alcohol.

It was time to leave. She had what she sought. So she rose from the silt, stretched, and stalked back silently through the willows toward the city.

As she passed, she did not see a man rise from his bindle to jam his hat onto his head and stoke the fire with driftwood. He was dressed all in gray, and even the red of the fire gave no color to his clothes nor to the hat which nearly covered his eyes.

She felt him watch her as she entered the willows and picked her way through them in the dark. Under the pressure of his eye, she scrambled up the bank toward the point at which the bridge floor met the street.

~

When she went down to the station to buy her ticket, she did not see the boy in his blazing jacket. He watched her from the corner, then from the sidewalk outside the station, and then as she was leaving, from where he thought he was hidden behind the fender of a standing cab.

~

She still remembered—and lately had begun to dream of—the man with the wide hat and duffel bag who had walked her father's fence line so many years ago. In her memory, he was still dusty and tired; he still walked steadily into his disappearance. But in her dream, he was utterly faceless. His back was turned, or his face was averted, or the wide hat covered his eyes, so that she never saw his face. In each of her dreams, she watched as he stepped off a curb and into the street. That was all. She saw him and knew him by the wide hat and the duffel bag and by the gray jacket. His back toward her, he stepped off the curb and into the street. Each time the dream was the same and each time she was left with the feeling that she was to follow him, to step off a curb and into the streets of a city. In San Francisco, in Oakland, in the half dozen cities since then, she had seen old men who could have been such a man, but never had she seen him in the wide gray hat nor carrying the duffel bag nor walking in the same steady march. But she remembered him so clearly of late and had dreamed of him so hard that when she felt called to the window tonight she half expected to see him.

Instead, she saw Paul. Paul! Searching half blind among the coffin lid doors and graveyard windows of her street.

The sight of him there made her laugh.

~

An hour later, she looked around her room: It was nearly as bare now as when she had moved in. Working in the dark, she had set everything she was taking in a row by the door. The blue light from the street fell across the linoleum of the kitchen, scrapped and tattered at the corners and scuffed and blackened at each nail head. It dressed the Formica surface of the kitchen table, the painted shelves, and the bone-white sink. In the room where she had slept, the light had raised patterns in the floorboards, had textured even the sides of the dresser which stood in its corner.

She would leave the flowers in the mason jar. Whoever followed her into this room could keep the dresser and the kitchen table and the two chairs. She had given up the negatives, her ghosts. She owed nothing to anyone. She was taking with her no more than a nun would take.

Within the hour, while the lamps still softened the darkness of the streets, she would be waiting at the Greyhound station. Her bus would come down off the ramp from the dark highway bearing its own lights like fish at the bottom of a dark sea.

She stood in the middle of the bare, light-dressed room and breathed slowly and deeply. She enjoyed the thought a moment more: she owed nothing at all to anyone. Then she turned, picked up her bundles, and went down the stairs.

On the street, she stopped again and looked around her at the closed windows and blank doors.

She stood silent among the gray buildings and the gray morning mists. From the yards across the river, she heard a distant train. She waited until she felt the gray mist shroud her. Then she stepped off the curb and into the street.

12

PHOTOGRAPHS:

A Black woman in the white uniform of a waitress. She stands at her station behind a counter set with a napkin holder, salt and pepper shakers, menus. Behind her is another counter, shoulder high, which looks onto a kitchen. To her left is a pair of cylinders, one for coffee, one for hot water. Her arms are folded; she leans back against the high counter, but she does not appear to be at rest. She looks aside to a place off-camera.

The look on her face is skeptical and sad.

A small metal cross hangs from a chain at her neck.

~

Four people stand near the door of a bus. The head and forepaws of the running dog logo are to their left. They have just dismounted and they clutch their bags closely. Three are men and one is a woman; two of the men wear straw cowboy hats and the third, possibly the youngest, wears a baseball cap. The woman is bare-headed and her hair is pulled back in a braid that falls to her left shoulder. They are of a small, stocky build that speaks of poverty and hard work.

Each of them looks worriedly to the left, to a place to the side of the camera. They seem to be asking, *What sort of place have we come to?*

~

A man stands pointing to a set of glass doors to a building behind him. He appears to be agitated; it shows in his ribbed brow, in his wide eye, in the nervous way his arm stretches toward the doors, one of which has been shattered in a spiderweb pattern.

His jacket is open; we see, pinned to his shirt, an ID badge with his first name—Karim—in bold letters.

This man has an urgent story to tell.

AMY almost wished she had not set out like this. Almost, but not really. For now it was done, and though she was tired and cold and nearly in despair, she was determined to see it through. She was determined to reach Jenny before she went away. Though she knew her mother would be angry—no, past angry, furious—she was willing to take the risk. And though she was cold and tired past belief, she stayed hidden from the lights of the street in the doorway of an abandoned building.

The bus station's neon dog shone across the front of her building, but not across her, for she had pulled back from the light into the recess of the doorway where she was sure no one could see her. A woman stood on the corner nearby; she stayed fully in the light and watched each car closely as it passed. When there was a car to watch, which at such an hour was not often, the woman canted herself to one side and stood with her hand on her hip. When there was no car to watch, the woman wrapped her hands around her shoulders and stamped one foot.

Amy, in her hidden place, stamped her foot as well, for she was cold, and it was late, and she had nowhere else to go.

Twice already she had been to the bus station, on Jonathan's suggestion, to see if she could find Jenny among the travelers lining up. But no; there were all these sad people worn down with their bundles and suitcases and she wished she could take their picture though she did not have the nerve to ask them. It was an hour to the next bus, and she would have waited right there among them, but she had seen the security guard watching her and she had seen him talking to the manager and pointing to her, and when, finally, she had fallen asleep at one of the little chairs fitted with a pay TV, he had jabbed her three times in the shoulder.

"You can't sleep here," he said. She rubbed her eyes. "You can't work here either."

You're a stuck-up, stuff-shirt, redneck, rent-a-cop, too-ignorant-to-make-a-real-cop jerk, she thought. *You can back off right now,* she thought bravely. But she said none of these things.

Instead, "I'm waiting for a friend," she said.

"You can't sleep here," the guard said again. "Move on."

But where to go? It was cold, and she had never been on the streets at night. And to stand outside the station would invite more hassle from the security guard.

I can see it now, she thought. *If I get arrested for trespassing or something.* She was not sure what that something was, but she knew that coming home would be bad enough without that.

In quick succession, she thought of the warmth of her bedroom, her favorite books, phone calls to her friends. She thought of the inevitable argument with her mother, the punishment that would be heaped on top of what she already had to pay, and the eventual reunification they would have, the meals they would share. And she thought, *I could call. I could just make a phone call.*

But she had to see Jenny, just once before she went away.

~

After she left the station, she found a doorway where she could hide and wait. From there, she saw Jonathan, with his hands jammed into the pockets of his bright new coat, crossing from Broad and the station. The colors of his coat, under the flash of the dog, were achingly, unnaturally bright, as were the white high-top shoes on his feet.

That new jacket, she thought. *And that hard walk. Where's he going with that hard little walk?* He had a word for the woman on the corner, then skimmed down the street, looking back over his shoulder every few paces. The further he skimmed from the light of the dog, the more he became a shadow, in spite of his bright coat and shoes. He crossed the street at a point some twenty yards beyond the alley, then doubled back up the same way, still hugging the buildings. At the alley, he dove into the shadows, where he and another shadow seemed to talk, shake hands, throw out gestures, and trade small packets back and forth.

~

She expected silence to settle in at some point, after the roar of cars and buses had died and the traffic of bodies and voices from the bars and coffee shops up on Broad Street had begun to rest. But in the absence of that roar other sounds emerged, just as in a house growing dark and quiet, the mice scuttle out from their dark holes. Voices, radios, sirens, skittering leaves, truck engines, the highway half a mile off, the scree of the nighthawks that shadowed the streetlamps, other sounds unearthly and unidentifiable. All nibbled, scuttled, rustled, chittered, and scratched in the silence.

The stone and brick of the doorway seemed to suck the warmth from her body; the doorway had the cold breath of a cave. The damp of the stones slipped into her muscles and fixed itself in her bones. She shivered at times and stamped some more and shook her shoulders.

But she did not intend to move until it was time for the next bus. She knew no other way and had decided she would stay until she saw her. This is where I'll find her, she had decided, here at the corner where she first saw her and the seven laughing men.

~

Three times she snapped herself awake and had to wonder how long she had slept. After the third time, even the bar had closed. The woman was gone from the corner. The stiff neon dog still flared above the station, but the lights were out in all the houses around her. She had dreamed, she knew, but the dream was banished by the suddenness of her waking and by the thorough and sudden-seeming darkness.

The streetlamp cast a blue glare down against the gray street, the darkened windows, and the granite steps, a half-toned, washed-out light in which all things seemed to be under a murky sea. The alley sucked down light, black as a grave. In the darkened puzzle of signs and windows, sidewalks, parked cars, doorways, litter cans, mailboxes, curbstones, channels of asphalt, brick walls, stone lintels, iron railings, flickerings of hidden televisions, scuttering rats, night lamps shadowed over with moths and nighthawks, scraps of paper, and shards of broken glass, the alley was the only thing of clarity and form. Geometrically black, the alley blazed with darkness.

She dozed again, in moments.

~

She woke when she became aware, as an animal might, of someone standing near her. She woke, but she did not dare move, no more than to barely open her eyes. It was Daniel, leaning against the opposite doorpost.

"Wassup," he said.

She pulled back; she was aggressively silent.

"It's cool, man. I ain't like that." He sat down opposite her and leaned against the opposite wall. "Little J told me you was here."

"Little J needs to be home in bed."

"That's what I told him, get his skinny ass home."

"You said you don't want him dealing."

"I told the little motherfucker, better never let me catch him slinging that rock."

"Well, what do you think he's doing out at this hour?"

Daniel was silent for a moment.

"Where do you think he got that new jacket? I mean, put the pieces together."

"Naw, man. He ain't on that."

"I stood here and watched him, not more than an hour ago."

He whispered what seemed to be curses. "I know the motherfucker that's got him started."

"You don't think you had something to do with it?"

"Like I said, I told him don't never let me see him slinging."

"So what does that mean when he sees you do it?"

He shrugged, shook his head, and was silent.

"So what are you here for?"

"I come down to check on you."

"I didn't ask you to come check on me."

He nodded.

"I don't want to be checked on."

"So you, like, want to find that lady?"

"She's no lady to you. She's a wine-sucking lowlife, something-or-other to you."

He nodded again and did not seem to disagree.

"I mean, you act like somebody with a problem is some kind of dirt."

"I didn't ask her to drink that wine."

"She's got, like, a disease. That's all. It's not like she can help it."

He remained some moments in an unconvinced silence. Then he asked, "So you gonna, like, just sit out here and wait for her to show up?"

"Do you have a better plan?"

He spat again. This time he arced his spitball down the steps and nearly to the street. "Come on up to my crib."

"No. No thanks." She shook her head. "I mean, I'm not into that."

"I don't mean . . ." He threw out his left hand and touched his heart with his right. "Man, it's like, you don't give nobody a chance or nothing."

"So what do you mean?"

"It's like, you just think, He just wants to do me. You don't even know what I'm saying."

"So what are you saying?"

"Come on up to my crib so you can stay warm and won't nobody mess with you. My granny's up there. She can give you something to eat. You can stay on the couch. It's too crazy out here. You don't know what can happen to you out here. There's crazy people out here."

"You help make them crazy."

"I ain't on that."

"How can you say that?"

"How can I say that? I just said it."

"You know what it does. You won't use it yourself. But you sell it."

"Shit." He shook his head.

"I'm right. You don't like it 'cause I'm right."

He waved his hand at her dismissively. "That's it again. You don't never give nobody credit. You just want to believe the shit." He looked to the street with his chin on his fist, slowly shaking his head. "It's like that all the time," he muttered.

"So what is it? You sell, don't you?"

"I said, I ain't on that."

"How can you say that?"

He threw open his hands.

"I mean, I see you out here, day after day. And I see the people that . . ."

"So I quit. I ain't on that no more."

"For like, what? Two days?"

"Man, I like threw it down." He swept his right hand downward for emphasis.

"Yeah, right."

"Yeah. Be like that. Can't give these lowlifes credit for nothing." He stared out toward the alley. "Nothing."

"So you don't?"

He raised both hands with a shrug.

She stopped to ponder this a moment, then asked, "Did you stop because of Little J? You did. Didn't you?"

He said nothing, but pointed toward a trinket of light far up the street. "Here comes the bus," he said.

"You did," she said. "I know you did."

They crossed to the station and watched a group of Mexican men in straw cowboy hats dismount the bus. They were silent and somber, as if there were something sacred about the night. No one came to board, and after a few minutes wait, the bus pulled out and dropped into the night like a stone.

"So let's go back to my crib," he said.

"But I don't want to miss the next bus."

"The next bus don't pull in here for another three hours. I checked."

"But if I go to sleep . . ."

"That's what they make alarm clocks for."

~

She followed him off Broad and onto a side street. He remained stonily silent for half a block more when he surprised her by asking, "So what you gonna do? You gonna save her or something?"

His tone made it sound as if this were something wrong.

"And you don't think I should. Because she's a wine-sucking so-and-so."

He shrugged.

"She's my friend." Then, after several paces more, she said, "Besides, you're out here trying to save me."

He did not seem to notice what she said. They walked two more blocks in the silence that was not a silence.

In the darkness that was no true darkness, the buildings around her were transformed. The swing sets and jungle gym and teeter-totters of the playground had taken on lurking, reptilian shapes. The vacant lots, which by day teemed with rubble and vegetation, now seemed black and unfriendly as nightmare. An occasional hall glowed with empty light, but the buildings around them seemed to have drawn back just as flowers draw back their petals. All the colors had resolved themselves into shades of black, the colors of smoke, the colors of a negative.

She followed two paces behind him for another block, until he stopped, turned, and nodded toward a doorway flanked by a pair of empty shops: padlocks on the doors, soap on the windows, a trellis of fire escapes climbing to the top floor. The fire escapes crossed the front of the building and darkened it like a veil. Above the hallway door and above each dark window was a carved stone block. She gazed a moment, then asked, "Is this it?"

A rat scuttled out from the black hallway and along the front of the empty store to the right, then stopped in front of her.

She gasped; it was so close that if she fell forward she would have landed on it. It posed, a three-legged, waiting stance: forepaw dangling, incisors bared, eyes shining like black beads.

Daniel turned and saw her frozen to the spot. He laughed. "That rat ain't nothing," he said, then charged on it with his heavy shoes. The rat turned back into shadow and disappeared.

She followed him into the gloom of the hallway, straight down the center of the passage to avoid stepping into the path of another rat. For a moment, she could not see Daniel at all and could follow him only by the tread of his shoes on the concrete of the hall.

In a few steps, they entered an open courtyard. A lamp fastened high up on a post formed enormous shadows out of the garbage cans and formed black mouths of the three doorways, left, center, and right.

"Welcome to the get-o," he said. "You want to know the get-o, this is it."

She followed him across the yard toward the left-hand door, then followed him down a dark hall and to a set of stairs lit by a dim bulb.

"You sure this won't bother your grandmother?"

"My granny's cool," he said.

~

Earlier, when she was taking the photographs, she had had only a glimpse of the old woman. "Daniel," she had called from a back room.

He had ignored the voice. Amy had lowered the camera to allow him to answer, but he had remained on the couch, staring out the window.

"Daniel," the woman said again. The voice was thin as gauze.

"She's sick," he said. "She don't come out from her room some days."

Later, before she left, she glanced down the hall and saw the woman bathed in white light. She raised the camera quickly, but thought, *No, I can't,* and lowered it again.

~

There was no sign of the grandmother when they entered the apartment. The living room light was still on, the bare couch and television even more stark under its yellowing light. "This is yours," he said, pointing to the couch. "Won't nobody bother you."

No one did, though she could hear the boy talking and the gauzy, gravelly sound of the old woman's voice and, a few moments later, the sound of the boy arguing with someone on the telephone. In the final minutes before she fell asleep, Amy heard a cottony noise of slippers from the hall and saw, in the dim light that entered from the courtyard lamp, the dim face and form of the old woman. She stood a moment by the hallway door in a white, ghostly gown, her face darkened under the cowl of her white hair.

When Daniel woke her, the woman was gone. It was still dark and silent. "Come on," he whispered.

She rose quickly and together they went out into the predawn streets.

ROGER Nolan looked out onto Broad Street and saw nothing that he wanted to see. Hours had passed, night had fallen, and the lights of the bars and nightclubs and coffeehouses had flared. He had parked his car near his alley and walked to the corner of Broad, several blocks down from the white dog of the bus station. There he watched, as if it were a wild, disordered dream, the stream of well-dressed, laughing people, in from the suburbs or down from the heights around the university as they thronged the sidewalk and crowded the street with their gleaming cars. Others, who did not know what Nolan knew, might see only the laughing people and the gleaming automobiles or the bright new galleries and shops with their exhibits of pastry or shoes or abstract sculpture lit up in the caged windows. These others might see only the white-shirt attendants of the valet parking for the bars. Or the women in tight skirts and spike heels with their escorts leading them like thoroughbred horses. They might see all the movement and the money, all the lights and the proud and excited traffic. But he saw behind all this. He saw, just out of range of the lights, the grimness of the side streets and the despair of the wineheads and the addicts in the shadowed alleys.

He knew what others did not know. He knew that by closing time, just a few hours away, when the last of the bright couples drove off for the suburbs in their glossy, high-step SUVs, after the musicians snapped shut their guitar cases or packed up their drum kits, after the valets and waitresses and busboys drove back to the heights around the university, after the lights left the facades, and the padlocks were snapped into their hasps and the iron gates drawn over the doorways, then all this glare, all this fashion, all this strutting and show, all this neon and incandescence, all this falsehood would be gone. The streets would be left with an almost primitive darkness. The dark side of the dollar would emerge.

Nolan left the brightness of Broad Street and entered a side street. He had been roaming for hours—and would continue to roam for hours, troubled with thought since the moment he had discovered his product stolen, his trust broken. The product, as he had told the slender dope boy, was no real problem. The money was no real problem. He could make more money; he had product stashed here and there like a squirrel. He had always played his game carefully—never trusted all his money or all his product to any one place or person. Even the breach of his shop was no big problem. He had figured out the window where the young man had slithered in, though it was hard for him to imagine how the boy could have narrowed those shoulders small enough to squeeze through. Nolan had sealed the window even tighter now than it had been before. He had poured a belly full of rage and a pocketful of nails into the plywood sheets; the window was now nailed so tightly shut, from within and without, that nothing could force it loose until the building came down to rubble.

But other things he had nailed down carefully for years were now flying loose. The doors and windows were open and a bone-cold wind sifted through the halls.

~

Again he hesitated on the brink of the alley. Again the light on the rounded bricks of the alley floor was like the light on dark, hidden water. The pigeons were all gone to roost. The wind had sucked in its breath. Voices, sirens, the groan of motors, the crackle of radios—all were muted and distant. By a dim lamp at the head of the alley, he could make out the windows of the rooms where he had grown up. His mother, so frail and bitter, was gone. And his father, who taught him that no place is safe, who taught him to live life ready to dodge a blow, was gone also. Everything he remembered was gone but the scuttle of the rats. He knew there was no good reason for him to come back here tonight. The windows were nailed down. The doors were padlocked; no one was getting in. It made no sense that he should be here, prickling as always with fear. Fear ran down his back and all in his arms and hands. *This is bullshit,* he thought. *I got to be out looking for that backstabbing motherfucker.*

But if the boy had come here once, he could come back again. And he might find him. That thought steeled him through the entry and down the first, always harrowing steps of the alley.

It can't hurt to check one more time, he thought. Anybody might try to come back here and try, now that the word was out, as it surely must be, that he could be taken. *Ever little dope boy wants to get himself up to dealing kilo level. They all gonna be trying to do what he did.* So it would not hurt to check one more time, and that thought steeled him through the middle of the alley to the turn.

The alley lamp had been stoned out long ago. But he knew his way by habit and by the feel of the bricks beneath his feet. He felt along the bricks for the casement of the first window and found it. The new plywood was tight as the head of a drum. And so were the others. And the padlock was secure on the door. He pulled out his keys. Looking to the right and left into the shadows, he snapped open the lock and pushed open the door.

By instinct, he shifted to one side of the doorframe to listen, as always, for any sound of movement. It was as if the room were a great lung, holding its breath. By some trick of perception, the great, pale, beast-like shapes of his appliances emerged from the darkness as if they, too, waited, as if they, too, held their breath.

He reached in its place for the flashlight, but stopped in mid-reach. He heard no sound. But he felt a presence. He sensed a darker space among the dark spaces against the walls and in the spaces between the appliances. In an instant, the darkness congealed. He sensed a movement—bat-shaped and silent—threatening as dream. In a single movement, he dropped, pulled out his pistol, and squeezed. All in one were the noise, flash, smell of carbide, and ring of sheet metal as the bullets tore into the innocent hearts of the dryers and cabinets.

He knew immediately that there was nothing and no one there. Calmly, with a wash of embarrassment and anger, he turned to the light switch to examine the wounds on his walls and appliances.

~

Back on the street, folded into the doorway of a shop, Roger Nolan pulled at a cigarette and watched in the shadows and the scraps of mist for any sign of the boy who had betrayed him. The traffic lights at each corner marched through their cycles of red, amber, and green, hazily visible through the mist. He was still nearly as jumpy as he had been in the alley, and he prickled each time a person crossed at either light. A woman, bundled to her eyes in a heavy cloth coat and in the white skirt of a waitress, came padding down the sidewalk in her tennis shoes. He knew her, in spite of the way she clutched her coat across her face. She was on her way to the breakfast shift at one of the downtown restaurants. It was obvious she did not see him, for she walked so close to the shop fronts that her shoulder clipped any little tatter of poster or any mailbox nailed to a door. She must have noticed him by the flare of his cigarette, for she dodged out toward the street with a sudden hissing in of her breath. He made no move other than to draw in his smoke and to follow her with his eyes, but a barely visible twitch to her shoulders and a brief skip to her walk told him he had frightened her.

I know her, he thought. *She's got no reason to be scared of me.* But she had quickened her pace and shifted her course to the middle of the sidewalk.

Damn, he thought. *I must have scared her bad.* The thought angered him, for he thought again, *She knows who I am. I done her some favors through the years.* When she was down between jobs. When her old man kicked her out. When she needed some smoke. *But she didn't even speak.* And he ran through a course of thoughts involving a crowd of people for whom he had done favors and who, in one way or another, had disavowed, disowned, or repudiated him. Dope boys, ex-wives, partners, parole officers, cousins, people he thought were friends.

He looked back up to watch the woman again. *She got a twitch to her step just like her little boy.* She had padded far up the block by now and was near the corner, still with the little hitch in her shoulders and the fearful skip in her step.

He thought, clinically, *She must be back off the pipe.* She was walking so purposefully. *But she's jumpy. It won't be long.* He thought over how he had frightened both mother and son and a wave of bitterness came over him.

It's like I'm everybody's pet monster, he thought. He shot the butt of his cigarette out into the street, fired up another, and sucked in and huffed out a stream of smoke. *Not even a damn dope boy wants my money.*

He had been too long at this and he knew too much. The burden of his knowledge was like a hod of bricks on his back. His burden was like that of a priest, for he knew the secrets of many, but no one knew what was in him. None of the wives knew what he knew, none of the girlfriends. He had no friends, no trusted ones. The world in which people shared a life seemed very far from here. All he had ever known was these streets, and all he had known of these streets was failure. It was failure he saw as he watched the woman hitching and skipping away from him in her fear. It was failure he would see when the woman, hitching and skipping, came back to him for something to calm her fears. From the time he first saw light, he had walked these streets, and he knew every brick, each granite curb, each iron star. He knew these streets better than a monk would know his cell, for he had watched closely and he had listened well. He knew who visited the whores, and who had become the whore. He knew who went straight and who fell. He saw the woman in the bright couple leave with her proud escort, and he saw her return, looking for the boys on the corner. A man might come to him and say, "Please don't tell my mother." And he would agree. He would not tell the mother.

Then the mother would come.

~

Roger Nolan had been out for hours, and he was tired. He could still smell the burn of his pistol. He had carefully cleaned it and reloaded it, but the smell, and even some of the warmth, still clung to it, and he sensed the weight and smell and heat of it against his side. It had been a foolish thing, he knew, to fire at the innocent appliances. And now, tired as he was, this whole search seemed foolish.

How did he know it was Daniel? He had thrown out the word onto the street in the midst of his anger without thinking it through. And so he knew he had to talk it out with him first. He would let no one punk him out. But he could bite back his pride long enough to talk.

But when? He did not want to drag this out. The boy had to come around some time soon. And when he did, Roger would ask, *What's up? Did you break in my stash? After I trusted you? He'll be selling wolf tickets,* he thought, *but I'll just stay calm. I'll just ask him. I'll say, Did you do it? Why did you do me like that? I'll talk to him like a brother.*

He would leave the pistol in his pocket while they talked.

He checked his watch and he checked the hint of daylight now breaking on the street. If the boy did his usual, he would be here soon. Roger stepped out of the narrow place where he had been hiding and looked down the dawning street. A woman with dark hair crossed at the corner; she carried a suitcase in each hand and bore a pack on her back.

LOOPY with exhaustion, Paul Lewis ran down to the corner after the woman with the luggage. He was not used to running, and as he reached the corner, he felt a stitch in his side. He bent to reduce the pain and he swept the street with his eyes. Gone: she was gone as surely as if she had been carried off by a wind. The lamplight fell onto empty bricks and blacktop. He had no reason to believe that the woman with the luggage was Jenny. But still, there was a chance.

He searched each passage and duckaway of the street as the light of morning gradually dressed the air around him and turned up more and more of the yawning streets and alleys. The glass in a doorway shivered with silver lights. An abandoned grocery cart, canted over, lay glinting and skeletal among the weeds of a vacant lot. A pair of stone lintels, thrown down from a demolition like Samson's columns, were not the luggage as he had first thought. He continued to scrabble from street to street, looping through each path and shortcut he knew until he came out, finally, onto Broad.

I should have known, he realized. The bus station. The white neon dog shed light across the faces of the buildings. A cabbie, fareless and bored, leaned against the wheel of his cab. Paul pushed on, in spite of the stitch which stabbed him with each breath and in spite of the cramps that had formed in one leg.

A block from the station, he saw the woman with the bags and knew the girl was right. It was Jenny. She had stopped to read something, perhaps a schedule, by the light of the neon dog, and as he approached, he became even more convinced. In spite of the years and the damage done, and in spite of the fifty yards between them, he could see that the squarish, familiar shoulders, bent and dragged low by alcohol and luggage, were no other shoulders. The same high cheekbones. The same spiky, up-and-downhill walk. The same half-moon eyes. She folded up her schedule and bent to pick up her suitcases. She made seven brisk, separated steps toward the door of the station. There, in the steadier light of the door, she stopped and set down her bags. As she bent, her hair swung down across her eyes, and as she rose, she pushed it back with a motion he knew to belong to no other.

My God, he thought. *My God.* She spoke to the cabbie and the cabbie checked his watch. It was too far to call to her and be heard. So he continued, limping by now from the cramp in his leg and sucking in his breath, carefully, from the stitch in his side.

She thanked the cabbie, moved several steps closer to the door, and then stopped again. In a quick, purposeful, undrunk movement, she pulled the bag from her shoulder, opened it, and pulled up what, at this distance, appeared to be a ticket. Her brow and eyes compressed as she tried to read it in the broken light.

Into the same light stepped the girl in her black coat and black hat. Behind her, like her shadow blown against a wall, stalked, into the same light, the boy who dealt drugs on the corner, arrogant, stony, and square.

What happened next happened in his full and impotent view.

~

Roger Nolan continued to try to sort this thing out in his mind as he searched for the boy who had betrayed him. He thought his way through two packs of cigarettes, smoked one after the other, and he continued to sort it out through three cups of coffee he had bought at three different all-night places. He continued to sort driving and he continued to sort walking. And finally he landed on what he truly wanted to say: It was over. It was done and he could put it all aside, no matter what they said on the street. He could handle anything, if only he could ask him, *Why did you break my trust? Why? I trusted you. So why did you do me like that?*

If only he could ask that; if only he could get on an answer that satisfied him, he could let it go.

Roger had driven around and around the blocks from downtown to the hillsides and up Broad and down, searching every side street until, finally, he realized: he'll see my car and bail in a hot minute. He took the car around to the alley and parked it, then walked around to where the boy stayed with his grandmother. Smoking and tossing one cigarette after another into the street, he watched the house with its dark stone face. Lights flipped on or off in various windows, and a television flared red, now green, now yellow and blue against a curtain. But he did not know which window was the boy's. And he knew there would be no marker inside to tell which door was the boy's. And he knew it would not do, at such an hour, to go knocking on doors.

He waited, smoking through a first pack and burning deep into a second. At one point he thought, *Maybe he's taken the money and dipped. He might be gone like Lost John.*

The anger rushed up and colored him again, so he pushed that thought quickly aside.

He waited long enough, finally, that he tired. A little while longer, he told himself. Just a little while longer. But twice he had to snap himself awake. He had fallen asleep standing, like a horse in pasture. The third time he woke to hear a scuffle of shoes and a murmur of voices. He looked up. There was no one at the mouth of the building, but a motion at the corner caught his eye. The boy, together with a smaller girlish figure, was already halfway up the street.

Damn, he thought. *I could have slept right through.* He walked briskly to the corner so as not to lose them if they turned.

Who's the girl with him? he wondered. She was small and birdlike, so small that, to keep up, she skipped every third or fourth step with a flutter of the wings of her coat. He could have caught them if he ran, but he did not want to come on the boy all of a sudden. That could be a fatal error. *He'll be strapped,* he thought. *He'll be carrying a nervous pistol.*

The boy looked out to the street every few steps. But he did not look behind him, Nolan noted. He did not yet always remember to watch his back. If Nolan still wanted to see the boy dead, he could do it easily. Just run up and pop him from behind. If he had to, he could drop the girl as well, and there would be no one to see.

But he only wanted to talk.

He followed them until it became clear that they were headed to the bus station. There was the white pulse of the neon greyhound; there was the door.

That motherfucker's rolled my product over for a pair of bus tickets, Nolan thought. *He's gonna take this little girl off to Florida or someplace.* He pondered, *Is that what this is all about? A girl?*

The two of them stopped at the door of the station, and Nolan took a moment just beneath the hanging lighted sign of a hairdresser. The sign was an old-fashioned type, the letters painted onto sheets of glass that sandwiched a twist of neon tube. For some reason, the light was still on at this hour, and the sign left a little pool of light on the sidewalk. To make sure he would be seen, and to be sure there were no surprises, he stepped into this pool of light and waited for the boy to see him.

~

Jenny did not want to see that girl. She did not want to see anyone at all. But there she was. "Just let me get on this bus," she murmured. "Let her not see me. Let me leave here as if I had never been."

Yet here the girl was, bounding out of the dark street with a tall, stalking boy behind her.

"I'm so glad I found you," Amy cried. She stood right square in the way, no way to dodge her. The light from the neon dog above the door flashed and the girl's eyes were abrim with tears. She had the momentum from running and would have got her in the crush of a hug. Instead, the girl held back. She brushed tears out of each eye. "I am," she cried. "I missed you so much. I've been so worried about you."

"Don't be worried about me, babe," she told her. "I'm okay. Don't worry about me."

"But I have been worried, for days. I thought maybe you . . . I've been looking all over for you and . . ."

Jenny wanted to tell the girl: *There's nothing to worry about. There's nothing here to worry about.* She wanted to tell her that any face she thought she saw in her was hollow, false, and empty. She wanted to tell her to hold and treasure herself.

"So you're, like, leaving?"

"Yeah, babe. I got to go." Jenny tried to get around her, but the girl held up her arms.

"Why? I mean . . ."

There was no way she could explain it.

The girl looked sad for a moment. But then her eyes grew wide. "I know," she cried. "Let me come too. I'm almost eighteen. And they won't blame you because you didn't snatch me up. I'm, like, going on my own. And, like . . . Just wait . . ." She held out one hand, palm up, like a traffic officer. "One minute." She raised a finger of the other hand.

"Babe, no," Jenny tried to tell the girl. She wanted to tell the girl so many things. Suddenly, she wanted to tell her secrets, stories, lessons. She wanted to tell her the message from the river if it could ever bear telling. But there was no time. No time at all, for the girl had turned to say something to her looming friend, the boy in the enormous coat.

But the boy had something else on his mind. He began suddenly to curse, looking past them into the street.

"What?" the girl cried. "What's happening?"

The boy reached into his coat, pulled up a pistol, and pointed it with his curses into the side street toward a man standing under a hanging sign.

"No!" the girl cried. And she dropped her hands and turned.

~

Jenny flinched when the girl called out. She tried to pretend she had not heard, but the girl put herself in Jenny's way and called out with such broad relief in her voice and face that Jenny turned her head as if to dodge a blow. Quickly, she stuffed her ticket back into her pack, turned aside, and reached for her luggage. But the girl raised the loose black arms of her coat. She would not let Jenny pass.

Words flew between Jenny and the girl, much pleading from the girl and much shaking of the head from the woman.

Paul slowed. He had time now. He could pause and let the stitch in his side ease. He was still some twenty yards away and in full view of them, though neither had seen him. The boy, standing flat as shadow against his wall, watched him in every step without moving his head. Paul knew it could be dangerous to approach someone like him too quickly, so he stopped.

Suddenly: In a single breath: The boy pushed himself up from the wall. Amy did not see, but Jenny startled and pulled back as the boy erupted in curses and pulled a pistol from his coat. He faced to the right, down the side street, and leveled the pistol.

"Don't even move, motherfucker," the boy called, at the end of a string of curses.

All of them followed with their eyes the long, pointed finger of the pistol. It was the man in the black leather coat, his palms turned out to show he offered no weapon.

All in a breath: Jenny hoisted up her baggage and tried again to dodge the girl. The girl, distracted, allowed her to pass.

The boy and the man in the black coat faced each other from across the street.

The man was standing beneath a hanging sign, his hands and brows open. He spoke; he reached to the boy with his eyes.

The boy fired back curses across his leveled pistol. "You a lying, dick-headed, shit-mouth motherfucker."

The man's hands turned upward. He shrugged; he questioned; he took a step forward to the curb.

The girl stood suspended between the woman and the boy.

The man closed his crucifixion palms; he was done with persuasion. He reached into his coat with a curse of his own.

Then all images ran together with a furious intensity.

Pock! The boy fired his pistol. The sound stopped Paul where he stood and startled the drowsing cabbie up from the wheel of his cab. Glass from the shattered sign of the hairdresser showered across the man. He winced; his face narrowed down in fury and he brought up a pistol from his coat.

Amy cried, "No!" She lunged toward the boy. "No!" she cried again. But at that moment, the man fired.

It was as if a massive curtain had been torn. Paul flinched backward, startled by the enormity of the sound, the sudden mattermatter-matter, round after round that clouded the street with smoke and the smell of burn. Paul felt each explosion as a blow to the face and, to his shame, felt hammered smaller with each one. Brick dust and smoke erupted from the walls of the station. The boy jerked as if pulled by strings. The stone of his face cracked; it flowered with blood.

Amy stopped and slowly, very slowly, turned.

Her arms, and the black wings of her coat, stretched out at her sides.

Jenny dropped the bags she carried and came toward her. She caught the girl with her outstretched arms and lowered her to the sidewalk.

The man in the black coat pitched a final, inarticulate curse into the silence, then disappeared behind the smoke he had raised.

Paul stood for a moment, stunned with the suddenly silent desolation on the sidewalk before him. The cabbie, fully awake, stared wide-eyed, one foot out the door of his cab. A security guard stood at the door of his station with his pistol raised. A waitress, from behind the window, covered her mouth with her apron. In the distance, a siren began to wail.

For a moment, no one moved. Then Jenny's knees bent under the weight of the girl. The waitress pushed past the guard to kneel by the crumpled form of the boy. The guard spoke into a radio he had pulled from his hip. The cabbie ran to where the boy lay bleeding.

Jenny bent her face down over the girl and began to caress her back, ignoring the heavy lock of black hair that fell across her eyes. Paul, like the others, had run over to help. "Let's set her down," Paul said. He put his hand on her shoulder and felt the girl shudder, then sag. Gently, very gently, Paul helped Jenny ease her down, very slowly down, to the sidewalk.

The boy's breath growled through his blood, but the girl was already still. When Paul touched her face, she was already pale, already cold. The flash of the neon doglight turned up a bruise-colored shadow below her eyes.

The boy's growling seized and stopped.

He and Jenny met face to face across the body of the girl. But he did not look at her and did not know if she looked at him. He looked, stupidly, trying to remember what to do. Amy's face was pale; her lips were blue. The front of her coat was all ripped and bloody.

Then someone shoved him aside and moved the girl around for CPR. "Quick, check her pulse!" Jenny rose and slowly backed away. The girl's blood was all down her coat.

The cabbie and the waitress were tending the boy, but the bullets had shattered his face.

"No pulse. No breathing." It was the security guard. Paul helped arrange her limbs and counted the breaths, though he knew there was no point.

They tried and tried, amid the growing wail of the sirens.

When the life squad arrived and took over, Paul rose with his knees and elbows sore and turned to look for Jenny again. Early daylight silvered the sidewalks and walls. The red lights of an ambulance and the blue lights of a pair of patrol cars miscolored the light of morning. Half a dozen police and EMTs stood watch, talked into radios, or entered notes. The waitress knelt, keening into her apron over the shrouded body of the boy. The cabbie, in a vigorous African accent, was witnessing to an officer, pointing here and pointing there. A bus pulled into the station, its windows crowded with curious passengers. Watchers from the station and the streets stood in a ring, worrying, pitying, speculating:

It was that girl who . . .

It's all that gang-related . . .

Wasn't he the one that . . .

It must have been a drive-by . . .

But Paul could not find Jenny anywhere. She and her bags were gone.

CODA

IT HAD been a week since the shooting. Both the funerals were over and the talk in the newspapers and on the streets had died down. Paul's exhibit was on schedule, due to open in two days; everything was ready.

No one had seen Jenny. Paul assumed she had gotten onto her bus in the confusion and ridden away. The man in the black coat had disappeared as well. Though everyone in the neighborhood knew him, no one had seen him, and rumors took him to Texas, Kentucky, or Florida, where he had relatives or contacts or property. The police had questioned Paul and everyone else near the scene, and there had been a buzz in the papers and on the streets, some talk of what-is-becoming-of-our-youth. But it all died down quickly beneath the next set of headlines.

Night after night, Paul fell down onto his bed and dropped into sleep like a stone into a well, only to wake, hours before dawn, with the lights in his brain gone foggy and his eyes out of focus. He would tinker awhile in his studio, though the girl had done her work well and there was little left to do. Then, as if pulled by a rope, he would find himself dragged out onto the streets until the milky light of the morning poured out around him.

At this earliest of hours, he might see a lone dope boy, a trucker loading news boxes, or a gray-coated man in a wide hat staggering under a duffel bag. But he always saw the trash picker with his complaining cart, studying and selecting metals from the gutter, the garbage cans, and the alley floors.

Twice he saw the boy, Jonathan, standing, for no good reason, at the corner of Broad, looking restlessly in all four directions. His face was shadowed in the hood of his new jacket, but Paul knew him by the twist in his mouth and by the nervous way he turned to the four corners.

~

The night before his opening, he saw Jonathan, again at the odd foggy hour, standing on the sidewalk in front of his shop. He was framed in the doorway, looking aside at the dark street. He had knocked just a moment before, but already his hands were stuffed into the pockets of his jacket. His shoulders were slightly canted, one up and one down; his whole stance was tentative; his feet were on the step, but he leaned out toward the street.

"Hey," he called to the boy. "Come on in."

The boy turned, pressed the handle, and pushed open the door. Carefully, he pushed it shut again, taking care that the latch clicked. "You ought to keep your door locked, man," he said.

This was an old argument, but this time the boy's voice was flat as a board, hoarse and dusty as the cut of a saw.

"I'm sorry about your cousin," Paul said. "They told me he was your cousin. I was there when it went down. It was really bad. I'm sorry."

The boy shrugged. "People got to go sometime. It ain't no big thing."

He started to say, *It is. It is a big thing. I was there. I saw him die. I saw the two of them riddled with blood. I saw them die.*

But the boy had swung up his arms; his hands cupped his heart. "Dude goes down," he said with a sudden lift of his shoulders and a shaking off of the dust in his voice. His hands chopped outward. "Life's like that, man. It ain't no big thing." He pulled himself taller and stood, wise and defiant, daring him to argue.

Paul did not argue. He would have argued if he could. He would have told him, *No, it is. It is a big thing. It was terrible to see them. They were too young to die.* He would have reached out and touched the boy's hair if it were not for the bristled stance the boy had taken. The boy twisted up the side of his mouth and shook his head. He looked around him at the stacks of photographs in their frames and said, "So you gonna have that show?"

"Everything's ready. You should come."

"Naw, man. I ain't got time."

"Come by for an hour, man. It's right downtown."

"I got bidness, man."

He nodded. All right.

"Fact. I got bidness right now." He unzipped the jacket and pulled up a worn manila envelope.

"What's up?"

The boy held out the envelope. "Check this out, man."

"What is it?"

"You know."

Paul did not know. He opened the flap of the envelope carefully because there was little left to hold it together.

"Go on," the boy said.

He pulled out a sleeve of black-and-white negatives. Quickly, he shoved them back into the envelope.

"Where'd you get these?"

The boy shrugged.

He started to ask, *Did you steal them?* He settled instead for a skeptical glance. "They're negatives."

The boy rolled his eyes. "I know that."

"Where'd you get them?" he asked again.

"I found them." The boy lied as easily as ever, but without the enthusiasm he used to have.

He started to pass them back to the boy. But the boy held up his hands.

"I thought you collected old things," Paul said.

"I ain't into that now."

"So why did you bring them here?"

"I wanted you to have them."

"Why is that?"

The boy shrugged, as if to say, *You should know that.* He made a gesture toward the door. "Later, man."

"Hold up." Paul did not want to be alone with the negatives. He saw the boy as teetering on a brink, ready to fall into a terrible darkness. He wanted to hold him back just a moment longer if he could, to save him if it were possible.

"I can show you how to turn these into pictures."

"You already showed me that."

"I can let you do it yourself."

The boy gravely shook his head. "Later, man." He had his business to attend to. He stepped to the door like a man of business. With a small wave of his hand, he stepped out the door and into the crackhead night.

Paul stood in the doorway to watch him swimming blindly away, arrogant and lost.

In the days after, he saw no more of the boy in his bright jacket. He watched the clusters of young men on the corners and the boys waiting singly at the heads of the alleys with their hard-set faces and their narrowed eyes. But he did not see the boy's small, twisted-up face among them.

His exhibit came and went. He sold some pictures and the reviews were good. For a while, he noticed an occasional flash of eyes or heard a pleasant little buzz of talk each time he entered a coffeehouse. Then it was over. It made no difference at all to the workers at the warehouse where he still worked nor to the man who pushed the trash cart, nor to the woman draining french fries at the fast-food place where he got his morning coffee. At the end, he hung some of the pictures on the wall of his shop, gave some away, and stacked the rest in a corner under a tarp to keep them from the dust.

He did not see Amy's mother at the opening, nor did he expect to. He had dedicated the exhibit to the girl and the boy who died with her, and he made sure the mother was invited to the opening. But he understood why she did not show up. It would have been awkward. They lived in different worlds and he did not expect ever to see her again.

But he knew something had to change as a result of all this. He did not know what it was, but something had to change.

~

He heard the early morning knock at the insomniac door of his shop. By now he knew better than to be surprised when someone came knocking at such an hour. And he knew better than to be surprised that it was Jenny. He came out of the darkroom and saw her pressed into the frame of the doorway in the milky light, bent and distracted, as if she, too, had been wounded.

He hurried to the door and opened it, half expecting her to fall in. But she pulled herself erect and in her gravelly voice asked, "Can I come in?"

She smelled of cheap wine and mildew. She was wearing the same parka she had worn the day of the killings; the girl's blood had crusted across the front of it. Her face was punchy and raw; little red veins spread across her cheekbones. Mucus had dried in a white path under her nose, like the trail of a slug. Her swollen, chapped hands clutched the front of her parka closed. He could see the collar of another coat beneath, perhaps a third. There was a boozy gloss to her eyes. Her hair fell straight to her shoulders from under a dirty toboggan cap.

"Come in," he said. "Come in." He pulled her by the elbow to the stuffed chair next to the space heater.

"You look cold."

She stared into the grate of the space heater as if it were a log fire.

"I'll fix you some coffee."

"No," she said. "No thank you."

"Tea?"

She raised her eyebrows impatiently.

"Well?"

"I'm okay. I don't want anything."

"You're sure?"

"I just want to get warm."

"Stay! Get warm! Get comfortable."

She had not relaxed her hands. They still gripped the folds of her parka. She did not even appear to be conscious of the way they were twisting the folds of her parka or the way the blue veins stood up on the backs of her hands.

Neither of them said another thing for a full minute. Paul pulled up a chair and sat where he could face her. *Why is she here?* he wondered. *What should I do?* Every few seconds she twitched her shoulder or her leg. He worried, *Is she detoxing? Will she go into convulsions right here!*

"Do you need some help?"

She raised an eye to him, then looked back into the red eye of the space heater.

"I mean," he said, "I can call somebody. I could help you get in a treatment center . . ."

She did not move her eye.

"I've got a little money. I could help you out."

"Why now?"

He had no answer. Clearly she wanted him to feel guilt, and he felt it. He said, "Because now is when you're here."

"You didn't care about helping before."

"So what can I do to help now?"

"I never wanted your help."

"What did you want?"

She shrugged. "There wasn't really anything to want. I was going to do what I was going to do. You couldn't stop me."

Her hands began to twitch up and down, hammer-fashion, as if she were ringing a bell.

"Look," he said. "You're about to be real sick. I'm going to call someone to get you some help."

"You see . . ." She ignored him. "You never did understand."

"I understand that if you don't get some help real soon, you're going to be sick."

"You see," she said, the words alternating with the bell stroke of her hands. "I never—could quit—because—I never—" She had to pause a moment to control the shaking in her voice. "I never—could find—a bottom. You had a bottom. I never did. No matter how far down—I went—I never found one. Do you understand that? Do you understand that? I looked—for years. It's hard—you see—you have to go—you have—to go—so deep. That girl—the minute—she put her hand up to that gun—she found a bottom. You could tell. She just—put her feet down—and touched bottom. Do you understand that?"

The hands stilled a moment, so he waited.

"All those years I was searching—for that—one—thing. I looked. I searched. I searched so hard. Do—do you know what I found? Nothing. I found nothing. A big empty hole. No matter where I looked—I found nothing—at all. Do you know what kind of feeling that is? You can't know. In all those treatment—centers—they said, Be yourself. And I nodded my head—and fed some line back to them—to keep them happy. But inside, I asked myself: How? I never had a self to be. And the only way to bear it—was to drink. Ah, God, I drank. Because there's a bottom—to the bottle."

She stirred, as if she wanted to stand, but sank back down into the chair.

"But you can't understand this. This is all garbled talk. Drunk talk. I'm a drunk. And all this talk is garbled, nothing talk. I'm wasting your time."

"No. No. It's fine. It's just fine. Please don't talk about yourself like that."

"I told you—"

"What?"

"I don't have—a self. I looked. I looked all the time. And—I never—found a thing. It's hard for you—to understand. 'Cause you always knew who you were and—and what you wanted to do. But I've—I never had a clue. I thought, if I could find a self, I could find God. But . . ." She raised her hand. The words would not come. Her mouth was open, and a high-pitched noise almost like a laugh came out. But no words. She began to jerk again on the rope of her parka.

"Let me make a phone call. You're gonna get yourself real sick."

"I said! I don't—have a self! All these people in your pictures—they have a self. That's why you like them. They're strong. Even when—they're all beat down—they're strong. They have a self. But I don't. I don't have a self. I never had. I only had—what I thought you—wanted me to have. I tried to be—what I thought—you wanted me to be. Until—you showed me—you really didn't want me—to be—anything at all."

"That was a long time ago."

"You didn't really want a thing from me." She laughed, and the bell-pull motion started again.

"I'm going to call now." He rose.

She looked up at him and her eyes fixed him in place.

"I'm serious," he said. "You need some help." She was starting to convulse. In no time, she would be rattling across the shop floor.

"But you see—" She looked back into the red eye of the heater. "When that girl—died—I found out—I had as much—self—as anybody else."

"I'm going in back. I'm going to call somebody. I want you to stay right here."

She nodded slightly. She continued to stare and her hands continued to ring their silent bell.

He went into the back room and punched in numbers, listening for her through the curtain. He must have been ten or twenty minutes, for the first call referred him to a second and the second to a third and he was on hold for long stretches each time so that by the time he came back through the curtain she was gone.

Quickly, he went to the door and stepped out into the street. Nothing. Nothing. She was nowhere in sight. He searched up a block and down a block and made a circuit several blocks around, but she was gone. He saw nothing but black windows, sleeping doorways, and the empty heads of the alleys.

~

This was to be a long, dark night. But now he had a purpose, a direction. He went to the file where he had stored the negatives the boy had given him. He took the packet back to his darkroom, and for the next several hours, cast down through the brittle frames, one image after another: the turned marble jaw, the face full of sun, the black bell, the broken raven's wing, the bottle thrust like a pistol to the teeth.

ANN Taylor had already spent a brittle afternoon at her desk, her first afternoon at the office since the funeral. It was almost a relief to be here. Almost. Because for nearly two weeks she had been dealing with the shame and the shock of the death of her only child. All the stupid, numbing detail of seeing someone buried. All those negotiations with the funeral home, as if she were picking out carpet. And her poor, stunned parents. And that bastard David, who was out on tour and couldn't be reached so she had to leave a message with someone sounding slinky and young who acted surprised to know he had a daughter. And sending regrets to the opening at the gallery that had been dedicated to Amy. And all the articles in the papers. And the weeping students and sympathetic teachers. And the boxing and sorting and donating of clothes to the poor. After all that, it was good to work on something so particular, so regular and mindless as the report in front of her.

She had deliberately waited until noon, when most of the office would be out to lunch, to make her reentry, so that she could get into her office, close the door, fire up the computer, and begin, without sympathy and interruption, to pick away at her backlog of emails, contracts for approval, and proposals for review. She stepped into the lobby and made sure not to look in the direction of the window overlooking New Town. Everyone, as she hoped, seemed to be out to lunch.

Rebecca the receptionist was at her station, though. She was eating a lunch she had brought from home.

"I'm here but I'm not here," Ann said. She slipped past Rebecca to her office and shut the door. For the next four hours she picked efficiently at her backlog, feeling better by the minute, her mind thankfully numbed by the update, repair, and revision of dangling and uncompleted projects. It was her plan to work this way until the last person left the office, take herself out to dinner, stop in to see her parents (whom she visited now nearly every day), and take herself home when she was too tired to do anything but sleep.

It was such a relief to be so absorbed in something that was not related to a funeral that she felt almost normal, except that through it all she felt edgy, not-quite-there, brittle.

She still had not smoked. She thought that might be the cause of this feeling, just the hint of a feeling on the edge of her consciousness, that at any moment she might break right in half. She paused in mid-memo and thought, *I need to move around.* She decided to risk a bathroom break.

"I'm not here," she whispered again to Rebecca. And no one else saw her. Coming and going, she still managed to avoid the big window. On the way back, she put her finger to her lips and made it nearly to her office door when Richard came from around the corner and met her head on.

"Oh," he said. "Ann!" He appeared to stumble over what to say next. She understood it was awkward for him, so she waved briefly and started to dodge around him to her office. He righted himself, however, and said, "I didn't know you were back."

"Just for a while," she said.

"Because I have those prints for you."

"What prints?"

"You don't remember?"

She did not, at first. It was not until she got back to her desk and tried to find her way back into the memo she had been writing that she did remember. Then Richard tapped at the door and let himself in.

"I'm so sorry. I didn't know you were here. I would have brought them by sooner."

"It's okay, Richard," she said, only looking up halfway from her legal pad. "You can leave them on my desk."

With a half-raised eye, she saw him place a white parcel on the corner of her desk.

"Thank you, Richard. It means a lot."

She thought he would go then. But he stood, hesitantly, halfway between her desk and the door. "I was glad to do it. I was glad to do anything I could."

He had asked, at the funeral, if there was any way he could help. And she had told him, then, Yes. There were Amy's photos. Half a dozen completed rolls and a seventh still in the camera. She had no idea what was in them, but some were probably shot within Amy's last hours.

"Print these for me," Ann had asked him. "No contact sheets. Print each one. Five-by-sevens if you can, but four-by-sixes are fine."

And then she had pushed them out of her mind.

"I took some time with them," he said. They were, by the size of the packet, five-by-sevens. "She was good. She took good pictures."

Ann drummed her fingers on her desk for a moment. "Thank you," she said. Her voice was heavy. Had she been smoking, and had she had a cigarette, she would have reached for it, ashed it with a chopping motion, hit on it hard, and laid a shroud of smoke across the desk.

Richard said something else, but she had tuned him out and it did not register. "I'll be all right," she said, still staring into the contract. The words on the pad had been transposed into some ancient and unreadable script, but she would not move her eyes from them.

He nodded and turned for the door.

"You can leave the door open," she said.

She heard Richard and the others gather their things to go, and heard each one speak a word to her as each left for the night. To each she nodded and waved briefly, though she still did not lift her eyes from the page. When the office door at last clapped shut behind the last of them, the words on the page snapped into place, and she was able to work again.

She worked for an hour or more, enjoying the silence and the lack of chatter. She completed a memo regarding the excessive number of misjudgments in the report she had just reviewed, then finished correcting the report itself, reviewed the billing, emailed the corrections and the memo to everyone involved, and went to the filing room to fetch out a proposal she knew was due.

She carefully avoided the windows. She did not want to look out the windows.

Of course, the proposal was misfiled. She riffled through the file drawer, front to back. *Why do I have to stand over people here every minute?* she thought. *How am I supposed to do a job if I can't find the work?* She cursed the young wannabe model whose job it was to file. *Why did they even hire that silly little flirt?*

She slammed the drawer shut and jerked open the next. Nothing there either. She opened the first drawer again, just in case, and again, she flipped through the drawer and was again ready to slam it shut when the file appeared under her fingers, exactly where it should have been.

She turned back to her office, still avoiding the window, sat down with the proposal, penciled on it ruthlessly for five minutes, then pushed it aside.

Richard's white packet still waited on the corner of her desk.

She pushed her hands through her hair, shook her head, and pulled the proposal back to her. When she finished her review of it, the pages were pocked and hammered with penciled-in additions and corrections. She dropped it in the typing tray, turned back to her desk, and stopped.

What do I do now? She could not think of a single project. She knew of a dozen. She knew there were hours of work within a few paces of where she stood. But she could not remember a single one of them. Her mind had become blank and open as a prairie.

The keening of a siren rose up from the dark streets outside her windows. It wavered, grew thin and distant, and died. She paced the hall in from of her office, but the fat white packet was all that she could see. She folded her arms and stared at it for a moment, then, with a shudder, walked to her desk and sat down. Carefully, she removed everything from the desk: phone, in-out trays, penholders, coffee mug, note pads, pencils, address book, calculator. She pushed the computer and monitor as far back as they would go and put the keyboard and mouse on the floor. The desk had become a blank and open space. Nothing was there but the packet of photographs.

The wail of another siren rose up and fell again.

Do I really want to do this?

She guessed there were over two hundred of them, five-by-sevens, separated by rubber bands into seven sets, one for each roll of film she had handed to Richard. Her fingers invisibly trembled. She began to deal them out in rows straight from the top, as if laying out an enormous game of solitaire.

The first shots were of a set of strange, shaggy men, leaning against the fronts of old buildings or splayed over park benches. Yes, she was good. Not every shot, of course. But she had taken pains to plan those pictures. She knew what she was doing. The men appeared confident, comfortable with her. Next there were shots of women with hard, wary faces, and several of a shabby man with a cart full of junk.

Then there were shots of the boy who died. She flared with anger when she saw him and she had an impulse to snatch the pictures into a clump and fling them into the trashcan. Instead, she studied carefully each one and placed it, like the others, clinically, one after the other, in a row on the desk. By now, into the third packet, she realized that her desk was much too small; it would never hold them all.

She pushed her chair to the wall and the potted plant to the corner and the trash can under the desk. She picked up each of the photos she had laid out on the desk, then she knelt and began to lay them out on the floor. This time she arranged them in a wide half-circle around her, as if seating them at a theater.

There were more of that boy, and some of an old woman, and some of a Middle Eastern man at the cash register of a store. She found more of the strange man with the cart and more of the hard, wary women. But, starting with the fifth packet, the rest were all of children. Dozens of them. Portraits and groups, Black children and White children and foreign-looking children. On steps and in the sidewalks and streets and in the jungles of vacant lots. Some of them appeared in picture after picture. Others, just once. She recognized in several of them the boy who showed her the photographer's studio that night on the street. She studied each picture carefully and placed it, like the others, in a seat in the theater: Children with book bags slung over their shoulders. Children decked up smiling on the steps of a school. Children with bashful smiles. Children who stared into the camera with faces set to stone.

When she finished, the photographs covered a wide section of her floor.

She continued to study the pictures for a long time. The sirens continued to keen outside the windows, but she continued to study the faces and clothing and surroundings of the men and women and children in the pictures.

I should go, she thought. *I have things to do.*

But she did not move. Her body was achingly immobile; her eyes were drawn to the eyes in the rows around her. And her hands were heavy as sand.

ACKNOWLEDGMENTS

Many thanks to the staff and board of the Ohio Arts Council for their support of this work and to the staff, board, and readers of Swallow Press / Ohio University Press, who shepherded it to completion. Thanks to friends and family who have read this work in its various forms. Thanks to Jessie Sojourner Henson and Liv Kristina Henson for advice on the work of photography. And thanks, finally, to the documentary photographers whose work, which they undertook sometimes at great risk to themselves, informs this book, among them Walker Evans, Margaret Bourke-White, Armando Bravos, Dorothea Lange, Doris Ulmann, Michael Cunningham, Roy DeCarava, Gordon Parks, Tina Modotti, Fred Burkhart, Jimmy Heath, Roger May, Rachel Boillot, and many, many more.